THE

Dragon

GUARDIAN

(Lochguard Highland Dragons #2)

Jessie Donovan

The Dragon Guardian
Copyright © 2016 Laura Hoak-Kagey
Mythical Lake Press, LLC
First Paperback Edition

Cover Art by Clarissa Yeo of Yocla Designs.

ISBN 13: 978-1942211358

For Scotland

Every time I visit, your people are kind, funny, and full of life. I only hope I do them justice in my stories since I will never be able to portray the depth of your beauty in words.

Other Books by Jessie Donovan

<u>Stonefire Dragons</u>
Sacrificed to the Dragon
Seducing the Dragon
Revealing the Dragons
Healed by the Dragon
Reawakening the Dragon
Loved by the Dragon
Surrendering to the Dragon (May 2016)

<u>Lochguard Highland Dragons</u>
The Dragon's Dilemma
The Dragon Guardian
The Dragon's Heart (Summer 2016)

<u>Asylums for Magical Threats</u>
Blaze of Secrets
Frozen Desires
Shadow of Temptation
Flare of Promise (March 2016)

<u>Cascade Shifters</u>
Convincing the Cougar
Reclaiming the Wolf
Cougar's First Christmas
Resisting the Cougar

CHAPTER ONE

Fergus MacKenzie sat on top of one of the hills surrounding Loch Shin in his dragon form and adjusted his grip with his talons. Despite waiting for the last hour to see the redheaded human female, she had yet to step outside.

That shouldn't surprise him given that it was January in the Scottish Highlands. The wind and chill in the north wasn't for the fragile. While everything he'd learned about Gina MacDonald over the last few weeks spoke of her strength, she was also heavily pregnant. For all he knew, she could be giving birth right that second.

Fergus's inner dragon spoke up. *Look. Her door is opening. Maybe we can actually talk to her today.*

Fergus watched as Gina stepped outside and headed for the chicken coop. The wind whipped her long, curly red hair behind her and the human pulled her jacket closer around her body.

His beast spoke up again. *Today might be our last chance for a while. We should speak with her.*

Fergus wanted to talk with the human more than he would ever admit to anyone. Not even his twin brother knew how Gina had invaded Fergus's dreams since the very first day he'd seen her. Dreams that more often than not had both of them naked and tangled in the sheets.

Pushing away those thoughts, Fergus answered his dragon. *We have no claim on her. I can't risk a confrontation with the father of her child.*

His dragon huffed. *We haven't been able to find out anything about him. If he's unwilling to protect his female, then he has no claim on her.*

Not true. What if he's in the armed forces and currently stationed overseas?

That is a very small possibility.

It could still be true.

Fergus debated returning to his home on Clan Lochguard when the female gripped her belly and hunched over. Without thinking, Fergus glided down to Gina's house. The sheep ran to the far side of one of the pens and he landed. Imagining his wings shrinking into his back, his talons changing into fingers, and his snout taking the shape of a human face, Fergus stood in his human form five seconds later. Uncaring about his nakedness, he rushed over to the female and shouted, "Are you all right, lass?"

The woman glanced over. Her eyes widened before quickly darting down to his cock and back up to his face. Taking a deep breath, she stood up and frowned. "You're the dragon who's been watching me for weeks."

He took a step closer. "That doesn't matter right now. If you need help, then tell me. I can ring a doctor or your husband."

"I don't have a husband." Gina rubbed her belly and then let out a sigh. "But the damn spell has passed, so care to tell me why you're standing in my yard buck naked?"

Just like the first time he'd heard her speak, he found her American accent foreign yet endearing. "Aren't you in labor?"

"No. I was trying to keep my food down. The smell of chicken scat makes me want to puke."

His dragon chimed in. *Get her inside. I don't like her out in the cold.*

Fergus had asked the same question a million times before, but decided to try once more. *Why do you care so much?*

Just get her inside first.

Fergus motioned with a hand toward the door. "Let's get you out of the cold, get me a blanket or a towel so I can cover some of my nakedness, and I'll answer whatever questions you might have."

The corner of Gina's mouth ticked up. "Oh, really? Whatever I want? I can't wait to make the big, bad dragonman squirm."

Ignoring her tease, he moved to her side and placed a hand on her lower back. Despite the layers of clothing between her skin and his, a small jolt shot up his arm. He couldn't remember the last time that had happened with a female. "I assure you I don't squirm. Now, let's get inside. It's bloody freezing out here."

Gina started walking and humor danced in her eyes. "Are you going to use that as an excuse for the size of your penis?"

He blinked. "What?"

"Well, just about every guy I've ever met says the cold makes him shrivel." She paused and leaned over. "But in your case, that makes me wonder just how big you are when it's warm."

Fergus cleared his throat. He wasn't about to allow the lass to disarm him. "The first time I met you, whilst in dragon form, you said you knew the dragon clan in Virginia back in America. I'm fairly confident the rumors about dragon-shifters and their cocks are the same there as here."

"Maybe. But I like the idea of making you uncomfortable."

He frowned. "Care to tell me why?"

11

Gina laid a hand on her stomach. "It's fun. And believe me, it's been months since I've had any fun."

~~~

Gina MacDonald wasn't sure what had come over her. The black dragon constantly watching from the hills had irritated her over the passing weeks. Who was he to spy on her? Not only that, but he never had the balls to talk with her so she could find out why he was there. She didn't think Travis had sent him.

No. She refused to think of that bastard.

And yet she was spilling her guts to the Scottish dragonman. Sure, it was true she hadn't had any fun since her mother had shipped her off to Scotland, but it was hardly something you told a stranger.

The dragonman pushed lightly against her back and Gina nearly moaned at his touch. She would give her left arm for a massage.

The mysterious dragonman spoke up, his yummy Scottish accent making her want to shiver. "Aye, well, sometimes fun has to wait. You're about to have a child, so get used to it."

She glanced over at the tall Scot at her side. "What, do you have a brood of five kids at home and are speaking from experience?"

"I don't have any children."

His tone was a little too controlled. The smart thing would be to drop it, but Gina didn't like unanswered questions. "But you do want them someday."

The dragonman faltered in his step. His dark blue eyes met hers and she drew in a breath. It seemed dragon-shifters were attractive on both sides of the pond.

Clenching her fingers, Gina pushed aside her attraction. After all, that was what had landed her in the current situation.

They reached the door and the dragonman turned the knob. Gina debated the negatives of inviting a strange man into her house. But then the wind gusted. Longing for warmth, she decided to trust her gut that the man wouldn't hurt her, and she stepped inside. "Come in, then, Mister...?"

"MacKenzie. Fergus MacKenzie."

Gina snorted. "You can't get much more Scottish than that."

Fergus clicked the door closed. "Fergus is a strong name. It means man of strength or man of force."

She put on a mock Scottish accent. "Aye, and it's a verra bonny name, too."

She didn't think it was possible, but Fergus frowned deeper than before. "We're doing accents then, aye?" His voice turned into a high-pitched Valley Girl accent. "I'm, like, so super cool. And, like, you're hella crazy."

She managed to keep it together until Fergus waggled his eyebrows and Gina barked out a laugh. "You should talk like that all of the time. It suits you."

His voice returned to normal. "But Americans love it when I roll my 'r's."

Not wanting to acknowledge it was true, Gina turned, picked up a blanket and tossed it at Fergus. "Cover yourself and I'll pour some juice."

From the corner of her eye, she watched Fergus wrap the blanket around his lean hips. The tattoo on one of his upper arms bunched and flexed as he did it.

Dragon-shifters really were too attractive for their own good.

13

Not now, Gina. We learned our lesson, remember? Keep it together.

Clearing her throat, she went into the kitchen. Just as she was about to lean against the counter and take a breather, Fergus waltzed into the room as if he owned it. Spotting her against the counter, he muttered, "Bloody stubborn female."

Before Gina could reply, he was next to her. Picking her up as if she weighed nothing, she cried out, "Put me down."

Fergus adjusted his grip. "No."

She slapped his chest. "As I told you when we first met, I have ways to defend myself against dragon-shifters."

"Aye? Well, if carrying you to a chair offends you, I wonder how any male came close enough to get you with child."

"Are you trying to insult me?"

Fergus gently rested her on the kitchen chair and remained bent over so his eyes were level with hers. His pupils flashed to slits and back before the corner of his mouth ticked up. "Lass, I have a younger sister and a twin brother. Believe me, when I insult you, you'll know it."

She opened her mouth and Fergus pressed her lips together with his warm, rough fingers—fingers that no doubt could do wicked things to her body.

Gina blinked. She needed to get Fergus MacKenzie away from her or she would most definitely do something stupid. Given her track record over the last year, she really didn't need to add any other mistakes to her list.

And spending time with Fergus would be a mistake she couldn't afford to make. Not with a child on the way she needed to protect.

Unable to speak, she raised her eyebrows. Fergus grinned and she stopped breathing. She loved how his eyes crinkled at the corners.

Fergus finally spoke up. "I'm going to release your lips on one condition—you promise to sit here whilst I fetch you some juice and a snack. Nod if you agree."

She should just nod and be polite. She really should.

Yet Gina didn't like Fergus's commanding tone. It was almost as if he expected her to follow his every word without complaint.

He may be taller and with a lot more muscle, but she hadn't come this far in life only to have someone try to take control.

Drawing on her high school years of drama club, Gina closed her eyes and moaned as if she were in pain. Fergus instantly released her lips. "What's wrong, Gina?"

Rather than think about how he knew her name, she hooked her leg against the back of his knee and yanked him forward. Fergus fell to the ground. Before he could make a move, she pinned his head between her legs. "Okay, dragonman. Let's get a few things straight right now. One, it's not nice to invade someone's personal space without their permission. Do it again, and I won't be so lenient."

Despite her best effort to sound badass, amusement danced in Fergus's eyes. "And I assume there's a number two?"

She growled. "You're going to tell me why you've been watching me and how you know my name."

"Actually, that's three things in total."

"Are you always this annoying?"

"There's nothing annoying about pointing out the details. I do it every day for my job."

For some reason, she wanted to ask what his job was. Fergus was a lot different from Travis, who had been a Protector.

Then she remembered Fergus shushing her lips like a child and Gina leaned closer to Fergus's face. "That's nice and all, but

15

how about you answer my questions? The longer you take, the greater the chance I could go into labor. You probably don't want to be under me when my water breaks."

~~~

It took every bit of strength Fergus possessed not to laugh at Gina MacDonald.

For whatever reason, Fergus enjoyed irritating her. The lass was a fierce one, but maybe a wee too stubborn. That stubbornness clearly clouded her judgment. She'd left his hands free. He could change positions and pin her to the floor, but he was rather enjoying the warmth and weight of her bum against his bare upper chest.

His dragon chimed in. *Too bad she isn't naked. I would love to feel her skin and wetness against our chest.*

Bloody dragon. She isn't ours.

She could be.

Ignoring his dragon's words, he focused back on Gina. "Although, judging by your size, it could be weeks before you go into labor." Gina growled and Fergus winked. "But, given that my cousin's mate would have my head if she knew I was needling a pregnant female, I'll answer your questions. However, if you want to focus on my answer, then don't turn around. The blanket fell off during the fall and we all know how you're distracted by my cock."

Gina's cheeks flushed and she raised her chin. "I'm clearly not a virgin, so I've seen a man's penis before. I'm much more interested in some answers."

Fergus's dragon snarled. *She shouldn't dismiss our dick so casually. I can tell from her pupils she wants us.*

Shut it, dragon. You're as bad as Fraser.

Aye, and your twin brother has all the fun.

Gina poked his nose. "Well? I'm waiting."

He chuckled, which only made the human poke him again. Not wanting Gina to carry out her earlier threat, Fergus answered her. "I know your name because I've asked the locals. You're American, so you may not be aware of how the humans around Loch Shin view dragon-shifters."

Gina waved a hand in dismissal. "My grandma lived here until she died and I've heard the stories about dragons being good luck. However, I have yet to be convinced any dragon-shifter is good luck, here or in America."

Fergus's job required him to gather intelligence and interview contacts. His years of experience told his gut she knew more about dragon-shifters than she was letting on.

However, Gina MacDonald wasn't his assignment. Truth be told, Fergus needed to return to Lochguard in the next hour. The sooner he placated the human, the better. "Well, believe what you wish. Is my interrogation over yet?"

She shook her head. "You still haven't told me why you've been watching me for the last six or seven weeks."

Damn. He'd hoped she'd forgotten that bit. The thought of lying to the human didn't sit well with man or beast, so he went with the truth. "I wanted to know your story."

Gina blinked. "What?"

"Your story. I know all of the humans around this loch, lass. You're new and I want to know why you're here."

She crossed her arms over her chest, which only plumped up her breasts. Bastard that he was, he glanced down at them for a second. He wondered how heavy they'd feel in his hands.

Gina cleared her throat and he met her gaze again. The female's cheeks were even pinker than before. It took everything he had not to stare at her lips as she replied, "Then why not knock on my door like a normal person? Do you know how creepy it is to have a giant, black dragon watching your every move? Despite my experience with dragon-shifters, I had begun to wonder if you were going to eat me."

His beast hummed. *Yes, I wouldn't mind eating her.*

Fergus nearly choked. He was trying to think of how to reply to that when Gina cried out and placed her hands on her belly.

"Are you faking again?"

Gina drew in a breath and shook her head. Both man and beast kicked into gear.

He gently took hold of Gina's shoulders and rolled them until she was lying on her back on the ground. Placing a hand on her belly, he felt the rippling of her abdomen. "We need to call you a doctor, lass. Can you stay here whilst I do that?"

Gina shouted, "No. Don't call a doctor."

He frowned. "Why not?"

He could tell when the pain passed because Gina's entire body relaxed into the floor. After a few beats of silence, she met his eye. "Because the baby is half-dragon-shifter. If you call a human doctor, they'll lock me up and eventually take away my son."

CHAPTER TWO

Gina had been working up the nerve for weeks to try to contact the one person who might be able to help her keep her baby, but had failed. She'd put off contacting Melanie Hall-MacLeod so long that she might not be able to seize a happy ending.

And despite the difficult life ahead for a human raising a dragon-shifter child, Gina desperately wanted to keep her son.

She cursed Travis for putting her into this predicament in the first place. His words of love and being her true mate had all been a lie. The second he'd known she was pregnant, he'd laughed and walked away. All he'd wanted was another child for his clan.

Tears prickled her eyes, but she willed them away. She wouldn't cry in front of Fergus, even if it killed her.

The dragonman assessed her with his dark blue eyes. He still hadn't responded to her secret. Just as she was going to ask for his thoughts, he replied, "I know someone who can help you."

Fear gripped her heart. "But will they take my baby away?"

"We can discuss that later. Right now, you need a midwife. Luckily for you, my sister-in-law is a bloody good one."

Fergus took out his mobile phone. Before he could dial, she grabbed his wrist. "I'm warning you, Fergus. If the person you're about to call will take away my baby, then I'll use my secret weapon to stop you."

Gina reached into her pocket with her other hand and closed her fingers around the precious tube of ground periwinkle and mandrake root. The substance had cost her a small fortune to obtain, but it was the only way to incapacitate a dragon-shifter. Not only that, it would prevent him, or her, from shifting for several days, too.

She had purchased it in case Travis, or anyone from Clan BroadBay, came after her. But she'd use it on Fergus if she had to.

Fergus lightly brushed a finger down her cheek. His touch helped to ease some of her tension. His voice was gentle, yet firm, when he murmured, "Holly won't try to take your child, lass. But you staying here in this cottage, on your own, is going to be a problem."

Gina's heart rate ticked up. "Does that mean you're going to turn me over to the DDA?"

He shook his head. "No. But I do think you should come back to Lochguard with me."

Clan Lochguard was the only dragon-shifter clan in Scotland. Gina had been trying to find out information about them for months, but still didn't know much about them since the locals viewed her as an outsider. All she had were the tidbits she'd learned from her grandmother before she'd passed a few months ago.

She wished her grandma was still alive. Marjorie MacDonald had spoken highly of some dragon-shifters being good. Maybe it had included Lochguard's leader.

But her grandmother was dead and Gina needed to sort the situation out herself. Gripping the vial in her pocket tighter, she gathered every bit of strength she had and made her voice strong. "I'm not agreeing to anything until I talk to your clan leader."

"You do understand that I could call the DDA right now and hand you over to them."

"And do what? I could just as easily report you stalking me for the last few weeks. The locals may not care about you lingering on human lands, but the DDA does."

As they stared at one another, Gina wondered if she'd pushed too far. Especially since if another pain came, she would be completely at Fergus's mercy. He could easily retaliate.

But then he smiled, and her fears eased away as he spoke up again. "A lass who uses her brain. I must admit I like it." Fergus waved the mobile phone in his hand. "Let me call my sister-in-law. After that, I'll call my clan leader and see what I can do. However, it's entirely up to Finn to refuse a meeting. You understand that, don't you, lass?"

"My name isn't 'lass.' It's Gina."

Fergus grinned. "Right, then, Gina. Same question."

The thought of living under an unknown dragon clan leader's rules didn't sit well with her. The dragon clan leader in Virginia, of Clan BroadBay, had determined that Gina's child belonged to BroadBay. His solution had been for her to visit the US Department of Dragons Affairs office in Washington, D.C. to sign a contract to hand over her child after it was born. When Gina had missed her appointment with the US DDA office, BroadBay had put a price on her head.

It was then she'd decided to run to where her grandmother lived, near Loch Shin. Memories were long, and despite keeping their secrets, many of the locals had helped Gina settle in without blinking an eye after her grandmother's passing. One of the few things they'd mentioned recently was that Lochguard's leader,

Finlay Stewart, might be a leader they could reach out to and work with. From what she could tell, Clan Lochguard was nothing like BroadBay.

While maybe not the best decision, Gina would take a chance for the sake of her child. She could always reevaluate her options later. "Go ahead and call the midwife."

Fergus dialed and put the phone to his ear. Gina only hoped she hadn't made another poor choice. The past year had seen too many of them.

~~~

Waiting for Holly to answer, Fergus studied Gina MacDonald. For a human, she had quite the backbone. Even with labor possibly looming over her, she had stood her ground to get what she wanted.

He wondered how such a lass could end up in the wilds of Scotland alone and pregnant with a dragon-shifter's child.

However, before he could think too much more on it, his sister-in-law, Holly, answered, "Hello?"

Fergus replied, "Holly, I need your help. How fast can Fraser bring you to the northwest shore of Loch Shin?"

"As much as I always want to help you, I need more details than that before I commit to anything."

He frowned as he studied Gina's face for any signs of pain. Luckily, the lass hadn't cried out again. "I have a human here who is pregnant with a half-dragon-shifter child. She's had some pain and I'm concerned."

Holly sounded confused. "Lochguard doesn't have any humans currently pregnant. Even Stonefire only has one, Samira

James, and I talked with her and Dr. Sid about thirty minutes ago. Who is this human?"

Fergus's dragon growled and he sent soothing thoughts to his beast as he lowered his voice. "If you trust me at all, Holly MacKenzie, then save your questions for later. All I know is the human is very pregnant and she had some pain in her lower abdomen."

Holly answered, "Okay, but I'll bring Layla with me. She's free right now."

Layla was Lochguard's junior doctor. "No, don't. The fewer people involved, the better. I'm calling Finn after this, so just hurry up. Tell Fraser it's the white cottage with a chicken coop right behind it. There's also a stack of firewood next to it. There aren't any other cottages around here with both those features."

"Okay, but—"

Fergus ended the call. Just as he was about to dial Finn's number, Gina sucked in a breath. Reaching a hand out, he cupped her soft cheek. "Tell me what's wrong, Gina."

"Pain." She closed her eyes. Fergus stroked her cheek and she leaned into his touch.

He wondered what it would be like to have a female of his own who always did the same.

Pushing aside that thought, he focused on the human. "Keep breathing, lass. I have help coming. If they fly, they can be here in the next five minutes."

Gina finally let out a breath. Opening her eyes, she touched his arm with her hand. "They won't try to take my baby, will they?"

Seeing the strong lass's fear made his dragon snarl. *She should never be unhappy. Cuddle her close. Our touch will help her.*

But we're naked.

Right now, does that matter?

His dragon was correct. A female with pregnancy pains wasn't going to be thinking of hot sex with a dragon-shifter. "No, they won't take the bairn, Gina. Has the pain passed for now?" She nodded and he continued, "Then let me hold you in my lap until they arrive. For whatever reason, my touch relaxes you. Don't deny it."

She bit her lip. His beast growled out, *Don't let her say no.*

What is wrong with you? I'm not Fraser. I don't give in to my dragon's tantrums.

It's not a tantrum. Our female must never be in pain, if we can help it.

She's not our female. Her male could be coming at any time.

His dragon remained silent. That meant his bloody beast was thinking of a plan.

Realizing Gina hadn't answered yet, Fergus stroked her cheek again with his thumb. "Come on, lass. I bet you're curious what it's like to feel all these muscles wrapped around you."

As if on cue, she narrowed her eyes. "Muscles mean nothing if you're a bastard. I don't know you well enough to make that judgment."

It was on the tip of his tongue to say he wasn't a bastard. But his dragon's possessive urge to hold Gina surged through his body, igniting his human half's own hidden desire.

Tired of playing nice, Fergus leaned over, placed his hands underneath Gina's armpits and maneuvered her to his lap. Before she could make a sound, he wrapped his arms around her and leaned his cheek against hers.

For a second, she tensed. Then she leaned against him. Fergus chuckled. "I told you."

She turned her head to meet his eye. "Only because you're helping me will I allow it this once. But don't get any ideas."

His dragon hissed. *We should be able to hold her whenever we want.*

Not now, dragon.

Ignoring his beast, he reveled in the heat and scent of the human in his lap. It reminded him partly of why he wanted a mate—so he could share this type of closeness every day.

But Gina wasn't his and most likely never could be. He needed to forget about her and focus on his clan's safety. There were too many unknown variables with Gina; she could be a potential threat to Lochguard. Not that he wanted to believe it.

Keeping his tone light, he answered, "You should be more concerned about the DDA. Or, hell, meeting with my clan leader for that matter."

"Exactly. Which is why you should be talking to him on your cell phone instead of keeping me captive in your arms."

He should call Finn that instant, but instead, he murmured, "I'm holding you captive?" He hugged her tighter against his body, loving the softness of her arse against his groin. "Then maybe I should start taking advantage of the situation."

"You wouldn't dare."

"Hey, you're the one making me out to be the villain."

Gina opened her mouth to reply when the baby kicked against his arm. A yearning he'd hidden for years, of wanting to be a father, flooded his body. Moving his hand to the same spot, the bairn kicked again.

He expected Gina to push his hand away, but instead, she placed her warm fingers over his. Gina's voice filled the room. "Strange. He's been a quiet baby. Yet with you, he's all but dancing and causing trouble."

Afraid moving would break the spell, Fergus kept his tone neutral. "Maybe he can sense another dragon."

Fergus met Gina's eyes. The lass searched his gaze while keeping hers neutral. For the first time, Fergus had the chance to admire her green eyes flecked with gold.

Those eyes held secrets he suddenly wanted to investigate.

He dismissed the notion as nothing more than his training as an information analyst. Fergus MacKenzie lived to find out the truth so he could help his clan. His brain was hardwired to always ask questions and demand answers. It was nothing more.

It certainly wasn't because he wanted to wake up every morning with Gina MacDonald at his side.

His dragon hummed. *Yes, we should have her every day.*

Care to tell me bloody why?

You're intelligent enough to figure it out yourself.

The only reasonable answer to his dragon's behavior scared the hell out of Fergus. Gina was carrying the bairn of another dragon-shifter. Not just any dragon-shifter, but most likely a male from one of the more unstable American clans.

Lochguard already had enough trouble fighting off dragon hunters, Dragon Knights, and old traitors who had been kicked out of the clan. Finn didn't need a new enemy.

And that would be exactly what would happen if Fergus pursued Gina.

No, he'd find a female in time. One who wanted him and wouldn't cause a danger to his clan. *What do you think of that, dragon?*

His beast remained silent, which was never a good sign.

THE DRAGON GUARDIAN

~~~

Fergus's words kept repeating inside of Gina's head. *Maybe he can sense another dragon.*

The last eight months had been about keeping her child away from Travis and Clan BroadBay. Yet, had it really been for the best? Her son would need help from the dragon-shifters; only they could teach him about shifting and controlling his inner beast.

Then her son kicked again and Gina smiled. She'd made the right decision. BroadBay may be full of dragon-shifters, but they would've trained her boy to treat humans as enemies that were little more than playthings. Gina would die before allowing that to happen.

Still, there was the issue of her son's upbringing. Thinking of her babe helped to break the spell of Fergus's warm, solid muscles at her back. Or, the feel of his large hand over her belly. "Maybe you should call your leader, Fergus."

Fergus instantly removed his hand from her stomach and she nearly grabbed his wrist to bring it back. For a split second, it'd been as if she'd had a husband who would care for her baby.

Clenching her fingers, reality washed over her. Most men wanted to feel their own child kicking inside the womb. Besides, she barely knew Fergus, let alone had a claim on him.

The Scot's warm burr caressed her ear. "I will, but then I'm going to try to make your son dance again. Maybe if I tire him out, he'll take a wee nap and give you a rest."

Gina's eyes grew wet. Fergus appeared to be the kind of man who took care of a pregnant woman. Hell, he'd probably treasure her. Why couldn't she have met someone like him instead of Travis Parker?

Yet she knew the answer. Before getting pregnant, Gina had been reckless. A mere dare from her college roommate had brought on all of this mess.

Forget about 'what ifs,' Gina. You can't change the past and your son needs you to fight for him. That is all that matters.

Taking a deep breath, she was about to comment but Fergus pressed a key on his phone and placed it to his ear. A beat later, he spoke. "No, Finn. I can't call you back. Something's come up." Fergus briefly explained Gina's situation and then added, "I want to bring her to Lochguard. But she will only agree to go if she could meet with you."

Fergus frowned and Gina resisted the urge to reach a hand up and smooth the creases away. No doubt, his clan leader was yelling at him. She didn't like the idea. All he was trying to do was help her.

Fergus gritted out, "Aye," before hanging up and clutching the phone in his hand.

Despite the whiteness of his fingers holding the phone, Gina dared a question. "I somehow don't think he congratulated you on finding a pregnant human, so what did he say?"

Fergus's face relaxed and a small part of Gina was pleased. "I guess it's too much to assume you're going to be treating me like a king for all that I'm doing for you. Right, lass?"

He'd used "lass" instead of her name on purpose. She would bet her life on it. "How would your clan leader feel if I started calling you King of the Scottish Dragons?"

Fergus grinned and Gina felt as if someone had punched her in the gut. "It would irritate him to no end."

"Then why are you smiling?"

Fergus leaned close and whispered, "Because Finn is my cousin and irritating him is part of the job."

"If you think being related to the clan leader means I'm going to start treating you differently, then you're in for a surprise."

The dragonman's hot breath danced across her cheek as he said, "Never change, Gina MacDonald. I like interesting females and you are unlike any female I've ever met."

She frowned. "Are you saying that to please me and help me relax?"

Fergus paused a beat, and then answered, "You caught me."

Gina pushed aside her disappointment. Keeping her voice strong, she tsked. "I hate false words and platitudes. If you want to remain on my good side, don't do either."

"I'm on your good side, then, aye? I had assumed the opposite."

"I never said you had made it to the good list. However, if you want to graduate to it, don't lie to me or tell me what I want to hear. That got me into this trouble in the first place."

As soon as the words left her lips, Gina regretted it. The less Fergus knew about her past, the better.

Fergus tossed the phone to the side and placed his hand back on her belly. Rubbing in slow circles, Gina forgot about everything but his warm, strong touch.

Unable to stop herself, she murmured, "Damn, what I wouldn't give for a massage."

The dragonman's hand stilled. Gina searched her brain for what to say when someone knocked at the door.

CHAPTER THREE

Thank fuck for the knock at the door or Fergus might've done something daft, such as give Gina a massage.

Rubbing her belly had been maybe a little too familiar. Yet the second Gina had mentioned her past, fear and anger had flashed in her eyes. Both man and beast hadn't liked it.

Bloody hell, all Fergus wanted to do was soothe away Gina's pain and take care of her.

His dragon spoke up. *As we should. Why you fight it, I will never understand.*

Because unlike you, I can put the clan first.

You say that now, but you'll change your mind. Wait and see.

Not dignifying his beast with an answer, Fergus raised his voice. "Who is it?"

Gina muttered, "I should be the one asking," right before his twin brother's voice boomed through the door. "It's us. Now let us in. It's bloody freezing out here. Not to mention I think the sheep are a wee bit angry at my landing. I'd like to get away from them before they jump the fence."

Fergus shook his head. "Always you and the bloody sheep. Just come in. It's open."

Removing his hand from Gina's abdomen, the door opened to reveal his twin wearing a length of tartan around his waist that looked like a poor excuse for a kilt. Before he could comment on his brother's near nakedness, Gina's voice filled the room. "There are two of you?"

Grinning, Fraser winked. "Aye. Though I'm the more handsome half."

Holly shoved Fraser out of the way and shook her head, causing dark strands of hair to fall loose from her bun. "Not now, Fraser."

Holly's dark eyes locked on Gina sitting on Fergus's lap and Holly rushed toward them.

Fergus resisted the urge to hug Gina close and growl at his brother. Instead, he waited for Holly to crouch down and he focused back on Gina. The lass had tensed the second Holly had squatted down. His poor human was afraid someone would take away her bairn.

Wait a second, Gina wasn't his female. He'd better not slip again.

Holly smiled. "Hello. I'm Holly MacKenzie." She waved at Fraser. "And that's my mate, Fraser. What's your name?"

Gina answered, "Gina."

Fergus noted the omission of her surname.

Holly reached out to take Gina's wrist, but Gina moved her arm away. "Why should I trust you?"

Fergus answered before Holly. "Because I trust her, Gina. Will that do?"

Gina turned her head to meet his gaze. Fergus worked on maintaining his kind and patient expression. He didn't want to scare her.

Finally, Gina answered, "Okay."

Holly shot him a quizzical look before focusing back on the pregnant female. "Okay, Gina. Are you still in pain, hen?"

Gina shook her head, causing her hair to tickle against Fergus's chest. "No. But if it follows the same pattern, the pain will come back any minute now."

Holly nodded. "Right, then let's get you to the bed." Holly's gaze switched to Fergus. "I need you to carry her."

The corner of Fergus's mouth ticked up. "I believe I need to ask Gina's permission first."

Holly's brows came together as she looked from Fergus to Gina and back again. Thankfully, the human remained silent long enough for Gina to speak. "Just this once, Fergus. I swear it's the last time."

He chuckled. "Keep telling yourself that, lass. Deep down, you love it when I carry you."

Gina raised her middle finger and Fergus laughed. Gina was a feisty one.

Holly stood up and bent to take Gina's hands. She talked as if Gina and Fergus had never spoken. "Right, then let's get you standing first."

A second later, Gina was on her feet, revealing a stark naked Fergus. Fraser growled from across the room. "Bloody hell, Fergus. Why are you naked? You know I don't like you naked around my mate."

Fergus ignored his twin. Standing up, he scooped Gina off her feet and turned away from his brother. "Where's your room, lass?"

Her answer was monotone. "Down the hall. First door on the left."

His dragon huffed. *I don't like her so distant. We should tell the others to go away.*

As Fergus made his way down the hall, he replied, *Don't be daft. Gina needs Holly's help. If all goes well, Gina will come home to Lochguard with us.*

His dragon paused a second before replying. *Okay. Then tell Holly to hurry up so we can take her home.*

The door for the room on the left was open. Fergus stepped inside. Weak light filtered in through the windows to highlight the clothes tossed everywhere on the floor. He carefully made his way through the mess. "Good thing my mum's not here, or she'd scold you for keeping your room such a tip." Gina pinched his neck and he cried out. "What the bloody hell was that for?"

"That was for criticizing my room. It's mine and I'm free to do with it what I will."

Fergus kicked a pair of stretchy leggings off to the side. "Aye, you can. But remember, I'm trying not to drop you."

Gina muttered, "I could've walked if I had to."

Fergus gently laid Gina on the unmade bed. "Keep pinching me or kicking me behind the knee and you may well have to the next time."

Staring into Gina's eyes, he realized he was leaning over the lass on a bed. The urge to lie down next to her and pull her close was strong. He didn't like the idea of Gina MacDonald sleeping alone in the huge bed.

Not only that, the human's flushed cheeks and deep green eyes made both man and beast want to do much more than carry her around.

Gina drew in a breath and his beast snarled. *She wants us too. Kiss her. Don't think. Just do it.*

His dragon's need pumped through his body and Fergus moved his head a fraction closer to Gina's face. Darting a glance to her pink lips, he contemplated kissing her. Surely one kiss wouldn't hurt anyone or risk his clan. Meeting Gina's eyes again, they were full of heat. Her heart was also hammering in her chest.

Raising a hand, he cupped her cheek. Just as he tilted his head to kiss her, Holly cleared her throat behind him.

It was as if cold water had been splashed over his body. What the hell was he doing nearly kissing a human female? Not only that, a pregnant one carrying another's child? It wasn't as if he could mate her. Doing so might anger the DDA and hurt his clan's chances of another female sacrifice in the coming year. And Lochguard desperately needed the new blood.

As always, he needed to think of his clan first and his cock second.

His dragon roared. *She can become part of the clan. Kiss her and take care of her. I want her.*

No.

Pushing himself away, Fergus avoided Holly's eye. "Take care of her."

Without another word, he strode out into the hall. When he reached the living room, Fraser opened his mouth to ask a question but Fergus cut him off. "Not now, Fraser."

Fergus needed to clear his head without his twin's infernal questions. The only way to ensure that was to go outside and stand near the sheep pens.

Walking out the door, he ran his hands through his hair.

Bloody hell. If his beast roaring inside of his head wasn't enough, his own heart was beating double-time. Even without the lass's scent surrounding him or her tempting lips right in front of him, all Fergus could think of was pulling the human close and kissing her.

34

Just thinking of Fraser in the room with Gina made his dragon snarl. *She's ours. Go back inside and claim her before it's too late.*

Damn, he wanted to say yes and rush back inside. But unlike his beast, Fergus had responsibilities to fulfill. *I can't.*

You'd put the well-being of the clan before seizing what we've both wanted for years?

For so long Fergus had yearned for his own female. Judging by his dragon's reactions, it was entirely possible Gina was his true mate.

Yet would fate be cruel enough to give him a female he couldn't have?

She could be ours, his dragon stated.

For a split second, Fergus toyed with the idea of charging back inside the house. Then he remembered the last time his clan had been attacked by an enemy. His sister has been gravely injured and confined to a wheelchair for over a month. The next time, it could be his mother or even his cousin, Finn, who was injured.

His beast spoke up again. *Talk with Finn and find a way. We shouldn't throw away our chance.*

Rubbing his hands back and forth through his hair, Fergus tried to figure out what to do. Could he accept the risk and have everything he'd ever wanted? Searching his brain, he tried to figure out a solution.

~~~

Gina watched Fergus's tight arse as he all but ran out of the room.

She was pretty sure Fergus had wanted to kiss her. There were a million reasons why she should've pushed him away when

35

he'd been hovering so close to her body. There was her son to think of, for one. There was also the little problem of not being part of the human sacrifice program, which meant it was illegal for her to mate a dragon-shifter.

Not that she wanted to mate Fergus. Of course she didn't. The last time she'd mingled with a dragonman, she'd had her heart broken. Gina refused to go through the same thing twice.

Holly's face moved into her line of sight. The woman's dark eyes studied hers a second before stating, "Roll onto your left side and then you can tell me about your pains as I start examining you."

She nearly sighed in relief at the distraction. The midwife wasn't going to ask her about Fergus. "They've been irregular over the last few weeks. But today's were really bad."

Holly lifted up Gina's hand. Taking the skin of her finger joint between her thumb and forefinger, she pulled lightly and watched as her skin held together. The other woman met her eyes again. "How far along are you?"

"Somewhere around eight months."

Holly took Gina's wrist at the same time as she glanced at the watch on her arm. A short time later, Holly released her grip. "I don't like the 'somewhere around' part of your answer. I need to get you up to Lochguard so I can have the doctor do a proper examination." Gina hesitated in how to answer that when Holly continued, "You'll be safe, hen. I don't know how the dragon clans are in America—I'm assuming that's where the father of your child lives based on your accent—but Lochguard will do anything to protect their clan or a guest on our lands. Finn will make the ultimate decision of your fate, but not without talking with you and weighing all of the options."

Gina fingered the sheet of her bed. Deep down, she wanted nothing more than to be part of a community again. The months of near isolation, running, and hiding had taken their toll. After all, before meeting Travis Parker, Gina had been one semester away from earning her bachelor's degree in marketing. Her life had been full of nights hanging with friends and study groups that were more social get-togethers than anything else. She'd also had two roommates who were her best friends. Giving it all up for her child had been the most difficult decision of her life.

With Lochguard, Gina might have a chance to fit in. And even if most of the dragon-shifters shunned her, she would have Fergus. He might also be able to help her contact Melanie Hall-MacLeod on Clan Stonefire's lands in England. Melanie was still her best chance at having a happy future; that woman had done so much for the dragon-shifters. It gave Gina hope that Melanie would help her as well.

Holly took her hand and squeezed. "If nothing else, think of the bairn. My job is to ensure both of you are healthy but I can't do that from this cottage, Gina."

Placing her hand over her belly, Gina nodded. "I'll do it for the baby. But if you try to take him away, I will do everything in my power to get him back."

Smiling, Holly squeezed her hand again. "A lass with a backbone. You'll definitely fit in on Lochguard." Gina frowned, but Holly continued before she could say anything. "We'll wait and see if the pains continue. But the best I can tell, you have Braxton Hicks contractions brought on by dehydration and probably a touch of stress as well. Once we get some water into your system, we'll see about moving you. Does that sound okay?"

Gina liked that Holly had asked her rather than ordered her to do something. "That sounds fine."

"Good." Holly turned her head and raised her voice. "Fraser, I need your help."

Two seconds later, there was a knock on the door. A voice that sounded a lot like Fergus's, except for its tone, carried through the door. "Are both of you decent? Not that I mind if you aren't, Holly. I'd much prefer if you worked naked."

Gina snorted as Holly sighed. She kept her voice low to Gina. "I apologize in advance for Fraser. He lives to tease me."

Fraser's voice filled the room. "I heard you, honey. Now, may I come in?"

"Hurry up."

Fraser strode into the room with a grin and stopped at Holly's side. As Fraser wrapped an arm around the woman, a twinge of jealously shot through Gina's body. At one time, she'd thought she'd had the same with Travis.

No. She wouldn't think of that asshole. Instead, she looked to Fraser. His blue eyes were the same shade as Fergus's, but the kindness mixed with steel was missing. Fraser's gaze was more one of humor and curiosity.

Fraser spoke up. "Hello, Gina. I would ask you why you were sitting on my brother's lap earlier, but I don't want to face Holly's wrath if I make you uncomfortable." He brushed Holly's cheek. "What do you need help with, honey?"

Gina should bite her tongue, but she blurted out, "I didn't think Scots used the term 'honey' as an endearment. At least, I never heard it in any of the TV shows I watched."

Fraser answered, "Aye, well, it's different with Holly. If you stick around long enough, I'll tell you the story of how I charmed this lass into being my mate."

Holly attempted to frown, but ended up smiling. "We'll talk about that later. For now, we need to figure a way to transport

38

Gina to Lochguard." Holly looked to Gina. "I saw a car parked out back. Does it work?"

Gina nodded. "Yes. Otherwise, I'd have to walk everywhere and the nearest store is hours away by foot."

Holly lightly patted Fraser's chest. "I don't trust your driving, so I'll do it." Fraser put on a mock expression of disappointment and Gina snorted. Holly winked at Gina before answering her man, "In the meantime, you can fetch some water and make sure Fergus is okay. One of you can fly ahead and one can ride in the car with us. I'll let the two of you decide amongst yourself. Just try not to start wrestling each other in the process."

"Wrestling each other?" Gina echoed.

Holly beat Fraser to the reply. "Oh, just wait. You might just meet the whole family together and you'll be begging to come back to this cottage for some peace and quiet."

Fraser squeezed his woman's waist. "Hey now. You're one of us now, too. And you know you love it." He leaned closer and whispered loudly, "Just as you love me. You'd wither and die without me, honey. You know it."

Gina blinked. She had thought Fergus's teasing was bad. But Fraser's would drive her crazy if he kept it up. How Holly dealt with it on a regular basis, Gina had no idea. She must really love the dragonman.

Holly gave Fraser a quick kiss and released him. "Go. And don't forget the glass of water."

"Yes, ma'am."

Fraser left the room and Holly removed the stethoscope from around her neck. "Let's have a wee listen to your son's heartbeat."

Gina burned with questions, but she managed to remain silent as Holly examined her. Maybe, just maybe, Lochguard would give her the answers she was looking for. Not only that, but deep down she hoped they might offer her a home as well. Gina was tired of running.

CHAPTER FOUR

Fergus gripped the fence posts and stared out at the choppy waters of the loch. He'd always loved sitting atop the wee island in the middle of the water to watch the locals. Be it cars driving down the road, humans visiting with their neighbors, or the shearing of the sheep, Fergus had always been careful not to frighten anyone. The everyday actions of humans fascinated him.

His interest was in part because of his love of the old human stories of the Highlands. But it was also because he'd always kept a look out for a female who could be his true mate.

Despite his years of searching, he'd never found her. Well, unless his dragon's recent behavior signaled he had.

His dragon roared. *Why do you doubt me? I've tried being nice about it, but I'm done. Go after her or I'll take control.*

Don't test me, dragon. I'm not in the mood.

His beast hissed. *She is our best chance for happiness. Don't waste it.*

Fergus pounded the fence post with his fist. *She can't be.*

His dragon spoke up again. *She is. You're the romantic who's dreamed of nothing but having a family. My instinct is to fuck and claim her. If you wish to woo her first, then stop denying the truth or we'll do it my way.*

Fergus growled. *Stop threatening me and think for a second. We know very little about the lass. She's running from something, and someone wants her child. If we claim her, she'll endanger the clan. Do you want Mum or anyone else to be hurt because of your desire to mate?*

Nothing will happen to them. Finn is a strong leader. He'll make things work.

Before Fergus could reply, something furry rubbed against his legs. Looking down, a pair of yellow cat eyes in the midst of a black face stared up at him with curiosity.

Then the cat meowed and his anger eased a fraction. Fergus had always had a soft spot for cats; only his sister's allergy had prevented him from having one. Keeping his dragon contained, Fergus smiled down at the wee animal. "Well now, who do we have here?"

The cat meowed again and Fergus noticed the collar. "Are you Gina's cat?"

As if understanding him, the furry beast swished his tail. Fergus slowly lowered his hand and offered it for the feline to sniff. The wet, black nose tickled the tips of his fingers. Moving slowly again, he scratched behind the cat's ear and it purred.

Fergus was about to pick up the wee beastie when the front door banged open. The feline ran away. If the black cat was indeed Gina's, Fergus would need to find it later.

His dragon broke free and spoke up again. *And why is that? Shut it, dragon.*

Turning his head, Fergus spotted Fraser. Great. Judging by the twinkle in his twin's eye, he was going to tease Fergus about the human.

His dragon snarled. *If he says anything bad about Gina, then punch him in the face.*

Fergus cleared his throat and greeted his brother. "How's Gina doing?"

Fraser tilted his head. "Curious about the lass, are you?"

42

He growled. "Fraser."

Fraser put out his arms and shrugged. "What? Considering she was sitting in your naked lap, I think we're past your 'I need to protect everyone because I'm an honorable male' excuse, brother."

Fergus kept his tone neutral. "I was perched on the nearby mountain and saw her double over in pain. An arsehole like yourself might look the other way, but I just want to help the lass."

His twin crossed his arms over his chest. "Your forced 'neutral' tone might work with strangers, but not me. What was it you asked me after you punched me a couple months ago for keeping the secret of Holly being my true mate from you? To just be honest? Well I'm bloody trying and I need you to try, too."

His dragon chimed in. *He's right. Tell him. Then Fraser will stay clear of Gina and let us claim her.*

While he hadn't agreed to claim anyone, Fergus paused a second and studied his twin. In their twenty-nine years, Fraser had always been able to keep the biggest secrets when asked.

His beast huffed. *Just tell him. Fraser will tell you the same as me—to hurry and claim Gina.*

Fraser raised an eyebrow. "Now you're arguing with your dragon? I really want to know what's going on and you know when I'm determined, I don't give up."

"Aye, but I can resist as long as necessary. Your tricks won't work with me."

Fraser's eyes turned concerned. "I don't want to use my tricks on you, Fergus. I want to know how to help you, if you need it. Is the lass your true mate? Even if she's pregnant, your dragon might still feel the pull."

Fergus ran a hand through his hair and decided to trust his brother. "Honestly? My beast wants to claim her right now. But it's not as if I can take the lass home and woo her. She's pregnant with a dragon-shifter's child, Fraser. I have the sense she's running away from the father of her bairn."

Fraser finished his thought. "And Lochguard has too many enemies already."

"Exactly."

"You're an idiot, Fergus Roger MacKenzie."

Fergus blinked. "Pardon?"

"I-D-I-O-T. Idiot. You've been fantasizing about finding your mate for years. I know you think you've hidden it most of the time, but I'm your best friend. I know you better than anyone in the world." Fraser leaned forward and searched his eyes. "If Gina is your chance, don't fuck it up."

Fergus's dragon preened. *He's on my side. That's two against one.*

It's not a bloody democracy.

Yet a part of Fergus was starting to think he could at least try to woo the lass.

His dragon snarled. *More than woo. Fuck, claim, and protect.*

When Fergus didn't answer his twin, Fraser rolled his eyes. "You're always so bloody logical. I don't know how your dragon puts up with you."

"Gee, thanks, brother."

Fraser ignored him. "If nothing else, it can't hurt to talk with Finn. Considering what he did for his mate, Arabella, and for my Holly, he might be able to work some magic for you, too. All of the MacKenzie men deserve love."

"Finn's a Stewart, not a MacKenzie."

Fraser shook his head. "Don't start, Fergus. You know what I mean—everyone we love should have the gift of a mate. I'm sure even our stubborn-headed sister will find someone eventually."

As he stared at the face so like his own, hope flickered in Fergus's chest. His twin might have a point.

His dragon huffed. *Will you listen now?*

At his beast's prodding, Fergus quickly tamped down his hope and used his logic again. "I don't know how the lass even feels about me. She barely knows me."

Fraser grinned. "Then woo her and kiss her. Even if she's your true mate, there won't be a mate-claim frenzy as long as she's pregnant or breastfeeding. You might have a rare opportunity to get to know her before you fuck her."

"You were always such a romantic."

"Bloody right I am." Fraser closed the distance between them and gripped Fergus's shoulder. "You thought Holly might be your last chance at finding a mate. But what if you've been given another chance? The lass clearly likes you or she wouldn't have allowed you in her cottage, let alone sat in your lap and let you touch her belly."

"You saw that?" Fergus asked.

"Aye, through the window."

With any other person, Fergus would explain away the situation. Yet as he looked into eyes the exact shape of his own, Fergus never wanted to lie to his twin brother ever again. "I'll test out the waters first with Gina before I talk to Finn. I don't want to give our cousin a new problem to solve if the human female feels differently from me and my dragon."

Fraser slapped his shoulder. "Good lad."

"But."

45

Fraser sighed. "Is this where you have a million caveats to add to make everything more difficult than it has to be?"

Fergus grunted. "Not all of us toss caution to the wind on a whim."

"I'm going to let that slide just this once since I promised Holly I wouldn't start a wrestling match. I'm sure punching you would also land me in trouble."

"Fraser," Fergus growled.

"Fine, fine. I'll behave. Just finish your bloody sentence so we can go back inside. It's fucking cold out here."

"My caveat is that I don't want any interfering. I won't ask you to hold the information from Holly, but don't tell anyone else, not even Mum. If either of you try to meddle, I'll tell Finn and Arabella about the giant hogweed you planted in their yard. Finn won't take it well."

Giant hogweed could cause a painful rash when rubbed on the skin and exposed to sunlight.

Fraser narrowed his eyes. "You said you'd keep that in confidence."

He shrugged. "Then don't meddle with Gina. It's as simple as that."

A gust of wind nearly blew off the material around Fraser's waist. "Fine. Can we go back inside now?"

"You're such a bloody lightweight. Dragon-shifters are supposed to be tough."

"I am tough, but there's nothing wrong with a little comfort. This isn't the bloody dark ages."

Fergus pointed over Fraser's shoulder. "Oh, no. Some of the sheep jumped over the fence."

Fraser whipped around. "Where?"

He laughed and Fraser realized he'd been tricked. Getting a hold of himself again, Fergus said, "Just because one of the rams hit you in the dick with their horns doesn't mean all sheep are out to get you. Being afraid of the animals ruins your alpha image."

Fraser gave him the two finger salute. "I'm going inside with or without you."

His twin turned and dashed into the cottage. Taking a deep breath, Fergus followed.

As per usual, talking with Fraser had led to Fergus possibly causing trouble.

Of course, Gina could tell him to fuck off and then he wouldn't have to burden Finn.

His dragon hissed. *Not before you at least kiss her. One taste and you won't be able to stop yourself.*

You wouldn't be able to, but I could. If she says no, I won't force her.

She won't say no.

I can't deal with your cockiness right now.

Ignoring his dragon, Fergus entered the cottage. If he planned to see if Gina not only wanted him but was worth the trouble of asking for Finn's help, then he wasn't going to hold back. It was time to pursue the human and see how she handled it.

~~~

As Gina sipped her glass of water, she watched Holly jot down something in her notebook. While no one had told Gina whether Holly was a dragon-shifter or not, her gut said the woman was human. This might be a prime time to ask how Lochguard treated humans.

Before Gina could say anything, Holly glanced up with a smile. "I can feel you watching me. If you have any questions, hen, feel free to ask. As soon as the twins come back, I'm not sure if we'll ever have a moment of privacy."

Despite sensing an undertone to Holly's words, Gina ignored it. After swallowing her water, she asked, "Are you human?"

"Aye, I am. I arrived on Lochguard as a human sacrifice a little over two months ago."

Gina should try to be polite and work her way up to the bigger questions, but she'd never been good at restraining her mouth. She blurted out, "So are you pregnant, too?"

Holly gave a sad smile. "I was, but I lost the bairn."

"I'm so sorry."

Holly waved a hand. "Don't worry about it. If Fraser has any say in the matter, we'll probably have ten kids in the next ten years, if stamina equates pregnancy."

Gina's cheeks flushed. Sometimes, she hated being a redhead with fair skin. "He's your true mate, then?"

"Aye, he is." Holly paused. Her voice was gentle when she continued. "If Finn allows you to stay, you can always come talk to me if you need it. The MacKenzies are a handful and sometimes it's nice to merely sit with a cuppa, a biscuit, and enjoy some human company."

She was about to reply about how she'd like that when the twins waltzed into the room. A quick glance told Gina both had material wrapped around their waists. She instantly met Fergus's eyes and the determined look made her shiver.

Clearing her throat, Gina pushed past her attraction. "I see it takes company for you to cover yourself, Fergus."

"Aye, well, Fraser threatened to walk around naked if I didn't cover up. And if you saw him, then I'd have to kick his arse."

Fraser shoved his brother. "More like I'd kick yours for showing Holly your goods again."

As the twins growled at one another, Holly clapped her hands. "Enough, lads. Did you decide who's flying ahead and who's riding with Gina?"

Fergus took a step forward. "I'm riding with Gina."

His words held a sort of dominance, as if Gina should meekly obey. "Maybe I want Fraser to ride with me. He has yet to invade my personal space, after all."

Fergus growled. "If he tries it, then he'll deal with me."

Holly frowned and looked to Fraser. Fraser nodded toward the hall. "Come here for a second, honey. I want to talk to you about something before I fly back to Lochguard."

Holly's gaze moved back to Gina. "Will you be okay in the room alone with Fergus?"

Fergus answered before Gina had a chance. "Of course she will."

Picking up a pillow from the bed, she tossed it at Fergus. "Stop speaking for me. I have a brain and know how to talk. I can make my own decisions."

His eyes flashed to dragon slits and back. "In this, I'm making the decision."

She barely registered Fraser tugging Holly out of the room and shutting the door. Gina scooted to the edge of the bed with her glass of water still in hand. Narrowing her eyes, she stood up. "What's wrong with you? If you're trying to act macho and alpha in front of your brother, then I really don't want to sit in a car

49

with you for who the hell knows how long. I'm sure Fraser and Holly will protect me."

Closing the distance between them, Fergus leaned close to her face. "I'm the only one who will be protecting you, Gina MacDonald."

Her voice was faint as she asked, "And why is that?"

He brushed her cheek and it took everything she had not to lean into his touch. "I know you feel the attraction between us."

Her eyes darted to his lips and back up again. "Attraction leads to trouble."

Raising his other hand, Fergus cupped her cheek. "I will hunt down the bastard who hurt you later, Gina. But right now, you shouldn't be thinking of another male."

She should push Fergus away and call for Holly. Instead, she asked, "And why is that?"

Fergus's eyes flashed and she swallowed. The predatory look in his eyes shot straight between her thighs.

Leaning a fraction closer to her lips, the heat of Fergus's breath tickled her lips. "Because you should be thinking of me. Let me kiss you, Gina MacDonald. I can think of nothing else but your soft, sweet lips or your warm mouth." He caressed her cheeks with his thumbs. "Kiss me and then decide what to do with me."

Her heart thundered inside her chest. Between Fergus's touch and heat, Gina was starting to forget why she should stay away from the dragonman in front of her. He wanted her. Not only that, thanks to him, she might have a future where she could keep her child.

Surely one kiss wouldn't be the end of the world.

Before she could change her mind, Gina whispered, "Okay."

In the next second, Fergus's lips descended on hers. His warm, firm lips sent a shiver through her body. Then he placed a hand on her back and drew her body closer until her belly lightly brushed his groin. The heat of his body against hers made Gina moan, and Fergus slipped his tongue inside her mouth.

Each stroke only made her crave more. Damn, his taste was addictive. Never had a man tasted so good.

He lightly pressed her tighter and she could feel his hard dick. The touch only made her wetter.

Fergus moved his hand to lightly tug her hair and took the kiss deeper. Her knees grew weak and only leaning against his muscled body prevented her from falling over.

Realizing she still had the damned water glass in her hand, she tossed it to the side and it landed on a pile of clothes. As she fisted Fergus's hair, the dragonman nipped her lips. She tugged and he did it again.

Her nipples ached and she moved until they brushed his chest. The fabric of her shirt only added to the delicious friction.

Growling, Fergus roamed a hand over her waist, her back, and finally gripped her ass.

Images of what his large, rough hands could do to her breasts and between her thighs flooded her mind.

Just as she was about to grip Fergus's tight butt, a knock at the door brought her back to reality. Breaking the kiss, she raised her fingers to her lips and met Fergus's eyes. They were full of heat and changing between dragon eyes and human ones.

The sight brought back a memory of another dragonman looking at her exactly the same way.

She was such a fool.

Turning her back on Fergus, Gina shut her eyes and took deep breaths through her nose. She needed to kill the problem with Fergus before it morphed into something dangerous. If he thought to kiss and fondle her in hopes of taking her to bed, he was in for a surprise. Gina MacDonald wasn't about to be fooled twice. She wouldn't trust her body, let alone her heart, with a dragonman again.

Fergus touched her shoulder and she flinched. His voice was neutral as it filled the air. "What's wrong, lass? Is it the bairn again?"

She was saved from answering by a more insistent knock and Fraser's voice. "Open the door, Fergus, or I'll start listing the reasons why you locked it."

With a curse, Fergus removed his hand. Gina let out a sigh. Without Fergus's touch or presence nearby, her brain started to function again. Good thing as she needed to think of a plan to keep Fergus MacKenzie and his delicious kisses far away from her. It was the only way to protect herself from a repeat of what had happened with Travis Parker.

Chapter Five

Fergus clenched his jaw as he walked toward the door. The lass had flinched at his touch and he didn't like it.

His dragon spoke up. *We need to erase her bad memories. The American clan hurt her. We will need to replace those memories with good ones.*

Humans, especially females, are different than you, dragon. They need time to trust again.

Time is what we don't have. If BroadBay wants the bairn, it's only a matter of time before they find her.

Not sure how to reply to that statement, Fergus unlocked the door and tugged it open. He met Fraser's eyes. "What the bloody hell do you want?"

Fraser grinned. "My, my. Someone's testy."

Clenching his fingers into a fist, Fergus debated hitting his brother. But Holly stepped between them before he could act. "Fraser's about to leave and just wants to check with Gina in case she has anything she'd like to pass on to Finn."

Gina's voice filled the room. "No need. Fraser's riding in the car with us. Fergus can fly ahead."

Fergus blinked and looked over his shoulder. "What? Why?"

Crossing her arms over her chest, Gina raised her eyebrow. "You have no say over me. I'm not your family or your wife. I appreciate your help in getting Holly here, but now it's time for you to leave."

Fergus barely heard his twin whistle as he turned toward his human and narrowed his eyes. "I'm not about to let the flirty bastard in the car with you. I'll be riding in the backseat next to you. It's the only way I can protect you."

"I'm sure Fraser can protect me just as well. Unless you're going to tell me your brother is a useless piece of crap who can't take care of himself, let alone anyone else?"

Fraser walked toward them. "Hey now—"

Fergus cut his twin off. "After what just happened, I thought you'd want me to protect you."

The second he said it, surprise flashed across Gina's face. Then her jaw tightened. His dragon roared in the back of his head to stop it, but Fergus ignored his beast.

Holly moved to Gina's side and wrapped an arm around her shoulders. "Fergus, fly ahead."

He growled and looked to his sister-in-law. To her credit, she didn't so much as raise an eyebrow. "No."

"I'm the midwife and you're causing Gina stress. Fly your arse ahead or I will involve both Finn and Lorna in this."

Fergus didn't back down. "I'm not a teenager. I'm not afraid of my mum."

Fraser laid a hand on his shoulder. Fergus swiveled his head to the side. "Now is not the time to touch me, brother."

"Bloody hell," Fraser murmured. "Fly ahead, Fergus. You're both frightening and pissing off your human."

Gina spoke up. "I'm not his human."

Fraser never took his eyes from Fergus's. "If you want what we discussed, then leave. I swear on our mother's life, I won't touch her."

Fergus's dragon snarled. *We can't leave Fraser alone with her. He may try to claim Gina.*

At the mentioning of his brother pursuing Gina, the angry haze lifted a fraction from his brain. *He has a mate.*

Maybe he'll revert to what the dragons did a millennium ago and take multiple mates.

The ridiculous statement cleared his head further. Fergus glanced around the room. Everyone was staring at him, waiting to see what he'd do next.

What the hell had gotten into him?

Before his dragon could poison his thoughts and push him over the edge, Fergus gave a curt nod. "I'll fly ahead."

With one last look at Gina, Fergus stormed from the room. Her pregnancy may prevent a mate-claim frenzy, but it was clear his dragon wanted her. He'd thought she'd wanted him too.

Maybe he'd been too domineering. Fergus had always been the respectful and patient twin. Losing sight of that might have cost him his lass.

And yes, after Gina moaning into his mouth as she leaned against him for support, he finally agreed with his dragon. Gina was his female and true mate. After all this time, he'd finally found her.

However, the kiss had spooked her. Fergus needed to find out more about the bastard father of her child so he could think of how to handle the situation. While patience was usually one of his best traits, his dragon paced in the back of his mind. The action reminded him of what might happened if he took too long.

His dragon hissed. *Exactly. I will take her and claim her. She is ours. We should keep her away from the others.*

I agree, but I need some time.

Hurry up. Even without the mate-claim frenzy, I want her. No, I need her.

Fergus reached the clearing outside and took off the material around his waist. As chilly air brushed against his skin, Fergus weighed all of his options. Surely one of them would give him a way to win over Gina's trust.

Not only that, he was going to have to talk to Finn. Secrets had nearly torn his family apart two months ago. Fergus wasn't about to chance it again. The only question was whether his clan leader would be able to help the human or not.

~~~

Despite her show of bravado, Gina's heart thundered inside her chest.

She was alone with Holly and Fraser. Despite the fact that was what she wanted, the room felt emptier without Fergus's presence.

She never should've kissed him. Deep down, she would admit it was the best kiss of her life, even better than with Travis. But a kiss didn't equate caring and love, only lust. Just like with Travis, Fergus would discard her in the end.

Wouldn't he?

Holly touched her arm and Gina met the woman's eyes; the midwife's gaze was calm and collected. "Are you okay?"

Taking a deep inhalation, Gina nodded. "I'm fine. A little tired and anxious about my future, but fine. Give me five minutes to pack and we can leave. Oh, and we need to find Coal."

Holly blinked. "Who's Coal?"

"My black cat."

Fraser and Holly traded knowing glances and smiled. She was about to ask what was going on when Coal strode into the room as if he owned it. As her cat rubbed against her legs, she tried to figure out how he was inside.

Squatting down carefully so she wouldn't lose her balance and fall over, Gina scooped Coal up and held him close. As she breathed in the scent of cat and outdoors, another faint scent greeted her nose.

Fergus. He'd brought in her cat.

Stroking her pet, Gina's uneasiness faded. Coal hated all of the men in the area and had bitten more than a few. Yet Coal had trusted Fergus enough to allow the dragonman to pick him up. Maybe there was more to Fergus than she'd thought. After all, before Holly and Fraser had arrived, he'd been rubbing her belly and talking about her son.

The only question was whether she wanted to risk her heart by trying to get to know the real Fergus MacKenzie or not.

Holly cleared her throat. "I can fetch the cat carrier whilst you pack."

Pushing aside thoughts of a certain dragonman, Gina smiled. "Oh, no need. Coal likes riding in the car."

"Pardon?" Holly asked.

Gina hugged her pet close. "He may look like a cat, but he acts more like a dog. You'll see." She kissed the top of Coal's head and placed him on the bed. "Still, let me toss a few things together and we can leave. But Fraser, can you go to the closet in the living room and find the wooden cradle there? It was my grandmother's and I want to bring it with me."

Fraser nodded and left the room.

Once they were alone, Holly spoke up. "If you ever need to talk with me about dragon-shifter males, I'm here, Gina."

Gina glanced over at Holly. The midwife was more perceptive than she'd given Holly credit for. "The only thing that matters right now is my upcoming meeting with your clan leader. He's the one who will decide my future."

Holly opened her mouth but then promptly closed it. As the woman retrieved clothes from one of the drawers, Gina wondered why Holly held back. It conflicted with everything Gina had seen thus far.

Before she could think of how to poke without being obvious about it, Fraser returned with her grandmother's cradle in one hand and a cat carrier in the other. Coal growled at the sight of the carrier and Gina stroked his back. "He really doesn't like the carrier. But if you can get him in there, then we'll take him that way."

Holly's voice was full of laughter. "Aye, Fraser. It's good practice. After all, you promised me ten cats."

Fraser winked at his mate. "No worries, honey. It should be easy."

Gina blinked. "Ten cats? Am I missing something?"

Fraser ignored her. After setting down the cradle, he made clicking sounds at Coal. "Here, kitty. You know you want to help me out. Us males need to stick together."

As the dragonman inched toward her cat and stuck out his fingers, Coal sniffed a second before butting his head against Fraser's hand. The sight of the tall, muscled dragonman scratching her cat's ears made her smile. Coal was very picky about who he let pet him, not that a person could tell from his recent dealings. Could it be that not all dragon-shifters had hidden agendas?

Fraser set the cat carrier on the bed, opened the door, and retrieved something from inside the carrier. Once he held it up, Gina saw it was a piece of cheese.

Waving the piece, Fraser whispered, "Here, kitty, kitty."

Scrunching his nose and sniffing the air, Coal moved toward Fraser. Gina watched in awe as Fraser finally coaxed her cat into the carrier and clicked it shut. Fraser looked up with a grin. "He doesn't seem bothered to me."

Holly chuckled and rubbed Fraser's arm. "Good. Then I don't see why we can't adopt a cat or two once we're back." Fraser opened his mouth to reply, but Holly beat him to it. "Unless you're doubting your cat whisperer abilities?"

Fraser stood up taller. "Of course not. But let's take care of Gina first." Fraser met Gina's eyes. "We'll help prepare you for my cousin. A few tricks might help your case with him."

Gina frowned. "Why are you so interested in helping me? You barely know me."

Fraser shook his head. "The American bastards must've done a number on you. Just know that us Scots are different. We like to help someone in need."

She sensed there was something he wasn't telling her. But her baby kicked, garnering her attention.

Okay, little one. Thanks for reminding me of what's important. Gina needed to figure out her future. Dealing with the MacKenzies and sorting out their secrets would have to wait.

~ ~ ~

Fergus snatched one of the spare plaids tucked into the wall of Lochguard's main landing area and wrapped it around his body. Once he finished, he headed toward Finn's cottage.

His dragon paced at the back of his mind. *Finn had better agree or I will challenge him.*

Finn will do all he can. But not even he will do something to endanger the clan. That's the best we can hope for.

His beast snarled. *Why are you so calm? Even now, she rides with your brother. Until she is our mate and living in our cottage, the others might try to take her.*

Your desire to claim the lass will scare her off.

But I want her.

Aye, I know. But let's try my way first.

His dragon sniffed. *You're one to talk. You fucked up pretty badly back near the loch.*

Because of you. If you would just bloody calm down, I could think properly.

I would say it was your own hidden desire, but you'd deny it. I'll just say this—if I don't see any progress in the next few days, I'll try it my way.

Taking a deep breath, Fergus merely shook his head. *It won't come to that.*

I see someone's confidence has returned.

Ignoring his dragon, Fergus picked up his pace.

Clenching and unclenching his fingers, he was impatient to put his plan in motion. If Finn agreed, Fergus might have enough time to win over the lass before the bairn arrived.

Of course, his dragon's need to fuck Gina continued to course through his body. At this rate, he'd meet Finn with a hard cock.

Since telling his beast to stop would fall on deaf ears, Fergus imagined some of the older dragonwomen in bikinis, and his dick softened again. *Good.* He'd keep the images handy for the next time he saw Gina. They might help him better manage his dragon's desire.

60

He approached the two-story cottage with overgrown shrubs in front of it. Knocking on Finn's door, he schooled his face into a neutral expression.

The scarred face of Arabella MacLeod, Finn's pregnant mate, greeted him. After scrutinizing him a second, she stepped to the side and motioned with a hand. "Finn's waiting for you."

Fergus nodded. "Aye, I expect he is." Arabella said nothing as he rushed past, but her eyes were full of questions.

Finn opened the door to his study just as Fergus approached. His cousin's amber eyes were hard, which never boded well. "Get your arse in here, Fergus MacKenzie. I had to reschedule our meeting with both Bram and the human soldier and let me tell you, neither were happy about it."

Finn retreated into the room and Fergus followed, shutting the door behind him. "You didn't tell them about the human female, did you?"

"No, of course not." The irritation eased a fraction from Finn's eyes. "Fraser texted to say the lass is better now."

Fergus let out a sigh of relief. "I'm glad. I didn't like seeing her in pain."

Finn steepled his fingers in front of him. "I imagine not. But let's cut to the chase, cousin. I need more details than the fact Gina is carrying a dragon-shifter's child and is in hiding. I can understand wanting to be cautious over the phone, but if I'm to decide the lass's future, I need a lot more information."

Fergus's dragon growled, but he ignored his beast. "The lass's name is Gina MacDonald. She's American and on the run to keep her child. The first time I met her, she mentioned Clan BroadBay."

"Fuck," Finn muttered. "I hope the father isn't from BroadBay."

Fergus nodded. "If it's truly them, I wouldn't blame her for running. Their brutal and narcissistic reputation precedes them. The only question is if you'll offer her protection and allow her to stay."

"I think the bigger questions are how do you know so much about the lass and why were you watching her in the first place?"

His dragon spoke up. *Tell him the truth. It will give Gina the greatest chance for safety.*

Give me a chance, you bloody beast.

Finn crossed his arms over his chest and remained silent. Standing up straight, Fergus answered, "My dragon wants her."

His cousin raised his brows. "And how do you know this? If she's pregnant, she won't stir the mate-claim frenzy."

"Aye, but my beast is insistent. Even more so after I kissed her. You of all people should understand the significance."

Finn's dragon had wanted the nearly uncatchable Arabella MacLeod. Only through perseverance had Finn won Arabella's heart. "You've mentioned your dragon, but what about the human female? I won't keep her here against her will, Fergus. Do you think she'd want to stay with you, too?"

"I don't know, but I have a proposal, if you'd like to hear it."

Finn motioned a hand. "By all means. The fewer plans I have to devise, the more time I can spend with my mate."

"I didn't plan to burden you with this, Finn. I hope you know that."

His clan leader smiled. "Of course I do. Our dragons are unpredictable at best. And considering you're here talking to me about it, you're already doing better than your brother."

Fraser had kept the secret of Holly being his true mate from everyone and had caused a lot of trouble in the process. "Aye, well, I think we all learned from that." Finn nodded and Fergus continued, "I'm not sure if you've paid attention over the years, but I've been collecting human myths about our kind."

"It was mentioned, although I can't say I paid too much attention."

"You always were more interested in talking with people in the present than learning about the past, so I can't blame you."

Finn shrugged. "We all have our strengths. Your obsessive attention to details has helped the clan more often than you know."

Fergus gathered intelligence for Finn and the Lochguard Protectors. "Well, it's going to prove useful in this instance as well. Have you ever heard of the Dragon Guardians of Scotland?" Finn shook his head and Fergus explained. "Back when the humans lived together in clans, dragon-shifters had much closer relationships with humans than they do today. The humans even fostered their own kind of sacrifice system by marrying off daughters of the lairds to some of the dragon-shifters. That way, the dragons wouldn't try to attack them and would even help protect the human clans from invaders."

"That much I do know. Get to the bit about the Guardians."

Fergus hated to be rushed, but Finn was a busy dragonman. "Since there wasn't a DDA, the lairds set up a type of protection for their daughters. A dragon-shifter acted as a Guardian to the female during the first year she lived on a dragon clan's lands. If anything happened to the daughter, the Guardian would be held responsible and be executed by the human laird."

"Sounds like a fun job," Finn drawled.

Fergus ignored Finn's comment. "The best Guardians performed their duties for their entire lives. They earned reputations in the Highlands as protectors of humankind. While the truth is somewhat less brilliant, the job was an important one. Only those with patience, strong wills, and an innate desire to protect were selected."

"And how do the Guardians relate to the human female?"

Standing up tall, Fergus answered, "I want to bring the practice back and be Gina's Guardian. For the first year, I will guarantee her safety and watch out for her and the bairn. At the end of the year, we'll see if she still requires my protection."

His clan leader studied him a second before finally replying, "How often did the Guardians of old take their charges as mates?"

"Not often. Leaders weren't as concerned about true mates and happiness as they were survival in those days. Alliances were often more important than love."

"Aye, but this is the 21st century, Fergus. You say your dragon wants the lass, yet you want to protect her. The most important question is if you can protect her from yourself?"

His dragon growled. *We would never hurt her.*

Clenching his fingers, Fergus took a step toward Finn's desk. "If I feel my dragon seizing control, I will tell you. In that instance, I'm sure Faye and my mum would look after her. Faye may no longer be a Protector, but she still has all of the training."

"I'm sure this sounds fantastic inside your head, but what if the lass rejects you? She's been hurt and may not open up for quite some time. Hell, for all we know, she might still love the father of her child. Even if fate decrees you as true mates, there is the possibility Gina will fight it and deny you."

Only through sheer force of will did Fergus keep his dragon in check at the mention of Gina loving the bastard who hurt her. "Did you let that stop you with Arabella?"

Finn smiled fondly, no doubt at the memory of pursuing his mate. "Good point, cousin." His clan leader paused a second and continued, "Before I even attempt to convince the DDA of allowing the human to live here long-term, I want to meet this Gina MacDonald and assess if she's a threat to the clan. If she passes my check, then you still need to convince the human to accept you as her Guardian."

"I'm fairly sure I can convince her. But, if I can coax the lass to agree, BroadBay might try to take her back. Can the clan handle another threat?"

Finn waved a hand. "You always worry too much about the clan. In this, you focus on Gina and I will deal with BroadBay if they show up." His clan leader gripped his shoulder. "You are one of the hardest working and least recognized clan members, Fergus. You deserve a chance to seize your own happy ending. And not just because you're my cousin. You're a fine male, Fergus MacKenzie. Any female would be lucky to have you."

Fergus had never been good with praise, so he didn't acknowledge it. "So when will you have a decision?"

"That anxious to have the female to yourself, eh, Fergus?"

Fergus frowned. "Not all of us think solely with our cocks. She's alone and on the run. I bet she wants to know what her future holds for both her and her son."

Finn sighed dramatically. "You always were the logical and noble one, Fergus."

Grinning, Fergus winked. "Well, someone had to be. My mum needed an ally to help with the responsibilities, and you and Fraser weren't about to do it."

"We were a bunch of wild teenagers, weren't we?" Finn's mobile phone beeped with a text message. "Sorry to cut short our walk down memory lane, but that's probably Grant wanting to talk about Gina's background check. Go home and put on some clothes. I'll let you know when and where to meet Gina after I talk with her."

Fergus nodded. "Okay, but just don't scare the human too much. She's quite pregnant and Arabella will have your hide if she finds out you scared a pregnant woman."

"Hey, now, I don't scare people. I just hint that it's in their best interests to behave."

The door opened before Fergus could reply. Arabella stood in the doorway. "Grant's pestering me to the point I had to get off the couch. Call him, Finn, so I can take a nap."

Finn's expression turned concerned as he walked to his mate's side. "Are you okay, Ara? Do I need to call Dr. Innes?"

Arabella sighed. "No, for the tenth time today, I don't need the doctor."

Placing a hand over the small bump of Arabella's abdomen, Finn whispered, "Come on, babies. Give your mum a rest. Otherwise, she's cranky."

"Finn," Arabella growled.

Having heard Finn and Arabella's back and forth over the triplets before, Fergus motioned toward the door with his head. "Call me when you're ready, Finn."

His cousin nodded and Fergus rushed out of the cottage. Breathing in the cool winter air stirred his dragon. *I wish he'd stop being overprotective with Arabella. It's really irritating me.*

Fergus snorted. *As if you'd be any better. If we can convince Gina of the Guardian idea, you'll be just as protective.*

Maybe. But it won't matter because then she will be ours.

Not quite, dragon. Protecting her and winning her over are two different things.

If you say so.

Despite the possible danger to his clan and the very real chance Gina would tell him to fuck off instead of agreeing to his being her Guardian, there was a small flicker of hope in his chest. The thought of waking up next to Gina in his bed and feeling the kick of a child under his palm sent a rush of warmth through his body. He'd nearly given up hope he'd ever have a family of his own. And now, he might have one.

The trick would be in convincing the headstrong American to stay with him.

CHAPTER SIX

Gina waited inside the Protector's security building at the main gate and willed herself to sit still.

Yes, she was a tad nervous about meeting Lochguard's clan leader, Finlay Stewart. But being surrounded by the well-toned, imposing forms of Lochguard's Protectors made her want to run out the door and never look back. Not because they could snap her in two without breaking a sweat. No, it was because it reminded her of Travis and his buddies back in the US.

No. Forget about him.

If only Fergus had made an appearance, she might be able to do that. Yet the dragonman had yet to walk through the door and she doubted if he ever would or not. She was still torn between her fear of him using her and being interested in the dragonman who was able to coax her kitty into the house.

Flexing her fingers, Gina wished she had her pet right now. She'd adopted Coal from a neighbor shortly after arriving in Scotland, but the large black cat with golden eyes had won her heart quickly. The very first night, he had cuddled at her back as she fell asleep and purred. Her hormones had made her cry and snuggle with the cat for comfort. With Coal, she'd never be completely alone in Scotland.

Since one of the Protectors in the room was allergic to cats, her pet was at home with Fraser. However, Holly hovered at her shoulder. Looking up, Gina smiled. "It's okay. I haven't had another contraction. I think I can handle sitting in a chair."

Holly frowned. "It's not the sitting I'm worried about. Keeping you here is causing unnecessary stress. I'm going to have a word with Finn later. Failing that, with Arabella."

Lowering her voice, Gina whispered, "But can you do that? If anyone had challenged Steven Roberts, the dragon leader back in Virginia, they would've been punished accordingly."

One of the Protectors stopped studying his tablet and met her gaze. The dragonman's dark brown eyes were full of hatred. "Roberts is a right bastard and gives dragon-shifters a bad name. Don't ever compare Finn to him."

Gina blinked. "Okay."

Holly squeezed her shoulder and glared at the black-haired dragonman. "Leave her alone, Shay. If BroadBay is all she's known, then we should do everything in our power to change her opinion. Barking at her isn't going to help."

Before the dragonman could reply, a tall, blond dragon-shifter walked into the room and everyone fell silent. Gina debated standing up or not when the man smiled at her. The kindness in his eyes helped to ease her tension. There was something familiar about him, but she couldn't place it.

The blond dragonman stopped in front of her. "Sorry to keep you waiting, lass. How about you come with me and we can chat a bit?"

"You're the clan leader?" Gina blurted out.

"Aye, although you don't have to sound so surprised about it." He lowered his voice. "After all, attracting flies with honey is far easier than with vinegar."

Before she could stop herself, Gina asked, "What the hell are you talking about?"

JESSIE DONOVAN

Slapping a hand over her mouth, she held her breath. If she'd done the same back in Virginia, she would've been reprimanded or banished from the clan's lands. Would the Scottish leader do the same?

Then Finn winked at her and put out a hand. "I prefer not to dance around an issue, and I admire the Americans for doing the same. Come, lass. We'll talk in private."

Holly spoke up. "I want to come with you."

Finn shook his head. Holly opened her mouth, but he beat her to it. "You can sit outside the door, Holly. If anything happens, I'll shout for you, aye?"

Holly looked about ready to argue and Gina didn't want to risk upsetting Finn.

Standing up, Gina turned toward the midwife. "It's okay, Holly. If Finn tries to harm me in any way, I have a few moves to stop him."

Amusement danced in Holly's eyes. "Oh, aye? Someday, I'd love to see them."

Finn muttered, "What is with the females tossed my way over the last year?"

Holly flashed a grin at him. "You love a challenge and I think the universe is testing you."

"Aye, well, let's see if I pass this test." Finn offered his arm. "Come, Gina. The sooner we chat, the sooner we can decide your future."

As she took the proffered arm, Gina held her tongue. There was no reason to risk blurting out something that could ruin her chances.

Finn guided her out of the room and Gina made sure to keep her chin high the whole way. While she didn't have a churning stomach as she'd done with Steven Roberts in Virginia,

70

she no longer trusted her own gut. Travis had been a good actor and she wasn't about to be duped again.

Once she and Finn finally entered a small office at the end of the hall, Finn released her arm. He motioned to a chair and she took a seat. Finn propped his hip on the desk before he spoke up. "So, Gina MacDonald. Tell me why I should allow you to stay here despite the risk to my clan."

Clenching the material of her stretchy, tunic-style shirt, she kept her voice even as she explained her situation to Finn. "I slept with a dragon-shifter and ended up pregnant. Afterward, he reported the pregnancy to the DDA in Washington, D.C. I was required to give up my child willingly or by force; I couldn't keep him. Not liking those options, I fled."

"Which means you can never return to America. At least, if you want to return with your son in tow."

She nodded, not trusting her voice to remain steady. Just thinking about how she'd never see the Virginia coastline or William and Mary's campus ever again made her heart ache.

Finn sighed. "I'm truly sorry for what happened to you, lass. If any Lochguard dragonman acted that way and took advantage of a female, he'd be exiled or worse."

Gina wanted to believe Finn's kind eyes, but she needed much more than that to secure her future. "The past doesn't matter. I need to know if my son and I are welcome here."

"Aye, I know you do. Your preliminary background check came back clean. Provided the rest of your story checks out, you need to prove yourself and contribute to the clan before I can guarantee any long-term future here."

She frowned. "But I'm not a dragon. How can I contribute to a dragon-shifter clan?"

71

Amusement tinged Finn's reply. "Humans have their uses, too. Holly is human and she nearly runs the show when it comes to pregnancies and deliveries. I'm sure we can think of something."

She bobbed her head. "And? What else? News of the attacks on Lochguard last year made it to the US and I imagine you don't trust someone that easily, even if she's a pregnant woman."

Finn chuckled. "Clever lass. That will be helpful too." The dragonman's expression turned serious. "Trust takes time, as I'm sure you well know." Gina nodded, not expecting anything less. "Good, because it might make this next part easier to accept."

Dread pooled in her stomach. "What does the next part entail?"

"If you wish to stay, then you must accept Fergus MacKenzie as your Guardian."

She frowned. "What? Like an adopted father?"

Finn snorted. "No, not in the human way. He will watch over and protect you. For the most part, you will become his responsibility."

"Like a bodyguard? If it means I have to follow his every order, then I might take my chances back at Loch Shin."

Finn shook his head. "It's not safe for you there. And trust me, if BroadBay's leader is determined to have your child, then he'll find a way. I've never met Roberts in person, but I've heard enough to appreciate the ocean between us."

"How do you know about BroadBay? I never mentioned the American clan by name."

"Fergus."

Placing her hands over her stomach, Gina leaned back in her chair. If she were back in the US, she would merely agree to

72

the clan leader's words rather than risk a backlash. Yet as she studied the kind yet steely Scottish leader, Gina decided to roll the dice and speak her mind. "Assure me that I don't have to obey every word he says, and I'll agree to it for now."

Finn raised an eyebrow. "For now?"

She smiled slowly. "Fergus may just have a change of heart after a few days with me."

Chuckling, Finn put out a hand to shake and she took it. He added, "Give him hell, Gina MacDonald. But I warn you, Fergus is one of the most stubborn, patient males I know. He most likely won't give up unless he's dead."

"Well, that makes it all the more fun. I always did like a challenge."

Finn barked out a laugh. "I hope everything works out with you, lass, because I think my mate might like you."

The word "mate" sobered her up. But she quickly hid it with a smile. "Then what's next, Mr. Stewart?"

"Call me Finn, lass." He motioned toward the door. "It's time to meet with Fergus. He'll take you to your new home and you two can settle in."

Her heart thumped harder. "I don't have to live with him, do I?"

"As much as Fergus would love it, no. You will be neighbors with two separate houses."

She let out a breath. Fergus being her neighbor was still dangerous, but she could manage it with walls and space between them.

~~~

Fergus paced the length of the small room. Finn had sent him a text message asking him to wait in the conference room of the Protector's headquarters. That had been twenty minutes ago.

His dragon huffed. *I want to see Gina. Finn is taking too long.*

Before he could reply, the door opened. His twin brother stood in the doorway with a cat carrier. "Hey, Fergus. I thought you could use some company."

A soft meow came from the carrier. Fergus pointed at it. "Why the bloody hell are you carrying around a cat? I assume it's Gina's, but the poor beastie must be terrified."

Fraser shrugged one shoulder. "Not really. He's a brave one, he is."

"Forget about the cat for a second. Why are you really here?"

"Finn's bringing Gina here shortly and I needed to bring the cat before you two left for your new homes."

Fergus frowned. "Homes as in plural?"

Fraser nodded. "Aye, you're going to share the old Sinclair place. One house for each of you. I'm sure Mum is going to be thrilled. With you out of the way, she'll have the freedom to dote on Ross more."

Ross Anderson was Holly's father and a permanent human resident of Lochguard. "I thought you hated the idea of Mum and Ross?"

Fraser shrugged. "If they get together, then I can watch people's expressions when I tell them I married my stepsister."

He sighed. "And Holly is on board for this?"

"Not exactly. But I have ways of convincing her."

Fergus put up a hand. "I don't need to hear about your magic cock again."

"Are you sure? It really is quite spectacular. I might even say it's the envy of all males on Lochguard."

"Treasure Holly, brother, because I don't think there is another female alive who can put up with your annoying behavior."

"Annoying? I prefer to think of it as charming. And Holly loves all of me."

Before Fergus could reply, Finn's voice filled the room from behind Fraser. "Sorry to interrupt your all-important talk of cocks, but I have a female here who's anxious to know her future."

Fergus's dragon roared. *It's Gina.*

Pushing Fraser to the side, Fergus craned his neck and met Gina's green eyes. The female's gaze was unreadable. Aware of everyone listening, Fergus nodded. "Hello, lass."

At the term "lass" her lips thinned. It took everything he had not to laugh.

Holly pushed in front of Gina and pointed at Fraser. "Fraser, stop talking about how charming you are and bring the bloody cat out here." She looked to Fergus. "We'll wait down the hall to give you some privacy."

Fraser sighed. "And I was looking forward to eavesdropping."

Fergus punched his brother's arm. "Get out. If I find out you were listening in, then I will challenge you in dragon form and win."

His brother opened his mouth, but Finn cut him off. "Everyone out. Gina's looking pale and if Arabella finds out we're keeping her standing whilst you two argue, she'll have my head. Not only that, Aunt Lorna will have a thing or two to say."

Holly nodded. "Aye, she always has the wooden spoon handy."

Instead of stating he was twenty-nine years old and wasn't afraid of his mother, Fergus reached out a hand to Gina. It was time to work on earning the female's trust. "Will you come, Gina? We have much to discuss."

Straightening her shoulders, she took a step toward him but didn't take his hand. "I'll come, but I want Coal to stay with me. He's been stressed enough for one day."

Fraser lifted the cat carrier. "I'd give him more credit, Gina. He's a braw one."

"Braw?" Gina echoed as she plucked the carrier from Fraser's hand. "I have no idea what that means."

Fraser motioned toward Fergus. "My brother can explain it to you. Judging by the look in Finn's eyes, I'd better leave or I'll end up with some sort of crap task."

Finn nodded. "Good you noticed." His cousin looked to him. "Don't take too long, Fergus. I want the human sitting down with her feet up within the next half-hour."

Finn and the others left the room. The second the door closed, Gina made a beeline for the table on the far side of the room. The lass laid the contraption on the table and cooed to her cat.

With her bum slightly out and Gina bent over, all he wanted to do was come up behind her and cover her with his body. His dragon growled and flashed an image of their cock pumping in and out of their female.

She's not ours, Fergus stated.

Then hurry up and convince her.

76

He cleared his throat to garner her attention, but Gina ignored him to open the door and pick up her pet. With Coal laying over one shoulder, she turned toward him and raised her brows. "Well? You said we had much to discuss, so start talking."

Taking a step toward Gina, he restrained himself from reaching out a hand to touch her. "How about you first tell me what Finn said."

As Gina stroked her pet, Fergus wondered what it would feel like to have her hands stroke him.

Thankfully, her voice cut off the thought before it went any farther. "Ah, so you don't know everything then. Judging by how you liked to order me around earlier, I figured you had all the answers."

The responsible half of Fergus would let the barb go and focus on the bigger issue. He would never win Gina's trust if all they did was argue. "Look, I'm sorry about earlier. I'm not sure how much you know about dragon-shifters, but we're protective."

"I didn't see you acting this way around Holly."

"I leave the overprotectiveness about her to my brother."

Something he couldn't read flashed in her eyes, but it was quickly replaced with casual indifference. "I don't care about dragon-shifter nature or some other excuse. I'm not a possession to be passed around, Fergus MacKenzie. If we're to ever get along, you'd best remember that."

His dragon spoke up. *We're going to do much more than get along. Not now.*

Gina tilted her head. "Your eyes flashed. What did your dragon want?"

His beast chimed in again. *I want to keep you, that's what.*

Fergus didn't react to his dragon. "Believe me, you don't want to know."

Still carrying her cat, Gina took another step toward them. The scent of woman and heather hit him. His dragon snarled. *Hold her against our body. I want to memorize her scent.*

Gina's voice was lower when she replied, "Tell me, Fergus. Consider it a show of good faith to treat me better in the future."

As they stared into each other's eyes, a sizzle danced down his spine. Before he could stop himself, Fergus closed the distance between them. Standing so close, he was surrounded by her scent. The heat from her body warmed his chest through his clothes. If he leaned two inches closer, her belly would press against his groin.

Do it, his dragon growled out.

Lost in the depths of Gina's gold-flecked green eyes, he barely heard his dragon. He focused on Gina's increased heart rate. Then her pupils dilated, tempting him to pull her close.

Raising a hand to her cheek, he fully expected for her to scurry away. Yet she parted her lips and tilted her head up a fraction. "Tell me, Fergus."

The heat of her breath on his chin made his cock go hard. No doubt, Gina could feel it pressing against her, but he didn't care. A pulsing need to brand the lass flooded his body.

He needed to win Gina MacDonald's trust—and soon—so he could make her his female.

~~~

Earlier, when Gina had been sitting in Fergus's lap back at Loch Shin, her pains had taken all of her attention. But now, there was nothing to distract her from the heat of his body or his hard dick pressing against her.

His flashing pupils should remind her of exactly why she should push the dragonman away. Yet as Fergus stroked her cheek, all she wanted to do was curl against his chest and ask him to hold her.

Parting her lips, she was about to raise her head in invitation when Coal meowed in her ear. The sound snapped her out of the moment and she took five steps back.

Fergus clenched the fingers that had been caressing her cheek moments before. She waited to see if he would come closer again. The irresponsible part of her brain yearned for the dragonman to walk up and kiss her.

Turning away from her, Fergus remained quiet a second. A rush of disappointment squeezed her heart and she laid her head on Coal's back. Fergus's rejection should make her happy. It really should. She didn't need any more complications in her life. Especially not the kind that involved a dragon-shifter who believed she might be his mate.

Yet his touch had reminded Gina of what she may never have—a man to call her own and a father for her son.

The dragonman's voice was gravelly when he finally spoke up. "The answer to your question is that my dragon wants you, Gina MacDonald." Fergus looked over his shoulder and she drew in a breath at the heat of his gaze. "While I know your body wants me too, I'll hold off."

Her voice was strangled to her own ears. "Why?"

He turned. "Because if you wish to stay on Lochguard, I am to be your Guardian. Keeping you and the babe safe is more important than pleasing my dragon's lusty thoughts." He took a step toward her and her heart rate kicked up. "You have nothing to fear from me, lass. I promise you. And I'll find a way to prove it."

As tempting as it was to say she very much wanted to live out his dragon's lusty thoughts, Gina could no longer think of only herself.

Still, she studied Fergus's face and tried to determine if he was sincere. From everything she knew, dragon-shifters took what they wanted, consequences be damned. Could it be that, despite the rumors and portrayals in the media, not all dragon clans acted that way?

Clearing her throat, her voice sounded a lot more even when she replied, "I'm curious to see how you prove it. Dragonmen tend to think with their dicks first and their heads later."

Fergus's eyes flashed and she held her breath. Now was the time to test the dragonman, what with Finn and the others nearby to save her if she screamed. Even if they didn't help, she had the vial of ground mandrake root and periwinkle in her pocket. The young guard who'd searched her had believed her story of it being a herbal tea to help with pregnancy symptoms.

The corner of Fergus's mouth ticked up. "I have an idea. How about I take you to my mum's house for tonight to settle in? My mum can cook for you and give you some tips about the clan. Between her and my younger sister, you should feel safe enough. Although your cat will have to stay with Fraser for the night. My sister is highly allergic."

Gina had seen but never talked with a female dragon-shifter before. Before Travis, she'd been fascinated with all things dragon-shifters and had even joined the fan club at her college. She was curious about how they acted. Her plan to irritate Fergus and drive him away could wait a day if it meant she could check something off her list of things to do. After all, she might be spending the rest of her life on Lochguard and she needed all the information she could get.

Nodding, she adjusted the cat on her shoulder. "Okay, but just for tonight. If your family is anything like you and your brother together, I'm not sure I could take more than one day there before I started kicking people."

Fergus grinned. "Feel free to kick my sister, although I'd watch out for my mum. She had to raise three hellions and an unruly nephew. She'll predict your next move five minutes before you even think it."

Gina really should keep her mouth shut, but she couldn't resist saying, "You act differently when you're around your brother or talk about your family. You're a lot less stuffy."

His eyes flashed again and Fergus's grin faded. "We can debate my stuffiness later. Right now, I should take you home and get you something to eat. You're paler than I like, lass."

She opened her mouth to reply and her stomach growled. *Thanks for betraying me, body.*

Fergus moved to her side and placed a hand on her back. Raising her head, she stared into Fergus's dark blue eyes. Damn, the man was attractive. It was a good thing she'd be around his family. She should be able to resist kissing him again in front of his mother.

Not that she should ever kiss him again.

She waved a hand. "It's no big deal. Another half-hour won't kill me."

"It might not, but it will drive my dragon crazy," he stated and picked up the carrier. "Let's get the wee beastie into the carrier. The sooner we leave, the sooner my mum can feed you."

As she and Fergus stared at one another, she wanted to know why he cared so much. Even if his dragon wanted her, it was for sex only. Travis had explained that to her.

Stop comparing him to that bastard. Considering Travis's trickery, it was highly possible he'd lied to her. Fraser and Holly were mates and there was a lot more than mere lust between them.

Fergus shook the carrier. Gina gave her cat one last stroke before she maneuvered Coal into the contraption.

The dragonman bent his head and locked the carrier door. The scent of something wild and male filled her nose. Damn, he smelled good. The memory of his warm, possessive kiss filled her mind and she shivered.

Gina shook her head to clear it. Would staying in the same house with Fergus for the first night be the best idea? All it took was one whiff of his scent and she ached for his touch. Hell, if he kissed her again, she'd probably strip and offer him her body.

Her son kicked and she placed a hand over her stomach. *Are you telling me you want Fergus around?* Her baby kicked again and she smiled.

"Why are you smiling?" Fergus asked.

Taking a deep breath, she met his dark blue eyes again. "My son is kicking again. My guess is that he's practicing in case your hard dick gets a little too close."

Chuckling, Fergus moved his hand until it was an inch from her belly. "May I?"

Allowing the dragonman to touch her was a bad idea for many reasons. Yet before she could convince herself of why, she nodded. "Sure."

The second Fergus's large, warm hand touched her stomach, her son kicked again. Fergus leaned his head close and whispered, "He's a strong lad already. I can't wait to see what he's like when he's here and kicking. I bet he'll be a handful and a half."

"As long as he's not like his father, he can be any way he likes."

Moving his hand from her belly to her back, Fergus rubbed in slow circles. Despite his gentle touch, she didn't miss the steel in his voice when he stated, "With you as his mum, he'll turn out well. Maybe a wee bit stubborn, but a good lad. I have no doubt."

As she stared in Fergus's eyes, she saw nothing but truth in them. He barely knew her, yet he had such faith in her.

Blinking back tears, she cleared her throat and managed to whisper, "Thank you."

Her dragonman opened his mouth, but then shut it. Stepping away from her, he offered her his free arm. "Let me take you home."

Home. It wasn't something Gina had truly had in nearly four months, when her parents had sent her away to Scotland. Her grandmother's cottage had been nice, but it had never had the sense of safety or comfort she associated with home, especially after her grandmother's death. Would Gina find it on Lochguard, provided she could stay?

More than being on the run or hiding in a foreign country, Gina hated the uncertainty. Maybe if she won over Fergus's mom and sister, they would put in a good word with Finn so she could finally have a home. "And what about Holly and Fraser? Will they be there?"

"As much as I wish I could keep my bloody brother away, he always finds a way to sneak in."

Gina heard the love behind Fergus's words. "At least you have a brother to annoy you. I only have a sister."

"Females can be worse and I'm sure your parents had their hands full with you as a kid."

"What are you implying, Fergus MacKenzie?"

He shrugged. "Oh, just that your mouth was probably washed out with soap a few times for talking back. Am I right?"

She paused and finally grunted. "Maybe." Fergus chuckled, and the sight of the big, muscled dragonman laughing made her smile. "But soap is better than a sore bum."

"Aye, well, Mum still had the infamous spoon. I'd be careful. Even if you're pregnant, she might give you a few light taps if you step out of line."

She straightened her shoulders. "I'm not worried about that. Compared to you and Fraser, I'm an angel."

Fergus snorted. "An angel with a bite, maybe."

She smacked his arm. "Didn't anyone ever tell you not to insult a pregnant lady?"

"No, I must've missed those days at school. You're out of luck, lass."

Smiling, Gina shook her head. "I'm starting to think Scottish dragon-shifters are unique."

"If you mean handsome, clever, and brilliant, then you'd be right."

Fergus winked at her and Gina laughed. It was almost as if they were back in the cottage before her pains had started and changed her life forever.

Then her gaze fell to Fergus's lips and the memory of their kiss rushed back. Maybe she should give Fergus a chance.

"Lass, my eyes are up here."

Gina's cheeks flushed and she met his gaze again. "Shouldn't we be on our way? Holly probably wants to check on me before we go to your mom's house."

"If you're going to live on Lochguard, lass, then you should start saying 'mum' instead of 'mom.' It has a nicer ring to it."

"You do realize the Americans won the war against the British hundreds of years ago, right? I think that gives us the right to speak how we want."

Fergus leaned down and whispered, "You might've won against the humans, but if the dragon-shifters had joined forces, you'd be saying 'mum,' 'lift,' and any other number of words."

She raised her brows. "Someone's a little cocky." Fergus grinned and Gina sighed. "Fine, let's say you're amazing. Will that get your butt out the door any sooner?"

Fergus tapped his chin. "I may need a few more compliments to manage that."

"I've hit my compliment limit for the next hour, so you're out of luck."

Her dragonman turned toward her and lightly brushed her cheek. "And yet your sassiness never fades."

"Damn straight."

As they grinned at one another, Gina's son moved about inside her uterus. Only when Fergus was around did her little boy dance and move as if he was having his own private party.

Her mistrust of all dragon-shifters faded a fraction. She didn't want to get her hopes up that Fergus was what he appeared. But she might have a better idea after seeing him around his family.

She cleared her throat. "Well, I'm leaving. Whether you follow or not is up to you. I can always ask Finn or Fraser to take me to your house."

Fergus growled. "No bloody way. I'm going to be the one to introduce you to my mum."

"Then you can carry Coal's carrier. Since I pretty much only waddle these days, it's quite a chore to keep my balance with a fourteen-pound cat on one side."

Snatching up the carrier, Fergus was at her side. He placed a hand on her back and pushed gently. "Come, lass. Let me take you home."

Opening the door, Gina half-expected Fergus to sever contact. However, he never moved his hand from her lower back. Once they were in the hall, he looped an arm around her shoulders. She glanced over. "You're invading personal boundaries again, Fergus."

He raised his brows. "Do you want me to release you?"

She bit her lip a second as she debated telling him the truth. *What the hell.* Snuggling against Fergus's side for warmth didn't signify anything but practicality. After all, it was freezing outside. "No."

His pupils flashed. "Good answer."

As her dragonman drew her closer against his side, Gina reveled in Fergus's heat and spicy male scent. For the first time in a long time, Gina felt safe. She tried not to think too much about the reason why.

CHAPTER SEVEN

Fergus would have to thank Finn later for sending Fraser and Holly away while he'd been in the room with Gina. Meeting his brother might've broken the spell he and Gina were currently under. He still couldn't believe she'd allowed him to hold her close. Even now, when they were nearly to his mum's house, she hadn't asked for him to remove his grip.

A small gust of wind blew and his female snuggled closer against his side. It was taking every iota of strength he had to keep his cock from hardening. Having the human's lovely curves and heat so close was both fantastic and dangerous.

What was even better was his dragon's contented humming at the back of his mind. It seemed both man and beast were happy for the moment to merely have their female nearby.

The silence didn't bother him as they walked. After all, Gina's face was pale and she had circles under her eyes. His lass was tired, but trying to hide it. He wouldn't hurt her pride by mentioning it. His sister and mum had taught him well about a proud female's limits.

Still, Fergus couldn't resist stealing a glance over at Gina, who was watching two dragons doing flight exercises in the distance. Judging by their clumsy dives and maneuvers, they had to be two adolescents not quite used to their larger dragon forms.

He pointed in the direction of the blue and black dragons. "I wouldn't judge the gracefulness of dragons on those two."

Gina tore her gaze away to meet his. "Why's that?"

"They're teenagers and their bodies are growing faster than they know what to do with in both human and dragon forms."

He paused and Gina looked back to the beasts. Fergus was about to nudge further when Gina murmured, "It's the first time I've been allowed to watch dragon-shifters fly together at such a close distance."

Frowning, Fergus stopped. Laying Coal's carrier on the ground, he gently touched Gina's chin with his free hand. "How is that possible if the father of your child is a dragon-shifter?" A thought entered his mind and anger coursed through his body. "Did he force himself on you? If he did, tell me his name and I'll bring the bastard to justice."

Gina studied him a second before replying, "No, he didn't force me. He was a lying asshole, but not a rapist."

Fergus tightened his grip on Gina's arm. "Tell me who he is and I'll teach him a lesson."

"No."

He frowned. "Just 'no'? As your Guardian, I should know as much about you as possible. Otherwise, I can't do my job properly."

She raised her brows. "I still haven't decided if you'd be the best guardian or not. Until then, I'll tell you what you need to know."

"Gina—"

She cut him off. "Look, placing my trust in someone too early is what got me into this mess in the first place. I'm not about to be fooled twice, Fergus. Not even a growly dragonman with kind eyes will change my mind."

"What if I shift into a dragon?"

Gina didn't so much as blink. "Try it and see."

His dragon laughed. *She will never obey meekly. I like it.*

Aye, well, you're not the one who has to protect her without knowing all the facts.

Use your heart and gut to guide you.

Fergus grunted. He lived on acquiring information and forming a plan. Winging it wasn't exactly his style.

Gina poked his arm, but before she could do more than open her mouth, an all-too-familiar voice filled the air. It was his younger sister, Faye. "Fergus Roger MacKenzie, stop dawdling and get a move on. Mum won't serve her latest batch of scones until after you've brought home the human."

He sighed. "How does she even know about Gina?"

Faye ran up to them. "Finn told her." His sister looked between Gina and Fergus. "Well? Aren't you going to introduce me?"

Motioning between Gina and Faye, he made the introductions. "Gina, this is my annoying sister, Faye. Faye, this is Gina."

Ignoring him, Faye smiled at Gina. "Has my stuffy brother bored you to death yet?"

A faint flush filled Gina's cheeks. The sight pumped up his ego a notch. Maybe, just maybe, she was thinking of their kiss earlier, which had been the farthest thing from stuffy.

Gina put out a hand to shake and Faye took it. "Nice to meet you. And to answer your question"—Gina glanced at him and then lowered her voice—"Fergus is too much of a contradiction to be stuffy."

His dragon perked up at that. Faye opened her mouth, but Fergus beat her to it. "What do you mean I'm a contradiction?"

89

Amusement danced in Gina's eyes. "Do you really want to have this conversation in front of your sister?"

Faye's eyes widened. "Oh, this just became interesting. Tell me, Gina. What happened? Ever since Fraser mated Holly, it's been quite boring around here. I could use a good story."

Fergus stepped between Gina and Faye. He growled out, "Go home, Faye Cleopatra. We'll be along shortly."

Faye crossed her arms over her chest. "You're not the boss of me. I'm staying."

He hated to make a deal with his sister, but he wanted to find out more about Gina's comment. Both man and beast burned to find out the truth. "Leave now and you can have all of my scones for the next two weeks."

His sister loved food almost as much as flying. Since an accident last year had made flying difficult for her, Faye relied more on food to keep her happy. Only because of her dragon-shifter genes was she still thin.

Faye finally nodded. "Deal. But don't stay away too long or Mum will have your head."

Fergus grunted. "Fine, fine. Just go."

Faye craned her head around Fergus's body. "Nice to meet you Gina. Don't let Fergus keep you away too long. The MacKenzie household is a riot, you'll see. And once you're settled, you can tell me all about America. I've dreamed about going there since I was a little girl."

"Faye," Fergus growled in warning.

His sister rolled her eyes. "Fine, fine. I'll go. No need to try and use dominance on me."

Gina waved and Faye jogged away. He was finally alone with his human again.

His dragon hummed. *Find out why we're a contradiction. And more importantly, why our human blushed.*

Taking a deep breath, Fergus turned toward Gina. He stood only a few inches away, which was too bloody close. But he wasn't going to allow the proximity to distract him. "Explain yourself, lass." Gina raised an eyebrow and he added, "Gina. Explain yourself, Gina."

The human smiled and he felt as if he'd been punched in the gut. With her curly red hair blowing around her pale face, she was beautiful.

Kiss her, his dragon urged.

Fergus's gaze dropped to Gina's pink lips. Even now, he remembered how soft and warm they were next to his. And damn, her taste. He could drink her in all day.

His beast added, *Just wait until we lick between her thighs.*

The image of Gina naked and at the mercy of his tongue flashed into his head. What he wouldn't give to caress every inch of her body. She deserved to be treasured and he had a feeling the American bastard hadn't done so.

No doubt, the Yank arsehole had hurt her. Maybe Fergus could win her over slowly and prove he was different.

His dragon growled, but the human's voice interrupted his thoughts. "As much fun as it is watching your pupils flash and emotions dance in your eyes, either talk with me or I'll ask the next person I see to take me to my new home."

Fergus grunted. "I can't help it. My bloody dragon lives to irritate me. I love order and rules and he despises them. Imagine having a constant battle inside your mind, and that's what it's like."

Gina paused a beat before asking, "Then if it's so bad, how have you not gone crazy?"

His dragon swished his tail in the back of his mind. Fergus ignored him. "I may complain, but my dragon is an essential part of me. No matter where I am or where I go, I will never be truly alone."

Gina's face softened. "That sounds nice."

"It's more than nice, lass. But just because I can't imagine living without the bloody beast doesn't mean it's easy. America has had its fair share of rogue dragons as well. Those who can't maintain control end up being a danger to more than just themselves."

Placing a hand on her belly, Gina looked into the distance. "I hope my baby will be okay."

The concern on her face shot straight to his heart. He placed his forefinger under her chin and gently tilted her head back toward him. When she met his eye, he should've dropped his hand. But her skin was soft and he couldn't resist lightly stroking it. "If I have any say in the matter, the lad will grow up to be strong and in complete control of his other half."

"You say that now, but once he's born and crying in the middle of the night, you'll bolt the first chance you get."

"No, I won't." She opened her mouth, but he moved his finger against her lips. "I will take care of you as long as you allow me the privilege, Gina MacDonald. I vow it."

The wind swirled around them, but all of his attention was on Gina's face. He willed for the female to grant him the honor of protecting both mother and bairn.

Gina's eyes grew wet and it squeezed his heart. Both man and beast wanted to do everything in their power to chase away the tears. Their human deserved to laugh and be happy.

More than that, she deserved to be loved.

~~~

Gina was about five seconds from turning into a blubbery mess. She wanted to believe Fergus truly meant what he said. Not only that, but that he also wanted to help raise her son and even take care of her.

Of course, Gina could take care of herself. She'd done it for months. But just the idea of having someone to lean on when things turned difficult made her heart warm.

The only question was whether Fergus MacKenzie was sincere or not.

Yet the longer she stared into his dark blue eyes the less she thought about her past or what trouble might lurk in the future. Her dragonman's fierce, intense gaze sent a tingle down her spine and heat between her legs. Fergus MacKenzie was focused on her and only her.

She could only imagine what would happen if she allowed him to care for her.

A familiar voice carried in the wind—it was Fraser. "Oi, brother, hurry up. Holly's impatient to see Gina inside and resting."

Fergus flipped off his brother, but never broke eye contact with Gina. He was the first to speak. "We'd better go or my mum will be next. The MacKenzies are, for the most part, an impatient lot."

Gina seized the change of topic and smiled. "Except for you, of course."

"But of course." He wrapped his arm around her shoulders again. She nearly sighed in contentment, but held back. "We're almost there, lass. Come on."

After Fergus picked up the cat carrier, they walked the last few minutes in silence.

Any time they walked past another dragonman, Fergus hugged her a little tighter. On some level, she was offended as she didn't belong to any man. Yet the action showed her that Fergus wasn't as controlled as he liked everyone to believe. She wondered what would happen if she broke that control? Would an unrestrained Fergus be as careful and considerate around her? Or, would his dragon have the upper hand and pursue her?

Maybe if she survived the evening, she could poke and prod at Fergus's self-control a little and find out.

Before she could think on why she wanted to do that, a large, two-story cottage came into view and the front door opened to reveal a middle-aged woman with blonde hair streaked with gray.

Fergus murmured, "That's my mum," right before the older dragonwoman spoke up. "About time, Fergus. I wanted the lass to have a hot scone. By now, they're only mildly warm."

Fergus answered, "Gina is extremely pregnant, Mum. Unless you wanted me to half-drag her home, we couldn't have come any sooner."

Gina felt the urge to be a little evil. "I was walking slowly for your benefit, Fergus. You're the one carrying the cat carrier."

Fergus sent her a glare and she grinned. Her dragonman murmured, "My memory is long and I'll get you back somehow."

She opened her mouth to reply, but Fergus's mom walked up to them and inserted herself between them. Fergus released his hold just as his mom said, "I don't care about excuses. Take the beastie upstairs to your room, Fergus. Hopefully it won't bother Faye there until Fraser and Holly can take the cat with them. There's even a litter box and food waiting for the poor beastie."

Fergus gave her one last glance and Gina read the question in his eyes. She nodded at her dragonman. "I'll be fine. Go. Coal probably wants a warm bed to nap on after the events of today."

He looked about ready to say something else, but then Fergus was gone. The woman next to her spoke up. "He's a fine lad, he is. Although a wee bit protective. I suspect that's because he's the oldest." Gina tried to think of what to say, but Fergus's mom continued, "I'm Lorna, by the way, but everyone calls me Aunt Lorna. You should do the same. Finn told me a bit about you, but if you prefer to go by another name than Gina, just tell me now, child."

Gina studied Lorna's face. While her amber eyes were different from Fergus's, the shape of the nose and brow were familiar. And much like Fergus, Lorna had kindness in her gaze. "Gina's fine."

"Right, then let's get you inside, Gina. You look about ready to pop as it is. Even if you're fortunate enough to not be carrying twins, we should get you off your feet as soon as possible. Your lower back must be protesting by now, aye?"

"A little."

Lorna snorted. "There's no reason to hold back and be polite, child. Act like that and my kin will eat you alive."

Gina wasn't sure if that was a compliment about Lorna's brood or a warning.

The dragonwoman guided them inside, her touch warm and comforting. It reminded Gina of her mother before 'the accident,' as her mom called it. After telling her parents about her pregnancy, they couldn't send Gina away fast enough. She missed the more loving version of her parents.

Damn it. She needed to stop thinking of the sad aspects of her life or she'd enter Lorna's house bawling like a toddler.

As anxious as she was to meet her son, Gina couldn't wait to be free of the extra hormones and become emotionally stable again.

Holly dashed out of a side room. "Are you still doing okay, Gina? I wanted to walk you home, but Finn ordered me away. I nearly challenged him over it, too."

"I appreciate your concern, but I took care of myself for months before you came. If I really need help, then I'll ask," Gina answered.

Lorna carried on as if Gina hadn't answered. "Holly, is Ara here yet?"

Holly motioned toward a different room. "She's in the dining room with Ross, Fraser, and Faye. Something came up for Finn, and Ara wanted some company."

Lorna nodded. "Good. It's about time she started admitting it."

Frowning, Gina looked between the two women. "I'm lost."

Lorna patted her shoulder. "I'll explain it later, child. Let's get you sitting and fed first." Gina opened her mouth, but Lorna beat her to it. "No, you don't get a say in this."

Considering she'd just met Lorna MacKenzie, Gina should hold back. Whether because she was hungry or just tired of people ordering her around, she didn't know, but Gina dug in her heels. "With all due respect, Aunt Lorna, I'm not a child. I've talked with people more today than I have in the last two months combined. I'm tired, hungry, and a little cold. I'm not about to enter a room and be confused about even more people. Either tell me what I need to know before entering, or I'll wait in the hall for Fergus and we can stay somewhere else."

Lorna and Holly shared a glance. Gina may have just lost the good word she needed to stay on Lochguard.

Then someone clapped slowly behind her. Looking over her shoulder, it was Fergus. And he was grinning. "And that, Gina MacDonald, is how you should handle every Scottish dragon-shifter you meet. You'll have more than me on your side before long if you do."

Gina frowned. "What the hell are you talking about?"

Fergus closed the distance between them and lightly ran his finger down her cheek. "Most of my clan acts like my family does. If you want to fit in here, you need to stand your ground."

"Right, and next you're going to tell me that you kept pushing my buttons on purpose to train me?"

Fergus winked. "But of course."

As they stared at one another, Gina couldn't help but smile. "So does that mean I can use you as my punching bag for self-defense practice, too? I'm sure you want me to be prepared against an attack as well."

Fergus's voice was husky as he answered, "We'll see, lass. You've tricked me once, but now you've lost the element of surprise. You'll have to show the rest of your abilities. A little one-on-one should do it. I look forward to pinning you in place."

At face value, Fergus's words were harmless. But the deepness of his voice implied more than sparring and she shivered.

Thankfully, she was saved by Aunt Lorna. "If you're quite done, lad, I'd like to explain about the other people in the room. Unless you'd like to do it?"

Fergus looked to his mother. "Aye, I'll tell Gina about Ara and Ross. Can you give us a second, Mum? Holly?"

The two dragonwomen shared another look before they were gone.

Gina was alone again with Fergus.

Fergus raised one arm up. "Come here, lass. I heard you were a wee bit cold. I have more than enough heat for the both of us."

Remembering his warmth from earlier, Gina went without another thought. As soon as Fergus wrapped his arms around her, Gina sighed. Whether she liked it or not, Fergus was fast becoming her safe haven in the middle of the Scottish Highlands.

CHAPTER EIGHT

The instant Gina rushed into Fergus's arms, possessiveness coursed through his body and his dragon spoke up. *We should take her upstairs and kiss her again.*

Not now, dragon. She needs something to eat.

We can bring her something upstairs.

Fergus was tempted to keep Gina all to himself, but that wouldn't be fair to the lass. *No. Arabella's waiting and I'm sure Gina has a lot of questions about being pregnant with a dragon-shifter baby. Arabella can help.*

His beast huffed. *Only because I like Ara will I hold back for now. But make sure Gina is sleeping with us tonight.*

I'm not going to jump her the first night on our land.

Now who's the randy one? I just want to hold her.

Gina's voice interrupted his reply. "So tell me about this Ara person. Is she important?"

He couldn't resist rubbing up and down Gina's arm. Thankfully the lass didn't tell him to stop. "Aye, she's Finn's mate. I don't know if they showed the interview with Jane Hartley and Arabella MacLeod on American TV or not. If they did, she was the scarred dragonwoman who talked about her torture at the hands of dragon hunters."

"I remember watching the video online. I thought she was with Clan Stonefire?"

"She was, but then Finn's dragon wanted her. The rest is history."

Gina looked up and met his gaze. "So if someone's dragon wants another, they pretty much don't have a hope of escaping?"

He stilled his hand. "I wouldn't put it that way. A female can reject a male if they wish. It's just harder for a male to move on if the female is his true mate."

"And what about female dragon-shifters? They are oblivious to all of it?"

An accent different from Fergus and the other MacKenzies filled the air. "Of course not. But I like to think we're a bit more restrained."

Arabella MacLeod stood a few feet away. Fergus snorted. "Aye, so I imagine you and Finn are talking about computer code and security threats when you disappear into your cottage and tell us to stay away?"

Arabella raised an eyebrow. "It's more like we need a break from you lot."

Fergus chuckled just as Gina cleared her throat. A quick glance showed his female clenching her jaw. She didn't like being ignored. "Sorry, Gina." He motioned toward Arabella. "May I introduce Arabella MacLeod, formerly of Clan Stonefire and now Finn's mate. She's pregnant like you, lass, so you have lots in common."

Arabella rolled her eyes. "Yes, because being pregnant is the only thing I want to talk about."

Fergus shrugged a shoulder. "The bairns pretty much force you to talk about it all of the time. Has the acute morning sickness passed?"

Arabella answered, "Mostly." Arabella motioned toward Gina. "But as fascinating as morning sickness is, I think you're forgetting something, Fergus. For a Guardian, you're not doing a very good job with your charge. You should introduce her straight away."

Fergus opened his mouth, but Gina spoke up. "I can introduce myself. Hello, Arabella. I'm Gina MacDonald. Nice to meet you."

Fergus muttered, "I was getting to that."

Arabella and Gina both ignored him. Arabella smiled. "Finn told me a little about your circumstances. If staying the night with the MacKenzies doesn't frighten you off, then maybe you can tell me a little more. My sister-in-law, Melanie Hall-MacLeod, has a penchant for helping people and she might be able to work her magic again to help you, too. Provided you're not a threat to either of our clans."

Gina's eyes turned bright. "I would never hurt either of you. But do you really think Melanie can help me?"

Arabella shrugged. "If anyone can, it's Mel. You might even give me the excuse I need to convince Finn to let me visit Stonefire. We can stay with Mel and my brother."

Fergus hugged Gina closer. "Gina's not going to Stonefire to stay with Melanie and Tristan."

Arabella waved a hand. "Tristan is mated, Fergus. He won't pose a threat to the human."

Fergus growled. "That's not the point."

Arabella looked to him and her pupils flashed. "Ah, I see. I hope it works out for you, Fergus. I really do."

Gina looked between them. "Hope what works out?"

His dragon spoke up. *Just tell her already. She deserves to know she is our true mate.*

Later. If Gina doesn't eat something soon, she might faint.

Then why are we standing in the hallway? Let's go.

Fergus met Gina's gaze. "I'll tell you when we're alone again, lass. I promise."

Gina searched his eyes and sighed. "I can see you're not going to budge, even if I push. But I'll hold you to your promise, Fergus. I want to know what's going on."

Arabella chimed in. "He will. If he doesn't, I'll see to it myself. At any rate, Aunt Lorna is probably about to have a stroke, so I say we best get inside. Gina's had a long day and could use a rest."

Before Fergus could say anything, Arabella went back into the dining room. Looking down at his human, he murmured, "Brace yourself, lass."

Gina raised an eyebrow. "Let's hope your family together lives up to all of the hype. Otherwise, I'm not going to believe anything you say."

"Oh, aye? Well, just for that, I may stir the pot a little."

"Bring it on, Fergus MacKenzie."

He grinned. "Right, then prepare yourself for war."

~~~

Despite her brave words, Gina's stomach churned in knots. From everything she'd witnessed thus far, Fergus was close with his family. If they hated her, would he still offer to be her Guardian? She didn't like the idea of a stranger watching her every move.

Fergus brushed her cheek. "Be yourself and stand strong."

I can do this. As soon as she nodded, they entered the dining room.

Inside was a large rectangular table with six people sitting around it. Only one face was unfamiliar, although the older man

102

in his fifties or sixties had the same eyes and nose as Holly. Maybe it was her dad.

Fraser raised a hand in greeting before swiping a scone off a plate and taking a huge bite. Lorna clicked her tongue. "I didn't say you could have them yet."

Not caring his mouth was half-full, Fraser answered, "You said we could eat them when Gina arrived and she's here."

Lorna rolled her eyes. "You lot act as if I never feed you."

Faye spoke up next. "You do, but it's as if we're on rations."

The unfamiliar man chuckled. "I'm not sure I want to see you all when you're actually on rations. I can just imagine Faye and Fraser in dragon form, rolling around outside, fighting for the last scone."

Faye stuck out her tongue. "I'd win."

Fraser shoved his sister, who sat at his side. "I've been going easy on you the last few months. Say the word, and I'll unleash my bloody amazing flying skills and have you begging for mercy."

Lorna shared a glance with the older man and sighed. "This is why we can't have company."

The man patted Lorna's hand. "The alternative is boredom, and I can't imagine you liking it."

Fergus cleared his throat and all eyes moved to him. "Forget about the bloody scones for a moment. You're neglecting our guest. Do you want us to be compared to clans such as BroadBay or even SkyHunter? A brief display of manners wouldn't kill you."

Faye scowled. "It would take some extra work to be like either of those arseholes."

Lorna motioned toward the chairs. "Have a seat, Gina. Oh, and before I forget, this here is Ross Anderson. He's Holly's father and a temporary guest in my house."

Fraser muttered, "I doubt he's temporary."

Holly smacked her mate's arm. "Fraser."

Ignoring the ruckus, Fergus pulled out a chair. "For you, my lady."

She smiled. "I see you act polite in front of the others. When will that façade wear off?"

Fergus took a seat next to Gina and leaned close to her ear. "Ask me that again when we're alone."

Gina dared a glance at Fergus. His eyes were full of heat and a touch of amusement. "Maybe I'll ask to stay with Faye for the night. Then I won't have to worry about your growly, dominant side coming out again."

Fergus growled. "You're staying with me, Gina."

"Because I'm your charge or something else?"

"Both."

Under the table, Fergus placed a possessive hand on her thigh. His touch sent a jolt through her body. If Gina were smart, she'd push his hand away and ignore her attraction to the auburn-haired Scot. Instead, she gave in to the urge to feel his warm, rough skin again and laid her hand over his. Fergus's eyes widened a fraction before he gently squeezed her leg.

For a split second, she realized how right the situation felt. Fergus at her side, a crazy family arguing in the background, and the smell of freshly baked scones filling her nose. Deep down, she longed to belong again, with the MacKenzies, on Lochguard, where she could raise her son. Even from the brief glances she'd witnessed so far, Gina's gut told her Lochguard was the opposite of BroadBay.

Unfortunately, her lovely moment with Fergus was interrupted by a chunk of butter bouncing off Fergus's cheek. With a growl, her dragonman zoned in on his brother. "What the bloody hell was that for?"

Fraser answered, "Either get a room or answer Mum's question"

Gina's cheeks flushed at being caught. She'd been so absorbed by Fergus's gaze, that she hadn't heard anything.

Thankfully, Fergus took charge. "What did you ask me, Mum?"

Lorna tilted her head. "I heard you're moving out. Is it true?"

"Aye. Gina and I are going to share the old Sinclair semi-detached houses."

Gina poked Fergus's side. "What? This is the first I've heard of it. Finn merely said we'd be neighbors, not sharing a wall."

He shrugged. "What can I say? You have the tendency to distract me."

Faye snorted. "Fergus distracted? That never happens. You'll have to share your secret with me later, Gina."

Arabella finally joined in the conversation. "I somehow doubt you'll want to do what Gina does. Unless you're going to flirt with your brother?"

Ross grinned. "Aye, that's frowned upon, Faye, my dear."

Faye shot Ross daggers with her eyes. "Thanks for clearing that up."

Lorna frowned. "That's not how I raised you to speak to your elders, Faye Cleopatra."

Ross chuckled. "You make me sound as if I have one foot in the grave, Lorna."

Ross and Lorna shared a smile and Gina couldn't contain her curiosity. "Are you two a couple?"

Fraser choked on a scone as Lorna and Ross moved away from each other. Lorna spoke up first. "No, child. Ross is recovering from cancer and needs constant care."

Ross nodded a little too enthusiastically. "Aye, Lorna's right. Without her help, I'd probably be cold and in the ground."

Holly stopped pounding Fraser's back to frown at Ross. "Don't talk like that, Dad."

As everyone else at the other end of the table bickered and argued about everything from death to flirting, Fergus leaned down to Gina's ear and whispered, "Are you ready to run yet?"

Grinning, she met his eye. "Are you kidding? This is better than TV." She paused a second, debating if she had the nerve to say her next sentence and decided what the hell. "Although I'm not sure if I want to spend the night here. I need almost complete silence to fall asleep and I somehow doubt I'll get it here."

Arabella's voice interjected, "If we leave now, they might not even notice."

Gina looked over to where Lorna stood between Ross and Fraser. Fraser was accusing Ross of taking liberties with his mother, and Ross was frowning and telling Fraser to respect his mother's privacy.

She looked at Arabella. "I think that might be a good idea." Moving her gaze to Fergus, she patted his hand under the table. "I already see concern in your eyes, but I can call Holly later and have her check in on me."

Fergus squeezed her leg again. "As long as that's what you want, lass. I don't want you to feel uncomfortable or lonely."

Staring into Fergus's blue eyes, she wondered how she could have ever compared him to Travis. Fergus was kind,

106

patient, and thoughtful in a way that Travis never would be. "I'll be fine."

"Right, then. Let's hurry." Fergus nodded slightly toward the door. "You and Arabella can leave first. If anyone asks, I'll just say you're using the toilet."

Gina looked to Arabella. Despite the scar running from her brow, down across her nose, and to her opposite cheek, Gina wasn't afraid of the dragonwoman. After all, Arabella had been through a hell of a lot worse than Gina and had survived. In a way, it gave Gina hope for her own future. "Okay. But don't be long after us."

Fergus winked. "Don't worry. Wild dogs couldn't keep me from following you, lass."

At the twinkle in his eyes and his smile, Gina's heart skipped a beat. "Good to know. I may try finding some wild dogs later, if you step out of line."

Arabella quietly slid out of her seat and moved to Gina's chair. "I hate to break up the flirting session, but it's now or never."

Fergus lightly brushed her arm and Gina stood up. Despite her words, she didn't want to leave Fergus's side.

Arabella placed her hand on Gina's back and guided them out of the dining room before Gina could change her mind. Only through sheer force of will did Gina not look over her shoulder at Fergus one last time. The dragonman might think something was wrong and she didn't want to bring attention to herself.

Reaching the front door, they took their coats from the hooks on the wall. A few seconds later, she and Arabella exited the cottage.

Arabella sighed in relief. "As much as I love my mate's family, I can only take them in small doses."

"Your family is a lot different?" Gina asked.

Arabella snorted. "That's putting it mildly. If you stay long enough, you can meet my brother. He's as growly as Fergus is patient. Add in overprotective and how he likes to order me around, and I'm somewhat grateful that he lives down in England."

"And yet, I think you miss him."

Arabella darted a glance at Gina. "You're perceptive."

She shrugged. "I have a younger sister who used to annoy me when we were growing up. But now that I don't get to see her, I miss her. I bet it's the same for you."

Arabella remained quiet for about a minute before she finally replied, "Did you sister turn her back on you when she learned about your child?"

Gina debated sharing too much of her past with Arabella. But as her gaze flicked to the dragonwoman's scars and burn on the side of her neck, Gina knew that if Arabella could share her past with the world, Gina could share a little with one dragon-shifter. "Kaylee was the first person I told, after the father. She offered to run with me, but I couldn't allow her to ruin her life. So I told her she would only slow me down." The image of her sister's hurt face flashed inside her mind. "Maybe someday I can see her again."

Arabella stopped walking. "Look, I know you just met me and have zero reason to listen to anything I say, but I'm still going to give you advice. It took me a decade to realize that pushing those you love away only hurts both them and yourself. You shouldn't make the same mistake. Find a way to contact her, Gina. It will help ease your heart."

She nodded, unsure of how to respond to the pain in Arabella's voice.

The dragonwoman nodded. "Right, then let's hurry up and get inside. I guarantee my babies will make me ill again before too much longer and I'd rather be inside when it happens."

They continued walking in companionable silence. Arabella's revelation had made Gina more comfortable in the dragonwoman's presence. Not only that, a flicker of hope burned in her chest. Maybe Arabella could help her find a way to contact her sister.

Kaylee. The wall she'd put up around memories of her sister cracked a fraction. An image of one of their late night gab fests flashed, with both of them in pajamas and sharing a pint of ice cream. She and Kaylee had been close once. They'd talked about everything from studies to boys to trips they hoped to take one day. Whenever one of them had been in trouble, the other had found a way to help.

Her heart ached to see her sister's smile or hear her fake, devious laugh again as they plotted how to sneak out of the house without being detected.

Inhaling deeply, Gina patched up and reinforced her wall around the memories. Kaylee was safer if she kept her distance from Gina. As much as Gina wanted to hug her sister, she wasn't about to get her hopes up just yet.

Suddenly, she wanted to feel Fergus's strong arm around her shoulders. His presence would help ease the pain of loneliness. Looking over her shoulder, there was no sign of her dragonman.

Arabella's voice filled her ear. "He'll find a way to follow us, Gina. Until he does, I'll keep you company. I'm completely fine with saying nothing, but if you want to talk more, then I'm here, too."

"Thank you." She hesitated before deciding to seize the moment. "How far along are you?"

Arabella sighed. "Four months. But it feels more like four years."

She frowned. "I thought dragon-shifter women had an easier time."

"You'd think that, but my bastard mate knocked me up with triplets."

"Triplets?" Gina echoed.

"Yes." Arabella looked off to the distance. Gina barely heard her whisper, "And I'm not sure I can handle it."

Gina sensed Arabella didn't want to elaborate. However, much like Fergus had supported her, Gina could support Arabella. "Well, our babies will be close in age and I'm sure we can schedule play dates. That should help. Even if they're crazy little hellions, mommies supporting each other with chocolate and maybe a glass of wine can alleviate stress for a little while."

Arabella met her gaze again. "What are you talking about?"

"I'm sure you have play dates in the UK, just like back in the US. Moms and/or dads get together with their children and let them play. It's usually under the pretense of socializing for the kids, but I think it's to help with the parents' sanity. With the kids playing with each other, it gives the parents a breather."

Studying her a second, Arabella finally answered, "I'm not the most social person in the world, but I'll think about it."

Gina smiled. "Good because I'm new here and I could use some friends."

"What about Fergus?"

"Well..."

Arabella gave a small smile. "You can think of how to answer that later. We're here and I want to get out of the cold. I think tea and biscuits will help warm us up."

Gina nodded and looked to the house in front of them. It was divided into two houses sharing a wall. They must call duplexes semi-detached houses in the UK.

For two countries that shared a language, they were a hell of a lot of differences.

Still, Gina wouldn't have it any other way. Scotland had been her new start and so far, it was paying off. She only hoped BroadBay wouldn't come after her. Lochguard was being kind, but there was only so much they would do to help a stranger if she brought trouble to their front door.

CHAPTER NINE

Fergus half-jogged toward the old Sinclair place. Extricating himself from his family had taken longer than he'd anticipated.

His dragon paced at the back of his mind. *I don't know why you bothered to be nice about it. Gina waits for us. We should've left directly.*

Then they would've come over and never left. Mum and Holly, in particular, don't want the lass alone. Besides, I needed to fetch Gina's cat.

His beast huffed. *We will protect her. That is enough.*

My biggest concern is protecting her from us.

I would never hurt her. But protecting her means taking care of her. She still hasn't eaten anything. I don't like it.

Fuck, she must be hungry. We're going to have to stop by the shop.

Fergus rushed to the closest shop. So much for being Gina's Guardian. He couldn't even remember to get her some food.

He would work on it. After all, Fergus had yearned for so long for a female of his own. He needed to take care of the one who was probably his true mate. Especially if he was to convince her to stay.

And after their interlude back at his mum's house, Fergus wanted her to stay. Just thinking about his hand on her soft, warm thigh as they flirted made his heart warm. He'd never felt so at ease with any female in the past.

Picking up a few things at the shop in the clan's central living and shopping area, he paid the clerk and ran the rest of the way to the old Sinclair place.

Very few houses shared a wall on Lochguard, mostly because dragon-shifters liked their space. However, the Sinclair brothers had been close and lived as neighbors for sixty years before they died. He wondered if he and Gina would be neighbors that long, or would he succeed in wooing the lass? If his bloody brother hadn't tossed the butter earlier, Fergus might've pushed Gina a little further. A hand on her thigh was a start, but all he wanted to do was hold her close and never let go.

As it should be, his dragon stated.

His beast may be certain, but Fergus was cautious. The last time he'd pinned his hopes on a lass, that female had fallen for his brother.

His dragon roared, but before he could throw a tantrum or worse, Fergus constructed a complicated mental maze and forced his dragon inside. Fergus hated to do it, but he wanted complete control of his first evening alone with Gina. If he couldn't manage a kiss again, then he at least wanted to find out a bit more of her past.

Coal meowed inside his carrier just as Fergus stopped in front of porch on the left, which was Gina's house. "Just a moment, Coal."

Knocking, Fergus waited. The door opened and he nodded at Arabella. "Is everything okay?"

She raised her brows. "I don't give advice to you often, but stop hovering, Fergus, or you might drive her away. She's far stronger than you give her credit for."

He growled. "Of course the lass is strong. She escaped BroadBay and took care of herself in a strange land, all whilst pregnant with a dragon-shifter's child. But when it comes time for the bairn, she'll need help."

"So you plan to take the child as your own?"

"If Gina will let me."

Arabella studied him a second before stepping aside. "She's in the kitchen." She reached for her coat. "Finn should be done by now, so I'm going home. Call if there's any trouble."

Arabella taking an interest in someone so soon was unusual. "What did Gina do to you?"

"Nothing."

He gave her a skeptical look. Then the scent of the ham and potato bake wafted up from his takeaway bag, reminding him of his female needing to eat. "Go, then. I'll keep her safe."

"I hope you can, Fergus. I hope you can."

Before he could ask any questions, Arabella was gone.

Making his way to the kitchen, he found Gina sitting at the table nibbling on a biscuit. He couldn't help but stare at the fleck of chocolate on her upper lip. What he wouldn't give to lick it away.

Gina swallowed. "Something smells good. Stop staring at me and give me some."

Blinking, Fergus handed over the takeaway bag. "I hope you're not a vegetarian. How some humans give up meat, I'll never know. My dragon would drive me crazy without it."

Gina opened the container and took a deep inhalation. "No, I love meat too much. And this smells good." She picked up the plastic fork and took a portion. Fergus watched as she slipped the food between her lips.

He would love to have those soft, pink lips around his cock.

His dragon roared inside his mental maze and Fergus quickly brought up images of older dragonwomen in bikinis.

Damn Gina MacDonald and her sensual lips. She had to be taunting him on purpose.

With a deep breath, he focused on letting the cat out of his carrier. "What did you talk about with Arabella? Because whatever it was, you've nearly won her over and that's quite a feat when it comes to Arabella MacLeod."

Gina answered as soon as her mouth was empty. "Not much. She hasn't decorated a room for her triplets yet, so I'm going to go over there tomorrow and suggest some ideas."

He frowned. "Ara doesn't strike me as the type to care about decorating things."

She pointed her fork at him. "You'd be surprised. Apparently, she loves picture of old doors. We can totally use that as a starting point and go from there."

Fergus couldn't care less about decorating rooms, but he loved the anticipation shining in Gina's eyes. He'd bet his life that this was the first time in a long time the lass had forgotten about her past long enough to be happy. He only wished it was because of him.

Stop it, Fergus. We're a grown male. That may be true, but there was nothing wrong with making his lass a little happier.

Walking over to her, he tucked a piece of stray hair behind her ear. "If you can get Arabella to vouch for you, then Finn will probably allow you to stay, lass." He took her chin between his fingers. "And I hope you'll stay."

As he stroked the soft skin of her jaw, Gina stopped breathing. She even leaned a few inches toward him.

If he were noble, he would release his grip and allow the lass to eat. Yet as her pupils dilated and her heart rate kicked up, Fergus didn't want to waste his chance. He squatted down until he was eye level and murmured, "You're so lovely, Gina. Between the sparkle in your green eyes and your wild, curly hair, you are most definitely the bonniest lass I've ever seen."

She moved back a few inches. Only through his ironclad restraint did he keep his dragon in check as she replied, "Don't do that, Fergus."

"Do what, lass?"

"Say things you don't mean. I know you're my Guardian and I'm pretty sure your duties include keeping me happy. But don't do it like that. A dragonman sweet-talked to me for several weeks before laughing in my face and abandoning me. Don't lie to me, too."

He growled. "I'm not bloody lying. I'm sorry the bastard American treated you that way, but don't compare me to him." He leaned closer to her face. "You are beautiful, Gina. Don't ever doubt it."

She opened her mouth, but not wanting to hear another excuse, he kissed her.

~~~

Gina had been about to tell Fergus to leave when he kissed her.

Part of her wanted to punch him in the dick for his audacity, but the other part of her breathed in relief. Ever since he'd had his hand on her thigh back at the MacKenzie household, her lips had pulsed with desire, wanting to be kissed.

As he sucked and nibbled, she let out a sigh. Fergus made her feel as if she were the only woman in the world and he would stop at nothing to devour her. If only she could start over and have Fergus be the dragon-shifter she'd met in the bar; her life would be in a very different place.

116

Yet as Fergus threaded his fingers through her hair and dug his nails lightly into her scalp, she forgot about everything in the past. They were alone with no one watching. Even if it was just this one kiss, Gina wanted to feel desired.

Fergus pulled away but stayed close. His eyes were filled with heat and wanting. "Was that enough to convince you of how much I want you?"

Say yes and dismiss him. Going any further could be dangerous.

However, Fergus lightly brushed her cheek with a finger from his free hand and she shivered. He smiled slowly and added, "Does my touch make you burn, Gina MacDonald?" His eyes flashed to slits and back. "It's taking everything I have not to carry you to bed and make love to you."

Her heart thumped as she saw the truth in his eyes. "I thought a Guardian was only supposed to protect me."

"Aye, in the old days. If you refuse me, I'll still protect you with my life. But"—he brushed her cheek again—"I want more. I want to hold you close and wake up with you in my arms." He moved his free hand to her pregnant belly. "I want to watch your son grow into a strong male." He lifted his hand to trace the curve of her breast. "And I want to devour every inch of your skin and make you come harder than you ever have in your life." He removed both hands from her. "The bigger question is, what do you want, Gina?"

Recklessness had cost Gina her degree, her freedom, her friends, and even her family. Every sensible iota of her being screamed to order Fergus away and close off her heart from being hurt again.

On the other hand, Fergus's mere presence eased her stress. Also, her son loved to dance in the dragonman's presence and Fergus had even volunteered to protect her with his life. True, he could be using pretty words to get into her pants, but her gut said Fergus MacKenzie was different.

The only question was whether she took a chance and listened to her instinct or if she played it safe.

As she debated the reasons to go one way or the other, her son kicked. Gina smiled when he did it again. Without thinking, she reached for Fergus's hand and placed it on her stomach. As her son continued to kick and move around, Fergus's deep voice filled the room. "I think maybe we should listen to the lad. He seems to like me and you don't want to disappoint the bairn before he's even born."

She snorted. "So you're using my baby against me?"

He grinned. "Aye. It's best to get him on my side early on. With his help, I might be able to convince you to be my mate."

She drew in a breath. "Mate?"

Rubbing her stomach in slow circles, his grin faded. "Not now, of course. I will take as long as it takes to win you over, Gina Louise. Even if it takes me years, you'll be worth the wait."

She barely acknowledged the fact Fergus already knew her middle name. "But you just met me."

"I've been thinking of you every day since I first walked out of the lake in dragon form and tried not to laugh as you threatened me."

She narrowed her eyes. "Hey, it wasn't an idle threat."

"That may be, lass, but from that second, I loved your spirit. Whenever it fades, I can tell it's because of the male that hurt you." He paused, and then asked, "Maybe if you tell me about him, we can think of a way to purge your memories of his bastard self."

"You're just saying that to eventually get me naked."

Fergus tilted his head. "If all I wanted was you naked, then you'd be naked already."

Gina tsked. "Someone's cocky."

He laid a possessive hand on her thigh. "I want you to feel safe, Gina. But without knowing about your past, I can't help you, let alone try to protect you and your son." He squeezed her leg. "Tell me and the information will go with me to my grave."

She paused before asking, "What if it endangers your clan?"

"Then I'll persuade you to talk to Finn. But I won't be the one to tell him."

As Fergus stared at her, Gina tried to decide what to do. If Fergus knew the extent of how much BroadBay wanted her child, he might run to his clan leader. She'd be on her ass outside Lochguard's gate before Gina could do more than blink.

Glancing down at Fergus's large hand on her thigh, she attempted to think of a reason to keep her secrets.

Fergus spoke up again, his accent thick when he said, "If you won't tell me because you don't want to burden me, then think of your son. I can't protect him, either, without knowing all the facts."

She looked up at that. "So you're guilt-tripping me into telling you the past?"

He winked. "If this is guilt-tripping, then you wouldn't stand a chance against my mum. She's the queen of making someone feel guilty."

Smiling, she laid a hand over his. "Then I'll have to ask Aunt Lorna for lessons the next time I see her."

"Aye, I'm sure she'll give them to you, too."

Fergus fell silent. He was giving her time to make a decision.

Tears pricked her eyes. Even in this moment, when Fergus could easily overpower her and demand answers, he was patient. Kindness and something else she couldn't name filled his eyes.

Truth be told, it was easy to imagine a life where she woke up to her dragonman's blue-eyed gaze.

He could be hers if she took a risk.

Before she could change her mind, Gina blurted out, "It started with a dare. Madison was my roommate. Whenever she'd had a little too much to drink, she always came up with the most ridiculous dares. For the most part, they were impossible.

"But that night, we were at one of the bars at the edge of BroadBay's land. Technically, the dragon-shifters weren't allowed inside. But the owners knew the presence of dragon-shifters could be profitable in drawing crowds to gawk, so they encouraged it.

"Anyway, Madison noticed a group of men with dragon-shifter tattoos. She was usually the one to go up to men and ask them to sit with us. This time, she was pretty drunk and dared me to do it since it was on my list of things to do before we graduated and there were only six months left."

Gina and Madison had written their lists as a joke during their freshmen year, but Madison had soon made it her mission to accomplish everything on that list by graduation.

Peeking up at Fergus, his eyes asked for her to continue, so she did. "Despite what you may think, I'm shy in large social situations. It's only when I'm alone or in small groups that I can stand my ground. Since the bar was packed, I took one last shot of tequila before approaching the table. I half-expected the dragonmen to sneer and dismiss me. But the tallest one with light brown hair and whiskey-colored eyes smiled at me before coaxing me to sit next to him. He made me laugh and even taught me a few things about his clan. Having been an admirer of dragon-shifters for years, it was like a dream come true."

In retrospect, Gina had been naïve. Only human sacrifices could live with the dragon clans, but deep down, she'd believed Travis's promise about finding a way to be together.

Alcohol and pent-up dreams had made her a temporary fool.

Fergus lifted her chin until she met his eye. "Tell me what happened, lass."

She placed a hand on her stomach. "As you know the aftermath, it's pretty obvious he wooed me into bed. He pretended to date me for a few weeks. Despite using condoms, they failed for us and I found myself pregnant. While scary, I was also ecstatic. As a mother to a dragon-shifter child, I really could have the chance to live with BroadBay and my charming dragonman."

Taking a deep breath, she tried to calm her nerves. The next part still upset her, but without it, Fergus would never know the truth. She only hoped he wouldn't pity her. "As soon as my pregnancy was verified, I tried to see Travis. I should've known something was wrong when he showed up with an impatient look on his face. I asked him when we could go to the DDA to see about a special license. I knew they were giving a few out here in the UK, so I imagined it might be possible in the US. That's when he laughed at me and told me I was a bet. His friends had bet him he couldn't get ten females pregnant in a year, and he took it. He accomplished it by poking tiny holes in the condoms he used. I was the tenth female, hence why he was so determined to get me into bed since his year was nearly up."

Even after all these months, just remembering Travis's sneer made her stomach churn. He'd told her about the bet as if he were talking about the weather; he didn't care for her. His clan needed new blood and he was finding a way around the red tape of the sacrifice system. Half-dragon-shifter children needed to be watched by other dragon-shifters. US law dictated accidental pregnancies in favor of the dragon clans.

Fergus's voice was steely when he finally spoke up. "What's his name?"

She met his gaze and blinked at the fury burning in it. Fergus had always been so kind and patient that she sometimes forgot he was half-dragon. "His name doesn't matter."

"It bloody well does. I would beat him to a bloody pulp and cut off his dick for what he's done to you. But doing that would land me in prison and I won't leave you unprotected. We need to involve the DDA in all of this. They will stop him."

Tears prickled Gina's eyes. "Don't you think I tried that? I filed an anonymous complaint and waited for weeks to see what they'd do. But nothing happened. Some of my friends saw Travis wooing other women in the same bar, as if nothing had happened."

"Travis of BroadBay. Good. Now I can find him."

Gina shook her head. "Don't, Fergus. You promised that what I told you would stay between us."

He cupped her cheek. "I won't do anything without your approval. But think of the other females, lass. You were strong and ran to keep your child, but how many of the others had to hand over their bairns or face a prison sentence? We owe it to all of them and any other victims to stop this bastard. At least think about it, Gina. Will you do that for me?"

Fergus wiped the tears from her cheek with his thumb and she melted a little. "I wish I had met you instead. I can't imagine you ever stooping to Travis's level."

Fergus's eyes flashed. "Don't mention his name. My dragon is already roaring to seek revenge and the name only prods him further."

Placing a hand on his chest, she stared into his eyes and made a decision. "Then do whatever it takes to help ease him. If it takes me sitting in your lap again, then I can do that."

His jaw tightened before he replied, "What he wants I won't do. It's bloody selfish in this moment, right after you've told me about your past."

She moved her hand further down his chest. "And what's that?"

Fergus gritted out, "Don't ask me, lass. Finish your dinner and I'll come back in a little while."

Her dragonman moved to stand up, but she grabbed his shoulder. "Don't leave me drowning in my memories, Fergus. Stay and help me make new ones."

His nostrils flared. "You don't know what you're asking, Gina. You're vulnerable and I won't take advantage."

Irritation flooded her body. "I'm twenty-two years old and aware of what I want. I holed myself up in that cottage thinking I could keep myself safe by blocking out the world. Then you glided down into my life and everything changed. I want you, Fergus MacKenzie. You're kind, patient, and more noble than anyone I've ever met. I want you to stay with me. Please don't go."

CHAPTER TEN

Fergus's honor warred with Gina's need. Clearly, she was upset and emotionally distraught. Making love to her would be taking advantage of her.

Yet as her eyes pleaded for him to stay, he wanted to do whatever he could to make her happy.

His dragon, who had broken free several minutes earlier, growled. *She wants to forget about the bastard. Let's help her.*

Fergus was teetering. *I don't want her to wake up in the morning and regret everything. We should woo her more. She should trust us first.*

Gina looped her hands behind his neck and whispered, "If you truly want to help me, then kiss me, Fergus." She brushed the back of his neck with her fingers and fire flooded his body at her touch. "Please."

Between her voice, her touch, and her scent, it was all too much and Fergus's restraint shattered. He scooped her up and moved toward the bedroom down the hall. Gina laid her head against his chest. Each step only strengthened his decision. The lass would be his if she allowed it.

Gently laying her on the bed, he let his eyes roam her breasts, her round belly, and her thighs. Starting at her bare ankle, he ran his hand up her calf, tickled the back of her knee, and stopped at the top of her inner thigh. As he stroked with his thumb, Gina moaned.

Fergus met her gaze. "This is your last chance to back out, Gina. What will it be?"

Irritation flashed in her eyes. "You don't always have to be so patient with me, Fergus. I know from your kiss earlier that your dragon is demanding. It's okay to embrace him sometimes." She opened her legs wider. "I actually look forward to it."

The scent of her arousal grew stronger and his beast roared. *I agree with the human. Throw caution to the side for once. I want her. Hurry up and fuck her.*

Fergus moved his hand to the edge of Gina's panties and teased her swollen flesh. *Not fuck, dragon. With Gina, I'm going to make love.*

His beast huffed. *Humans. I don't care what you call it. Just do it.*

He dared to run his forefinger through her slit. She was so wet and the urge to taste her coursed through his body.

On impulse, he sliced her underwear in two and spread her legs wider. She was pink and glistening. For him.

His dragon roared to claim her, but Fergus held his beast back. After lightly teasing her flesh, he leaned down and licked slowly from her opening up to her clit. As he swirled around the tight bud, Gina moved her hips. "Fergus."

The sound of his name from her lips destroyed his last vestiges of restraint and he plunged his tongue into her core.

Damn, she tastes good.

Caressing her thighs as he continued to swirl and lap her pussy with his tongue, all he could think about was putting Gina on her hands and knees and taking her from behind.

His dragon snarled. *Now.*

No. Fergus would make sure his female came first. After everything she'd been through, she deserved it.

He wished he could look into his female's eyes as he devoured her, but her pregnant belly hid her face. So he let her know he was with her by rubbing her thighs, her lower abdomen, and even her hips. With each stroke of his tongue, his female opened her legs wider and melted a little more into the bed.

He slowly licked up her folds and traced around her clit, never making contact with the bundle of nerves. He continued to tease but not touch and Gina wiggled her hips. "Please, Fergus."

His dragon snarled. *Make her come. It's the first step to claiming her.*

With a growl, he placed his hands under her arse and lifted before finally flicking her clit with his tongue. Gina sucked in a breath and moaned. The sound drove his beast crazy. *Taste her again first.*

As Fergus trailed his tongue back to her pussy, Gina made a sound of frustration. Before she could say a word, he swirled her opening before entering. Moving in and out, his lass relaxed a bit more above his hands. Both man and beast wished she could thread her fingers through his hair. But that would have to wait.

Pushing aside the desire, Fergus moved back to Gina's clit. Swiping back and forth, he increased the pressure with each pass.

Her moans grew louder. His dragon roared. *Make her come. I want to taste our mate's orgasm.*

Fergus agreed with his dragon. It was time.

He gently bit her clit before sucking it harder. Gina screamed. Wanting to push her further over the edge, he thrust two fingers into her pussy and moved them in and out as she gripped and released him.

His dragon hummed in contentment at their female's orgasm.

When Gina finally relaxed, he leaned back and stood up. The sight of his human's flushed cheeks and heavy breathing only made his cock harder. Needing something of his female to appease his dragon, he sucked her juices from his fingers. Gina's pupils dilated as she watched.

His voice was gravelly to his own ears when he ordered, "Get on your hands and knees."

~~~

Gina had barely blinked after experiencing one of the best orgasms of her life before Fergus told her get on her hand and knees.

Judging from his flashing dragon eyes, man and beast were nearly one.

As much as she loved Fergus's kindness and patience at any other time, she kind of liked the fact he took charge in the bedroom.

Despite her recent orgasm, her pussy pulsed when Fergus growled out, "Hurry, Gina."

After seven months of celibacy, Gina didn't waste time rolling over onto her hands and knees.

One second passed and then another. She heard something being tossed to the side, but Fergus didn't touch her. Looking over her shoulder, she bit out, "I know my ass is double-wide at this point, but you can stop staring."

"Don't do that," Fergus bit out before he sliced through her tunic top and the remainder of her underwear.

She was naked except for her bra and the sleeves of her tunic around her arms. Opening her mouth to scold him for destroying one of her few sets of nice clothes, he ran his warm, rough hands over her butt. He squeezed one cheek and then the other before rubbing her skin in slow circles. "I will always love your body. Every time you try to dismiss how beautiful you are to me, I will just have to work harder at convincing you of the truth."

If she wasn't so turned on, she might start crying. Stupid hormones.

Wanting to avoid that as it would destroy the moment, she wiggled her hips and whispered, "Then start convincing me or I'll just have to go through the list of things changed by my pregnancy."

Fergus roamed his hand up her sides until he reached the band of her bra. She half-expected him to slice it, but he unhooked it. Her heavy breasts dangled free in front of her. Gina loved the freedom.

But then Fergus took her breasts in his hands and gently squeezed them. The pressure was just enough to feel good, despite how swollen her boobs were. "You've changed here."

As he gently kneaded, it was hard to concentrate on anything but the possessive grip of his hands. But somehow she forced her brain to work. "Leave it to the man to focus on bigger boobs."

He released her breasts and placed his hands on her belly. "All of the changes will be worth it, Gina. Just wait until our son is born."

Her throat closed up at the word "our." Surely Fergus couldn't mean it.

As if sensing her doubt, he rubbed her skin. "Yes, ours. But until he's born, I'm going to focus on you and only you, Gina MacDonald. You're mine."

She shivered at the possessiveness in his tone. Unlike with Travis, she liked Fergus claiming her.

She stilled. *No.* There was no way in hell she'd let the bastard intrude and ruin her first time with Fergus.

Wanting to speed up the process, she leaned back and pressed her ass against Fergus's hard cock. Her dragon hissed and she smiled. "Just imagine how much better it'll feel inside me."

Fergus backed away a fraction and ran his dick through her folds. He teased her opening, but never fully entered. She growled. "You can draw it out and prove your super dragonman sex powers later. My pregnancy has made me really horny. Don't make me wait any longer."

Slapping his cock against her clit, she barely heard him reply, "Just one last thing. I have no diseases and you're already pregnant. But if you want me to wear a condom, I will."

His words warmed her heart. Even when she was naked and on all fours in front of him, Fergus wanted to make sure she was okay.

Her own desire to claim Fergus coursed through her body. "Take me just the way you are, Fergus. But don't make me wait any longer."

In the next instant, he thrust into her and she arched her back. Damn, he was long and hard. The fullness was almost too much, yet it felt just right.

She wiggled her hips and Fergus moved.

He kept her in place with his hands and slowly increased in pace. Each long, hard thrust only made her wetter between her thighs. "Faster, Fergus."

The sound of flesh slapping on flesh filled the room. Gina leaned her head on her arms, afraid that she might lose her balance. But she'd rather lose her balance than tell Fergus to stop.

If only she could see his eyes. Gina knew it was difficult for both her and Fergus to have sex face-to-face when she was eight months pregnant, but she wanted no doubt as to the dragonman behind her. Before she could stop herself, Gina asked, "Fergus?"

One of his hands rubbed her back. "I'm right here, lass. Are you with me?"

Lifting her head, she managed to look over her shoulder. The magnificent sight of Fergus towering over her greeted her eyes. "Yes."

"Good. Then hold on."

He pulled out slowly and then pounded in hard. "My name is Fergus MacKenzie." He repeated the motion. "I will protect you with my life." And again. "Live the moment with me." Another thrust. "And just let go."

Each motion had been as if he branded himself into her. There was no doubt who was behind her.

Gina raised her hips in invitation and Fergus growled. "That's my lass. Mine."

Leaning over her back to kiss her neck, Fergus quickened his pace. His arms framed her body, causing his scent to fill her nose.

She was just thinking how difficult a position it had to be for him when Fergus moved even faster and Gina lost all thought. Each stroke of his dick took her higher. Then one of his hands found her clit and she cried out. "Fergus."

"Aye. Say it again."

Through her pleasure haze, Gina swore she heard longing in his voice. But she quickly pushed it aside. "Fergus."

He pinched her bundle of nerves, and spots danced before her eyes. The combination of his cock hitting her g-spot and the increased pressure on her clit sent her over the edge. She screamed.

As she spasmed, Fergus stilled and roared out. Unlike any time she'd had sex before, she felt the heat of his semen inside of her. She barely registered it before she spiraled into one orgasm after another.

Her arms gave out, but a pair of strong, warm ones caught her. As Fergus held her against his chest, she lost all cohesive thought and simply embraced the pleasure.

~~~

Even though sweat dripped down Fergus's back, he wasn't tired. He held Gina against his chest as she came down from her high. And more than that, her reaction to his orgasm told him what he needed to know.

Gina MacDonald was his true mate.

Her pregnancy was preventing the mate-claim frenzy, but his dragon still roared inside of his head. *She is ours. I told you. We must mate her and protect her.*

We can discuss it later. Right now, I won't burden her with this news.

His beast hissed. *It's not a burden. It is a gift.*

In this, I won't capitulate to you.

Fergus tossed his dragon into a mental maze and nearly sighed at the silence.

Taking advantage of his beast's absence, Fergus nuzzled Gina's neck and inhaled deeply. He would never get enough of her scent of woman and something faintly floral.

After all this time, he'd finally found his female. However, that wasn't the hardest part. No, he needed to find a way for both her and her son to stay.

Or, rather, for both her and their son to stay.

There was no bloody way Fergus would allow that Travis bastard to take the child away from Gina. A female giving a dragonman her body was something to be relished, not a game. Just the thought of all of the potential females Travis could still use and toss away made his blood boil.

Gina's voice interrupted his thoughts. "Fergus, what's wrong? You tensed up."

He changed their position so that Fergus sat on the bed with Gina in his lap. He would discuss dealing with Travis later. For the moment, he wanted Gina at peace.

As soon as she met his gaze, he replied, "It can wait till morning." He leaned forward and kissed her gently. "For now, I want to make sure you eat properly and then we can go to bed."

Amusement danced in her eyes. "Bed, huh?"

He lightly slapped her thigh. "Yes, actual bed. It's been a long day and you need some rest."

"So, the cock comes out and you switch to Guardian mode. Good to know."

He growled. "Gina."

She grinned and his irritation evaporated. "We're going to have to work on lightening you up a little. After meeting your brother, I know for sure you've been teased before."

"Don't mention my brother when you're naked."

She moved a little toward him and placed her hands on his chest. "I knew you weren't immune to the possessive streak that all dragon-shifters seem to have."

"Would you want me to mention your sister as I fondled your breast?"

She scrunched her nose. "That's just gross."

He grunted. "Then you understand."

132

"Fine, I won't mention he-who-must-not-be-named." She plucked at his shirt. "But do we really need to get out of bed just yet?"

She looked back up at him. The longing in her eyes shot straight to his heart. Kissing her again, he laid his forehead on hers. "If you're afraid I'm not going to want you again, then you're sadly mistaken, lass. If you were fed and rested, I would be taking you until your voice was hoarse."

"Fergus."

He tucked a strand of hair behind her ear. "It's true." He traced her cheek with his finger. "But if you finish eating, then I might be persuaded to help you shower, if you like."

Teasing returned to her eyes. "Maybe I want to help you in the shower. After all, you've seen me naked but you're still wearing most of your clothes."

Fergus winked. "I need to keep up the anticipation, lass. Because once you see these muscles of mine again, I'll be wiping drool off your chin."

Gina snorted. "Good to see your humor is back."

"Oh, I'm not joking. I see lots of drool on your chin in the future."

As soon as he said it, Fergus realized what it sounded like. He debated apologizing when Gina's husky voice filled his ear, "I think we'll be seeing more of my wetness on your chin long before I have drool on mine."

From inside his mental maze, his beast roared in approval. Gina MacDonald was comfortable enough in his presence to tease about him going down on her.

In response, Fergus took her lips in a rough kiss and slid his tongue into her mouth. He stroked a few times as he lightly tugged her hair. When he finally broke it, Gina was panting. He put a finger under her chin and closed her gaping mouth. "Watch it, lass, or you may yet have drool on your chin."

Determination flashed in her eyes. "You might've won this point, but the next one is mine."

"Oh, aye? So we're going to keep score?"

Gina pulled away and closed her expression. *Fuck.* Keeping score must've reminded her of Travis and his bloody ten females.

"Gina, look at me." She met his eyes again and he cupped her cheek. "You are not a point or prize to me. Don't ever think that." She nodded, but remained quiet so he continued, "Let's heat up your supper and you can tell me all about your sister. We'll both be dressed, so it shouldn't be 'gross'."

She smiled at his poor imitation of her voice. "We're going to have to work on your mimicry skills, Fergus. I'm not a squeaky mouse."

"Aye, we can. After you have some food and tell me about your sister. I bet she has a ridiculous American name like Brittany or Taylor."

Gina raised an eyebrow. "Her name is Kaylee, actually. And it's not like you're one to talk. Fergus sounds like an old man's name to an American."

"Oh, aye?" Fergus leaned down to Gina's ear and nibbled her earlobe before he added, "Well, this old man, has already made you scream twice. What do you say to that?"

"I say that maybe you're using a little blue pill."

He put on a mock hurt expression. "I may not be twenty-two like you, but this twenty-nine-year-old has a few more years left in him before he needs any sort of pill." He lightly patted her hip. "But in all truth, if I'm with you, Gina, I'll never need one." Gina blushed and he chuckled. "Right, then. Let's put our little innuendoes to the side and put on some clothes."

"What, like the ones you've sliced to bits?"

Fergus smiled slowly. "I won't apologize for that."

Gina rolled her eyes. "Men."

He kissed her cheek. "We'll find you something. Even pregnant, you should fit into one of my shirts."

"It's January in Sutherland. I'm going to need more than a t-shirt."

"Aye, and what do you have in mind?"

She cupped his cheek and whispered, "I was thinking you could be my blanket."

"Good answer, lass. Good answer."

As he kissed her slowly this time, both man and beast settled in contentment. He was close to having what he'd always dreamed of having—a mate and family to call his own.

CHAPTER ELEVEN

The next morning, Gina held a cup of hot tea between her hands and simply watched the yummy broad back of her dragonman as he cooked breakfast for her.

Even though she'd pinched herself a few times already, Gina kept thinking it was all a dream.

Fergus was everything she'd never thought she'd have. True, she hadn't known him long, but she was at ease with the Scot. Talking, cuddling, even teasing came naturally to her when she was with Fergus. She'd never felt this way in her life with anyone, not even the asshole dragonman who'd charmed her back in the States.

Sipping her tea, she hoped she could stay with Clan Lochguard. Fergus mentioning the word "mate" had scared her the day before, but with time, she might even warm up to the idea. She desperately wanted to trust him, but was honest enough with herself to know it was too soon to trust him without question.

Fergus turned around with a grin. He hadn't bothered to brush his auburn hair and it stood up every which way. Combined with his morning whiskers, he was so handsome it was almost painful to look at him.

Her dragonman placed a plate in front of her with flair. "I think I finally managed pancakes for you."

Looking down, Gina smiled. "The hotdog-bun shape is pretty original."

He handed her a fork. "The appearance doesn't matter. Try them."

Fergus had spent the last twenty minutes trying to make pancakes. The first batch had tasted like salty bread and Gina had barely kept it down.

Still, Fergus motioned with his hand and she cut a piece. *Okay, son, work with me. Even if it tastes bad, let's not hurt Fergus's feelings and throw up.* With a deep breath, Gina placed the bite between her lips.

The light, fluffy consistency melted in her mouth and she sighed. "Now that's a pancake."

He leaned down and kissed her cheek. "Then let me make you some more."

Before he could turn away, she grabbed his wrist. "Not until you try some." She cut off a piece with her fork, dabbed it in some of the extra syrup, and held it out. Never breaking eye contact, Fergus leaned down and took the fork between his lips and slowly slid the pancake from the utensil. As he chewed, she noticed some syrup on his full bottom lip.

Damn. "How do you make eating pancakes sexy?" Since his mouth was still full, Fergus waggled his eyebrows. Gina laughed. "Lean close for a second."

As soon as Fergus's head was close enough, she slowly licked the syrup from his lip. His pupils flashed to slits before he swallowed. "Aye, I think you might have some syrup left on your lip too." He licked the corner of her mouth before nipping her bottom lip. "You really are messy. I see some more."

She opened her mouth to reply, but Fergus cut her off with a kiss. As he devoured her mouth, she forgot about everything but the sweet taste of Fergus and pancake.

He finally pulled away. She shivered at the heat in his eyes. "Don't look at me like that or I'll never find out about your surprise."

He caressed her cheek. "Maybe more of me is your surprise."

"Fergus."

He chuckled. "I guess I should give you a break after last night. That was a fairly long shower after supper."

The memory of Fergus lightly brushing her breasts with a warm, soapy cloth came rushing back. He'd cleaned every inch of her body thoroughly. Especially as she'd stood over him as he licked between her thighs until she'd screamed.

Clearing her throat, Gina tried to put on a stern expression but failed. "I have to meet Arabella after lunch and you promised we'd be done by then. I somehow doubt that will happen if we take another shower or anything else that involves both of us naked."

Fergus's pupils remained slits for a few seconds before he sighed. "My dragon is pouting now. You'll have to make it up to him later."

She shook her head. "I'm not so sure giving in to a tantrum is the best idea."

He brushed her cheek with the back of his fingers. "Finally, I have a female on my side. Together, we may yet tame my beast."

"So? What's this surprise?"

"Tenacious one, aren't you?" She raised an eyebrow and he sighed. "All right, then. Finish your breakfast and we'll get ready."

He placed a hand on her belly. "If the wee one cooperates, that is. Is our son giving you trouble?"

Fergus had called her boy their son several times, and each time it brought tears to her eyes. Not wanting to cry, she rubbed her eyes. "He wasn't a fan of the first batch of pancakes, but everything should be good. My stubbornness alone should keep him in line. I want to find out my surprise."

Fergus chuckled. "If stubbornness solved everything, then my family would be superheroes saving the world."

"Speaking of your family, maybe we can see them again soon. I probably got off on the wrong foot with you mother by sneaking out like I did."

The corner of his mouth ticked up. "If anything, my mum will be amused. She may frown or scold, but deep down, she loves when people take initiative. Even if it's to avoid her."

Gina tilted her head. "I'm really starting to wonder about your family."

He twirled a strand of her hair. "When you're ready, we'll see them again, but not before. I'm sure you'll grow to love them soon. Even Arabella couldn't resist the MacKenzie brood's charm."

She took and squeezed his hand. "They mean a lot to you, which means I need to get to know them, too. Besides, I'm sure your mom has some interesting stories to tell. And Holly keeps sending me text messages asking if I'm okay. Maybe seeing me out and about will ease her nerves."

He rubbed her stomach in slow circles. "You may be young, but you've become wise."

She placed her hand on the side of her belly. "Sometimes life forces us to grow up quicker than we may like."

He met her gaze. "I'm sorry for the circumstances that forced it, but I can't be sorry because it brought you to me."

She smiled. "That is pretty cheesy." Fergus opened his mouth, but she beat him to it. "But I'm glad, too."

After kissing the corner of her mouth, he murmured, "Now that's settled, eat your breakfast. Or I may have to feed you myself."

She pointed her fork at him. "Right, because you're going to tie up a pregnant lady and force her to eat."

He looked to her pancake and back to her face. "Don't tempt me, lass. Because I may just do it."

Rolling her eyes, Gina speared another bite of pancake on her fork. "If you're threatening me when I'm this pregnant, I hate to see what you're like when I'm not."

Fergus's eyes twinkled. "Then stay around and find out."

She laughed. "We'll see about that, Fergus MacKenzie."

"Good." He pointed toward her food. "Now, eat. The longer you resist, the less time we have for your surprise."

She stuck out her tongue and added, "Yes, Mr. Guardian."

Before Fergus could say anything, Gina stuffed her face with food. As she chewed, she pointed to her jaw and then gave a thumbs up. It took everything she had not to burst out laughing at Fergus's sigh.

She only hoped that when they left their little bubble inside the house, the easiness and teasing would continue.

It was foolish to dream, but as Fergus wiggled his hips and did a ridiculous dance, Gina laughed and wished it to be true with all her heart.

THE DRAGON GUARDIAN

~~~

Fergus threaded his fingers through Gina's as they walked away from the old Sinclair place.

Both man and beast were content. Between taking care of their female and the upcoming surprise, Gina should start opening up to them.

His dragon grunted. *Which means we need to tell her the truth soon.*

He didn't give his beast an answer. Fergus knew what needed to be done, but not until after his surprise. He only hoped she liked it.

As he strummed his thumb against Gina's skin, she looked over at him and smiled. "So that's why you didn't want me to wear gloves."

He grinned. "Maybe a wee part of the reason. Dragon-shifters males tend to radiate heat and I didn't want your hands getting sweaty inside a glove."

"Right, I'm sure that's the reason." She swung their hands a few times and asked, "Where are we going?"

He motioned toward the right. "Over there."

"You know, you could give a little more detail."

He winked. "And ruin the surprise? I think not. I like watching the wheels in your head turn as you try to guess what it is."

"Considering you told me to wear my warmest coat, it has to be outside. Unless you have secret dragon caves full of treasure somewhere."

He snorted. "And here I thought you were one of the more informed humans when it came to dragon-shifters."

She placed a hand on her hip. "Hey, most legends have a grain of truth to them. Considering all of the small mountains you have in Scotland, I'm sure you could easily hide things in some of them."

He quirked a brow. "Small mountains? The tallest mountain in the entire United Kingdom is right here in Scotland. If you want to get a Scot on your side, either human or dragon, you don't want to go around insulting our beautiful landscape."

"Oh, it's pretty. I won't deny it. My grandma always talked about how I should see the mountains on a clear day with the heather in bloom. But the Blue Ridge Mountains are in Virginia, and the rest of the Appalachian Mountains aren't that far away. Both are somewhat more impressive than the mountains here, I think." She met his eye again. "Have you ever been to America? You could see them and compare."

"I went once for a few weeks. I met with some other dragon-shifter intelligence analysts from friendly clans for training in Virginia. I've seen the mountains you're talking about, but while beautiful, it's not Scotland."

She tilted her head. "Now who's insulting someone's beautiful landscape?"

He stopped and tugged her close. "You're too clever for your own good."

"But would you really want it any other way?"

He murmured, "No," and lowered his head to kiss Gina when someone whistled. A familiar voice shouted, "I knew you had it in you, Fergus."

"Fraser," Fergus growled and looked over his shoulder. "Shouldn't you be at work?"

Fraser approached them and Fergus put an arm around Gina's waist. His brother noted the gesture and grinned.

"Considering you should be working yourself, you're not one to talk."

He grunted. "Finn gave me a few days to see Gina settled in. You, on the other hand, should be finishing up the new warehouses."

Fraser shrugged. "It's lunchtime."

"And you just happened to be crossing through this part of the clan's land, which is directly opposite of your construction site."

Fraser winked. "I may have heard you were spotted this way. But I wanted to make sure the lass is all right." Fraser looked to Gina. "How're you, lass? If you need a little break from my brother, I'd be happy to oblige."

Fergus growled. "You have a mate."

Fraser put a hand on his heart. "Is that what you think of me? Holly and I want to show her around together."

"I'm sure," Fergus muttered.

Fraser looked back to Gina. "So, how about it? Holly and I would love to take you out to lunch and tell you everything you want to know about my twin brother. Poking at his pet peeves can be fun."

Gina raised her chin. "No, thank you. Fergus is taking me to a surprise. So unless you know what it is and want to spill the beans, we'll be on our way."

Fraser blinked and Fergus barked out a laugh. "It looks like you can add another female to the list of those who can resist your charm, brother."

Fraser stood taller. "Then I'll just have to up my game. Next time, I'll have Gina giggling at my words."

From the corner of Fergus's eye, he saw Gina roll hers and say, "I was in college until very recently. Guys in their late teens and early twenties think they're charming, but in reality they're being ridiculous. You would be easy to resist in comparison, Fraser."

Fergus squeezed Gina's shoulder in encouragement and added, "She has you down to a T, brother. So how about you act ridiculous somewhere else?"

Fraser sighed. "Does the last twenty-nine years mean nothing to you, Fergus?"

"Of course they do. However, you irritating me isn't recent. Besides, we'll see you later on anyway. Let us go or we'll be late for Gina's surprise."

"If I must." Fraser gave a dramatic bow and looked up at Gina. "Until later, my lady."

They took their leave of Fraser. Fergus met Gina's gaze. "He might be irritating, but Fraser is not only my best friend, he's loyal and would sacrifice his life to save his family."

Gina patted his chest. "I know. His mate has been extremely kind to me and I'm in her debt. Still, I learned the hard way to deflect charm right away to save myself a headache later on, so I took that approach with Fraser."

Fergus frowned. "Just how many males did you have to chase away?" She tapped her chin and he growled. "How many, Gina?"

"My, my, I see your possessiveness is back. Will it ever go away?"

"Probably not. You still haven't answered my question."

She raised her brows. "Is this how you get information out of people to help your clan?" She poked his bicep. "It could be a bit off-putting."

"Only you bring this demanding nature out of me, Gina MacDonald." Afraid he might've scared the lass, he searched her eyes. But all he saw was curiosity. He sighed. "I can't help it. My dragon's mood is affecting my actions. He's the possessive bastard out of the two of us."

She placed her hand on his chest. "I knew about inner dragons, but I never really understood how much they could influence your human half."

He played with a strand of her hair. "Aye, they do quite a bit. Usually, I can control him. But it's hard to do with you, lass."

"Why?" she asked.

Knowing what he did of her past with the Yank arsehole, he wasn't sure it was the right time to tell her about being his true mate.

His dragon growled. *The longer you wait, the more difficult I'll become.*

A few more hours won't kill you.

His beast huffed. *It just might. Because of your surprise, a single, unattached dragonman will see her today and he may go after her.*

We've known Alistair Boyd our whole lives. Stop being ridiculous. The male likes to keep to himself and isn't about to charm Gina away.

But he has knowledge our female wants.

Fergus mentally sighed. *I'm done arguing for now.*

Ignoring his beast, he focused back on Gina. "I can either answer your question or take you to your surprise. If we don't hurry, we'll be late and miss it."

Indecision battled in her gaze. She finally nodded. "Okay, I'll let it go for now. But I won't answer your question until you answer mine."

The corner of his mouth ticked up. "Fair enough. Are you okay to walk a little faster, lass? I don't want to be late."

Gina picked up her pace. "Tell me, does Fraser drop his act once you get to know him?"

145

He was glad for the change of subject. "Aye, he can. The idiot risked everything to save Holly a few months back. Despite not being a soldier, he took on some traitors and brought her home safely."

Gina frowned. "What traitors?"

He debated answering Gina's question. He never wanted to hold back with her, but he made his living sorting out secrets and delicate information.

His dragon grunted. *Telling her about the traitors won't hurt anyone. Most of it aired on the news last year anyway.*

Some, but not all.

Then tell her what broadcasted and maybe a bit more. She may have trusted us with her body, but we need to win both her mind and heart.

And we will.

His beast growled. *Stop wasting time and get on with it.*

He answered Gina's question, "Well, not everyone approved of Finn assuming leadership of the clan and a few of them caused trouble. However, they made the mistake of putting Arabella's life in danger, so Finn exiled those who wouldn't stand with him. The only problem is that the ones who left the clan banded together and are looking for a way to bring Lochguard down."

Gina placed a hand on her stomach. "Are they an immediate threat?"

He rubbed up and down her arm. "No, lass. I haven't heard anything about an attack, nor has our head Protector, and we both take our jobs and duties seriously."

"You, take a job seriously? I never would've guess."

He lightly tugged her arm. "Hey, now. The clan's safety depends on it."

"I know, Fergus. I think I need to tease you a lot more often until you don't explain yourself each time."

For the first time since he was a wee lad, Fergus had the urge to stick out his tongue. But somehow, he resisted. "As long as it means you're staying with me, you can tease me as much as you like."

Gina grinned. "Good, then I'm going to hold you to that statement."

With her cheeks flushed pink from the cold and her green eyes sparkling, Fergus couldn't help but lean down and murmur, "Do whatever you wish, my bonny lass."

He gently kissed her and pulled back a fraction to meet her eyes again. His dragon preened at the desire in her eyes. *She will stay. She is ours.*

Gina stood on her tiptoes and kissed him again before whispering, "We're going to do a lot more kissing later. But right now, we're going to be late."

Fergus raised an eyebrow. "Now who's the responsible one?"

"Hey, I can be responsible and fun. But I don't do well with waiting when it comes to surprises." She took his hand and tugged. "Come on."

Kissing her nose, he answered, "We're nearly there." Forcing himself to turn away and start walking, he nodded toward the old, long two-story brick building in the distance. "Your surprise is in there."

"What's inside?"

Looking to her face, he answered, "A school. I'm taking you to a dragon-shifter history class."

Gina's eyes lit up. "Really? As in a real class with stories humans never hear about?"

He grinned. "Aye. After hearing about how you were so interested in dragon-shifters during college, I figured you might like some lessons. The stories will better help you understand your wee bairn."

She grabbed his hand on her arm. "Thank you."

Both man and beast drank in the sight of their female's happiness.

Clearing his throat, he nodded to the school. "But we'd better hurry. Alistair Boyd hates tardiness and since he was kind enough to allow us to sit in, we don't want to be late."

Gina nodded. "Then let's go."

As she tugged him toward the building, Fergus smiled. Maybe after the lesson, when Gina was in a good mood, he could finally tell her the truth about being his true mate. After all, what male wouldn't want the clever, stubborn, beautiful human for their own? He needed to claim her as soon as possible.

His dragon grunted. *You're not helping.*

Pushing aside his beast and any thoughts about other males, Fergus squeezed Gina's hand. She looked up at him with a smile and Fergus knew she wouldn't look twice at Alistair. For the moment, her eyes were only for him.

CHAPTER TWELVE

Gina's heart rate sped up as Fergus guided her through the school's main entrance. And not just because she was about to hear some actual dragon-shifter history. No, her heart also hammered because she would have the chance to see some of the young dragon-shifters.

BroadBay had never allowed their children to be seen by humans. Well, at least, beyond the sacrifices who gave birth to them.

Since Gina was about to give birth to her own in a few weeks' time, she wanted to prepare herself for the challenge. If Fergus had trouble controlling his own dragon, it had to be much harder for a child. Gina only hoped she could help when her own son's time came.

Yet as they walked down one empty hall and then another, she darted glances at Fergus's profile. Things were going well. Maybe Fergus could help her when she needed it. She had a feeling he would be a good father.

Fergus motioned toward a door on the left and she focused back on the school as he said, "In here. Follow my lead."

Turning the doorknob, Fergus inched the door open slowly without making a noise. She had a feeling it wasn't the first time her dragonman had snuck inside a place silently. Maybe someday he'd tell her about his past adventures with his brother.

As soon as Gina stepped inside the door, nine pairs of eyes turned toward her. Eight of them belonged to young teens and the remaining set was from the tall, dark-haired dragonman at the front of the room.

Before anyone could say a word, a bell chimed. The dragonman up front motioned toward her and Fergus. "These are our guests for the day. I'm sure you know Fergus MacKenzie as he and his twin have reputations at this school from more than a decade ago. He's brought along a human female named Gina MacDonald. I expect you to treat both of them with respect. If we finish the lesson early, they might even answer a few questions."

Various voices murmured, "Yes, sir," before tearing their gaze from Gina and turning toward the front.

Fergus gently pressed against her back and whispered, "Let's sit down."

Gina was debating how she could sit in the plastic chairs for any length of time without fidgeting when Fergus guided them toward two padded chairs in the back. With a sigh of relief, she sat down. Fergus took one of her hands in his warm one. Placing her other one on her belly, she looked to Alistair Boyd.

Alistair began. "While dragon-shifters mostly kept to themselves during the medieval period in England, when the Normans took over the country from the Vikings, one event divided all of the dragon clans and they scattered around the country—we call it the Harrying of the North. Has anyone heard of it?"

Gina had no idea. However, during her time at college, Gina had suffered through several professors who could put someone to sleep with their voices. Alistair's, on the other hand, was not only a yummy Scots' accent, but also deep and full of energy. She actually sat on the edge of her seat, eager to find out what it was.

One of the male students spoke up. "Didn't that happen in England? Why would we learn about it? Does it even matter?"

"Events often have consequences we can only see in hindsight. There might not even be a Lochguard today if not for what happened in 1069 and 1070 C.E.," Alistair answered.

Before she could check herself, Gina blurted out, "How?" All eyes turned toward her. She drew strength from Fergus squeezing her hand and added, "I don't even know what this Harrying is." She shrugged. "I'm curious."

Some of the students murmured, "She's American."

The corner of Alistair's mouth ticked up. "I'm not sure most of the students know, either, lass." He waved toward the boy who had answered. "But Rory seems to have an idea. What is it, lad?"

Rory straightened his shoulders and looked at Gina. She saw his pupils flash to slits and back before he answered, "It's when William the Conqueror killed a lot of humans in Northern England to teach them a lesson."

She frowned. "Why did he need to do that?"

Alistair replied, "The short answer is to prevent another revolt and establish his power there. He slaughtered families, burned crops, and destroyed houses. The most cited reference says 100,000 people were killed or displaced. However, historians dispute that number, saying there was no way William's armies could have accomplished that much destruction given their numbers."

Gina put together a theory. "Some dragon-shifters could've sided with the conqueror guy and helped him."

Alistair nodded. "Exactly. Now, let's get into why this is important."

As the teacher dragonman turned on a projector and preceded to tell the story of how different dragon factions helped William's Harrying while others took in refugees and helped rebuild communities, Gina soaked in all of the information. The media usually portrayed dragon-shifters as selfish, brutish creatures. While that might be true in BroadBay's case, she was starting to see it differently. Between Lochguard and the history of some dragon-shifters helping the human refugees in the winter of 1069-1070, her fear of her son turning out similar to Travis and the rest of BroadBay lessened. With Fergus and Lochguard behind her, she could easily see her son sitting in this very classroom, learning the lesson she was hearing.

For the first time, Gina had more hope than worry for the future.

~~~

Fergus had to give Alistair credit—the dragonman was much more engaging than the history teacher they'd shared as teenagers. Old Mr. Morrison had usually ordered them to read books silently while he scribbled notes at his desk. No questions were to be asked. If a student tried, Mr. Morrison's response had always been to find it in the book.

In a way, that retired dragonman helped make Fergus who he was since he always looked for answers on his own first.

Yet as Gina kept raising her hand and participating in the class, he soon forgot about his old school days and simply enjoyed watching his female's enthusiasm.

His dragon spoke up. *I wish she was this enthusiastic with us.*

She will be. Once we find out all of her favorites, we can surprise her all of the time.

You're supposed to be an intelligence analyst, so start gathering information and figure it out.

You know I already have. Just have some patience.

His beast huffed and fell silent. His bloody dragon wasn't much better than a spoiled teenager. Maybe once Gina agreed to be their mate, his dragon would mature and mellow a bit. Not that Fergus was holding his breath; if Holly's influence didn't help mature his brother, he doubted his dragon would do it alone.

The bell chimed, signaling the end of class. Alistair held up a hand and the students fell silent. "We ran short of time today, but maybe Ms. MacDonald can join us again and you can ask her some questions then. For tonight, I want you to write one paragraph on how the Harrying of the North helped to shape modern dragon-shifter society. You're dismissed."

One of the two female teenagers in the room turned and stared at Gina. Fergus tensed, in case he needed to protect his human. But then the teenager smiled and walked up to her. "I hope you'll come back, Ms. MacDonald. I've always wanted to ask about the American dragon clans."

Gina tensed under his hand, but she kept smiling and her tone was light. "I'd love to come back. I'm not sure what I can tell you, but I can give it a go."

Alistair's voice boomed out. "You'll be late, Lindsey. You can talk with Ms. MacDonald later."

Lindsey smiled one last time and left. Alistair closed the door and then leaned against his desk. "You're quite the student, lass. Come back any time you like. You tend to ask the questions the teenagers are often afraid to ask."

153

Fergus stood and helped tug Gina to her feet. Excitement filled her eyes. "Can I? I was worried about asking too many, but soon the others joined in and everyone got involved. It's just so interesting. Very little American dragon-shifter history is known, so it's nice to learn anything at all."

Fergus's dragon growled. *Keep her away from Alistair.*

Don't worry. Even if Alistair wasn't an honorable male, we have to leave soon anyway. He has a meeting in ten minutes.

So I'm not the only one worried.

I'm not worried. But I want more time alone with Gina.

Alistair nodded at Gina. "Provided Finn says it's okay, you can sit in any time. Maybe I can even drop by the MacKenzie house for supper soon and I can give you more answers in a one-on-one session, if you like."

Fergus growled. "That won't be necessary, Alistair."

Alistair studied him a second. "Like that, is it? I didn't know."

Fergus should've pinned a sprig of heather on Gina's coat earlier. Then he wouldn't have to go through this; everyone would know she was his true mate then.

Fergus nodded. "It is."

Gina looked from Fergus to Alistair and back again. "Like what? Tell me what's going on Fergus."

He looked down at Gina. "Let's go somewhere private and talk." Gina's eyes turned concerned and he cupped her cheek with his free hand. "Don't think of the worst possibilities, lass. I just have a bit of news."

Alistair cleared his throat. "Well, you two clearly have a very important conversation. I have a meeting in here with a few other teachers, so you should probably get going anyway."

Gina smiled at Alistair and Fergus prevented himself from growling again as she said, "Thanks for having me, Alistair. I'll be back and soon you'll be begging me to leave."

The corner of Alistair's mouth ticked up. "I doubt it, Ms. MacDonald."

"Call me Gina."

Fergus grunted. "Thanks, Alistair, but we should be going."

"Aye. And good luck, Fergus."

Gina shot Fergus a quizzical look, but he ignored it to guide his female out of the room. When they set foot in the hallway, Gina opened her mouth but Fergus cut her off. "Not here, lass. Dragon-shifters possess keen hearing."

Curiosity burned in her eyes, but she merely answered, "Okay."

They both walked in silence out the door and toward a protected rock formation. He ducked behind it, drawing Gina along with him, and then turned to face her. Gina frowned up at him. "Are you going to tell me why you were growling and grunting back in the classroom? Alistair was kind enough to answer my questions. He even invited me back. He deserved better."

"Aye, he's a good male. And he does deserve better. But there's a reason why I can't help it. He's unattached and my dragon doesn't like it."

"Why should that matter? I'm fairly certain the teenagers were mostly unattached, as you put it, and you didn't growl at them."

Taking both of her hands in his, Fergus took a deep inhalation. He couldn't put it off any longer. "I want to tell you something, Gina. But promise me you won't act strange or run away when I tell you."

"Why?" she drawled out.

"I'm not going to hurt you, if that's what you're worried about, lass. In fact, quite the opposite. I spent the whole lecture staring at your lips, wanting to taste them again."

Gina's cheeks flushed, but her tone remained strong. "Don't try to change the subject. And don't make me promise anything without all of the facts."

He released one of her hand to trace her cheek. "Then just listen to what I have to say. Can you do that?"

"I suppose so." She searched his eyes. "Tell me whatever it is, Fergus. You're starting to scare me."

His dragon snarled. Fergus told his beast, *Quiet or I'll never get it out.*

Fergus looked into Gina's green eyes and answered the unspoken question there. "Normally, I'm one of the most restrained and polite dragon-shifters in the entire clan." He traced Gina's bottom lip. "But then I met you."

She drew in a breath. "What does that have to do with anything?"

"It has to do with everything, lass. You're my true mate."

"What?"

Fergus moved closer and leaned his forehead against hers. "I know you were hurt by the other bastard claiming to be your true mate. But he was lying. My dragon wants you as mate, lass. And more importantly, I want you even more because of who you are, if that's possible. You're clever, strong-willed, and kind. Few would've offered to help Arabella the way you did, let alone worry about spending time with my family when you have your own bairn coming soon." He searched her eyes. "You can take as much time as you need. I know you have a child coming and he should be the most important thing in your life. All I'm asking is for you to think about it, and if there is any more room in your heart, to just give me a chance."

~~~

Gina's heart beat double-time inside her chest.

If Fergus were telling the truth, she was his true mate. Part of her wanted to hug him close and never let go. However, her life wasn't as simple as finding a man she could see herself caring about and staying with him. The DDA or BroadBay could show up demanding her child at any moment. Who knew what would happen if Fergus tried to prevent them from taking her son.

The sensible thing would be to put distance between them to protect Fergus. But just the thought of never seeing Fergus's smiling face or feeling the sizzle at his touch squeezed her heart. After what she'd been through with Travis, she wanted more of Fergus, much more.

Fergus smiled and garnered her attention. He whispered, "I see the wheels turning. Just think about it. But while you do, remember this."

He tilted his head and kissed her.

She leaned against him and melted into his kiss, loving how he tasted. She couldn't imagine ever getting enough of her dragonman. If only she could find a way to ensure everyone's safety, she'd jump into his arms and growl at any woman who looked his way.

All too soon Fergus pulled away and gave her one last, quick brush of his lips. "Did that help or hurt my case?"

She smiled. "Wouldn't you like to know."

Fergus growled and placed a possessive hand on her butt. "I wouldn't try teasing me about this, Gina. My dragon is a possessive bastard."

She raised her brows. "Oh, just your dragon, huh?"

He lightly slapped her ass. "Cheeky lass."

As they grinned at one another, Gina decided she needed to talk with Finn later. If there was a way to stay and keep Fergus safe, she would try it. "Of course."

He kissed her quickly and then released her. She nearly reached out to pull him close again, but resisted. She was already falling for Fergus MacKenzie. Gina didn't want to tempt herself or allow him to burrow any deeper into her heart until she knew her future.

Fergus's pupils flashed. "We should get you inside and out of the cold."

She pointed a finger at him. "You can tell your dragon-half that I'm fine. I won't break that easily."

"To appease him, I'll just do this."

Fergus drew her up against his side and she sank into his warmth. "Uh-huh. I'm sure it's just for your dragon. Your sensible human side would never use a ruse to hold a woman close."

He grunted. "Not with any woman but you, Gina."

Gina laid her head on Fergus's chest. "Good, because I'm feeling pretty growly myself today."

Her dragonman chuckled. "Then come on. We have some time before we have to meet Arabella. I have a few ideas of how to spend it."

As they walked, Gina looked up at him. "Oh? And what exactly are they?"

"Not out here. Others might hear."

"Come on. I'm curious." She lowered her voice. "You mentioned tying me up at breakfast. Is that one of your fantasies?" His dragon eyes flashed and she grinned. "It is, isn't it?"

He met her gaze and his voice was husky as he replied, "You're a tease, Gina MacDonald." He moved his hand to her ass and squeezed. A rush of heat flooded her body. "And I hope you live up to it. I'm sure I can find a few scarves somewhere." His eyes moved to her protruding belly. "Although, we may have to wait a bit for that."

She shivered at the promise in his voice. "As much as I love my son, I wish he were a little bit smaller right now. I want to try out that fantasy sooner rather than later."

"Aye? Well, then maybe we should start making a list. That way, we'll be full of ideas after the bairn is born and you're healed."

Not wanting to break the spell, she didn't point out how she might not be able to stay. Instead, she purred, "We might just have to do that. Then you can dream about them and have plenty of time to perfect how you'd take me."

Slapping her ass, he leaned down to nuzzle her cheek. "Oh, it won't be just me, lass. I'm sure I can think of a few situations that you'll be dreaming about for months to come."

Remembering Fergus's hard, warm chest against her back from the night before made her shiver. "I wish it were now."

He chuckled. "Me, too, lass. But anticipation will make it that much hotter."

"You're an expert now?"

He stopped and pulled her up against his body. "I don't claim to know the female mind, but I can already smell your

JESSIE DONOVAN

arousal. If I can do that with words, just imagine what I can do after months of planning and the use of my hands."

Her clit pulsed to attention. "Damn you, Fergus. Teasing you has backfired."

"Aye, it has. And I like it."

Lowering his head, he kissed her. His lips and tongue were slow and gentle, as if savoring her taste.

Not caring who might see, Gina threaded her fingers through his hair and pulled him close. Maybe, just maybe, Gina might find her happily ever after in the end. She just needed to use her brain to figure out a plan.

Then Fergus snaked a hand between them to her breast and Gina lost all rational thought. For the moment, she simply enjoyed the dragonman in front of her.

CHAPTER THIRTEEN

A week later, Gina still hadn't been able to talk with Finn. Every time she made an appointment, something came up. He'd actually spent the last two days down with Clan Stonefire, planning some kind of top secret mission.

And every day that passed only made her fall a little more for Fergus.

Even now, he stood next to the hospital bed and held her hand as Dr. Innes performed an ultrasound. Her dragonman had insisted on staying and the look of awe on his face as he stared at the picture on the screen would stay with Gina always. Given the chance, she knew Fergus would treat her son as his own. And Gina wanted to give him the chance.

That settled it. After her appointment was over, Gina would track down Finn and tie him to a chair if need be. Arabella might even help her since Gina and Arabella had been spending a lot of time together to plan the triplets' room. The dragonwoman was slowly opening up to her. And given Arabella's past and former hatred of humans, it was quite a feat according to Fergus.

Fergus squeezed her hand and she smiled up at him as he asked, "Are you okay, lass? You had a faraway look in your eyes."

"I'll tell you once the appointment is over." She looked down at Dr. Innes. He was tall, about forty, and nearly as protective as Fergus when it came to her son. Since Dr. Innes had lost his mate and baby during a delivery over a decade ago, Gina at least understood his concern.

Still, she forced herself to ask, "Is everything still well?"

Dr. Innes nodded. "Aye. Your son's heartbeat is strong and he's nearly in position for the delivery. He should be along any time now."

"But that's a few weeks early, isn't it?"

"It is, but dragon-shifter babies usually arrive a little early for human mothers." Dr. Innes flicked his gaze to Fergus and back to Gina. "I'm sure you're aware of the risks."

Gina nodded. "I've had a week to absorb all that you and Holly have told me." She shrugged. "There's really not much else I can do but sit and wait."

Dr. Innes' voice was quiet when he answered, "It's not a light matter, Gina. The risk is real."

Fergus growled. "Between you and Holly, Gina will be fine. Scaring her will only raise her blood pressure. After what happened with Evie Marshall down on Stonefire, I don't want to risk anything with Gina."

Gina tugged on Fergus's hand and he met her gaze. "Evie had preeclampsia. So far, all of my tests have come back normal."

Fergus grunted. "It could still happen. There aren't always symptoms."

Gina sighed. "You could be hit by a bolt of lightning tomorrow. Does that mean you're going to stay locked inside a lightning cage for the rest of your life?"

Fergus shook his head. "Don't be daft, lass. Of course not. But the odds of being hit by lightning are much better than a human dying when bearing a dragon-shifter's child."

Dr. Innes placed the ultrasound equipment on a side tray and stood up. "How about we stop talking about odds and focus on Gina and the bairn? Gina, lass, I know you're not going to like it, but I need someone to be with you at all times. I don't want you alone when your labor begins."

Fergus straightened his shoulders. "I can work from home. I'll watch over her."

Dr. Innes answered before Gina could. "Good. I'll probably have Holly spend some time at the old Sinclair place as well."

Gina sighed. "I don't get a say in this, do I?"

"No," both men answered at the same time.

"I swear you guys have been rehearsing behind my back. Are we done now?"

The doctor smiled. "Aye, we're done. Both you and the bairn are healthy. The next time I see you, it might be when you're in labor."

Gina placed a hand on her stomach. "I'm both anxious and afraid. And not because of the danger. I can't believe I'm going to have to do this without drugs."

Fergus brushed her brow. "I know, lass. But it could hurt the bairn if you have them."

She met Fergus's gaze again. "Considering how stubborn dragon-shifters are, I would expect them to fight it and just come out fine on the other side."

Dr. Innes snorted. "Just give your son a few years. He'll think his stubbornness can solve everything."

Despite his light tone, Gina noticed the sadness in the doctor's eyes. The poor man was probably thinking of his unborn child. How he dealt with birthing children as part of his career, Gina had no idea.

"Well, he'll have to deal with me. Just because I'm human doesn't mean I'm going to allow my son to walk all over me. Him changing into his dragon form won't affect my resolve one bit."

The doctor chuckled. "You'll do, Gina MacDonald. You'll do." Dr. Innes picked up his clipboard. "I wish I could chat longer, but old Cal and Archie have been up to their tricks again and I need to check both of them for broken bones." The doctor nodded to them both. "Don't hesitate to call me when you need it."

Gina murmured, "Thank you." And in the next second, she was alone again with Fergus.

Looking up at him, she asked, "Can you help me sit up?"

As he helped her off her back, he spoke up. "Do you remember old Cal and Archie?"

Gina grunted and swung her legs to the side. "How could I forget? They accidentally dropped a boulder into our yard."

Fergus grinned. "Aye, Archie's grip slipped. But those two have been at it for most of their lives and won't stop until they're dead. Even then, one will probably claim to see the other's ghost walking about and try to tease it."

Gina started pulling on her clothes. "Let's just hope they don't drop a boulder on top of our house."

Fergus leaned down to nibble her ear. "Our house, aye? I like the sound of it."

She shook her head. "Why you still keep your stuff in the other half, I'll never understand."

He kissed the corner of her mouth. "I don't want to rush you."

She raised an eyebrow. "And yet you speak for me with the doctor?"

"You know why."

164

Gina did. But since she hadn't had time to speak with Finn, she couldn't guarantee their future. As much as she wanted to claim Fergus as her own, she couldn't.

That reminded her. "I need to see Finn as soon as possible."

"But you have an appointment with him tomorrow."

"Well, it can't wait. I'm tired of him canceling. As my Guardian, you need to help me. Otherwise, I'll resort to my own tactics."

Fergus growled. "You're due any time now. Don't be daft, lass. As I've said before, you're safe here."

"That's not the reason. I need to talk with Finn. Believe me, you'll thank me later."

"And yet you won't tell me why?"

"I just need you to trust me in this, Fergus. Can you do that?"

Fergus studied her a second before his pupils flashed. "Fine. You can thank my dragon's incessant roaring. I think he's going to always take your side over mine from now on."

She beamed. "I guess me petting him in dragon form yesterday is helping my case. I might just have to scratch behind his ears again later."

Fergus's pupils changed to slits and back to round. "Thanks for that, lass. Next, you'll convince my bloody beast to take you for a ride in one of the baskets despite being eight-and-a-half-months pregnant."

"There's an idea." Fergus growled and Gina laughed. "You're so easy to tease."

"Aye, well, if you want my help with Finn, you might want to be nice to me."

Gina tilted her head. "Oh, you haven't seen anything yet. Wait until I can actually sneak about instead of waddle. I have a few surprises in store for you, Fergus MacKenzie. Unless you're too old for a little fun now and then?"

He moved to stand between her legs. "Twenty-nine isn't old. I thought I'd proved that to you by now."

Placing a hand on his chest, she fluttered her eyelashes. "I may have forgotten. After all, I have pregnancy brain and my memory is a little faulty."

Fergus cupped her cheek and strummed his thumb against her skin. "I say we rush home and I'll remind you again." Her dragonman leaned down and gently kissed her. All too soon, he pulled away and whispered, "What do you say?"

Gina leaned forward, but then caught herself. "Help me talk with Finn first. Then you can do a little reminding."

Searching her eyes, he sighed. "That stubborn glint is back. I don't stand a chance of changing your mind, do I?"

"No."

"Then aye, I'll help you. But, you'll stay with Arabella or my mum whilst I set it up. That's the condition."

The corner of her mouth ticked up. "Aw, there goes my idea to sneak off in black ninja garb and jump Finn out of nowhere."

"If I didn't lo— er, like you so much, lass, I would call you a bit crazy."

Gina's heart rate kicked up. She had a feeling Fergus had meant to say 'love' instead of like.

A small part of her was thrilled that he felt that way. But until she knew she could stay with Fergus, she wouldn't explore that topic. Gina had a grip on her feelings still, but barely.

166

Brushing off the comment, she offered up her hands. "Help me up, dragonman. Otherwise, it could take me a good twenty minutes to get to my feet."

His eyes flashed as he murmured, "Now I know how to keep you in place for a wee spell if I need it."

She snorted, glad that he was acting as if he hadn't misspoken. "Do that to me and it's game on, dragonman."

Fergus kissed her and answered, "We'll see, lass. We'll see."

The next second, Fergus tugged her to her feet and wrapped an arm around her shoulders. As they left the surgery, Gina snuggled against Fergus's warmth. Teasing aside, she hoped Finn would find a way for her to stay. After the last week, giving up Fergus might break her heart in two.

~~~

Fergus hugged Gina closer to his side. He was just glad she hadn't caught on to his near-mistake of saying "love."

His beast grunted. *Gina is clever. I'm sure she figured it out.*

Females tend to react when they think a male says love. She's close to her time, so she might be too tired to put it together like she normally would.

These human games are pointless. We should move our things into her house today.

Help me with Finn, and we might just be able to do it.

I would, but you won't like my idea. I'd just pin Finn down and force him to meet with your female.

Right, because Finn would just lie there and allow it to happen.

He might.

Ignoring his dragon, Fergus looked down at Gina. "Do you want to stay with Arabella or with my mum while I hunt down Finn?"

167

"As much as I love watching the MacKenzie Family TV show, I think I'll go with Ara, if she's available."

"Don't mention the TV show idea around Fraser. He might actually try to pitch it to Jane Hartley on Stonefire."

Gina frowned. "I thought she was a BBC reporter."

Fergus nodded. "Aye, she was. But after she mated Kai Sutherland down on Stonefire, she had to sever ties with the BBC. She's in the process of launching her own video podcast about dragon-shifters."

"Somehow, I can't imagine the reporter I saw interviewing Arabella launching a reality TV show."

The corner of his mouth ticked up. "Now who's being serious and stuffy?"

She lightly slapped his side. "As if you would allow it to happen. Although, a 'get-to-know Lochguard' special might be in order."

"Is that what you want to talk with Finn about?"

"Of course not. Although I could always bring it up." Excitement filled her eyes. "Actually, I might have a way I can help your clan. Remember how I told you I nearly earned my marketing degree?" Fergus nodded and his lass continued, "If I teamed up with Jane Hartley, I bet we could launch a campaign. Her videocast numbers could jump and we might even be able to do a little advertising. Then her venture could become sustainable for the long haul. I know I'll have to wait a few months until after my son is born and I've established a routine. But even working a few hours here and there, I could throw something together in four-to-six weeks."

He squeezed her tighter against his side. "Provided you get Finn's permission, I'll help you any way I can, lass."

She bobbed her head. "Awesome. Then I can mention that, too, when I talk to Finn today."

"If I can find him. He's due back from Stonefire in about an hour."

Gina opened her mouth to reply when a warning siren blared across the clan's lands.

Finn had had them installed after what happened with Holly and the rogue dragons. They signaled unidentified dragons approaching.

Fergus shouted above the noise. "Come, I need to get you to safety."

"What's happening?"

"Unknown dragons are flying toward Lochguard. It could be nothing, but it could be the rogue dragons trying to take us down. Come on. We need to hurry."

Fergus changed direction and headed toward the warehouses at the far end of the clan's land. Thanks to Fraser, Fergus was one of the few that knew security bunkers had been installed underneath the new warehouses. The key players knew to meet there in the event of an emergency.

Gina may not yet be considered one of them, but there was no bloody way he was going to leave her above ground and risk her being injured. Or, worse, being taken.

Because Fergus still needed to find out if the unknown dragons were the rogue traitors or if they were with BroadBay. Either way, they would have to kill him before he allowed them to take Gina or their son away from him.

CHAPTER FOURTEEN

No matter how much Grant McFarland zoomed in the security cameras, he couldn't get a clear enough picture of the oncoming dragons to try and identify them. The dragons might be friendly and nothing to be concerned about, but Finn had entrusted Grant with the clan. There was no bloody way he was going to chance an attack.

His dragon growled. *Let's fly up and surround them. There are more of us than them.*

And what if there are others waiting for the signal to join them?

I still say we go.

Not everything requires confrontation. Shut it and let me think.

His beast snarled and retreated to the back of his mind. Grant looked to Iris, Lochguard's best tracker. "Take a small party and search out any other dragons from the ground. I need to know how many we're dealing with."

Iris nodded, her short black hair bouncing around her jaw. "Keep someone manned on the radio." She pointed at two lower level Protectors. "Come with me."

As the trio left, Faye MacKenzie burst into the room. "What's the situation?"

For a split second, Grant was distracted by her pink cheeks and the strands of wild, curly hair that had escaped her braid. He'd been so wrapped up on instituting new protocols and surveillance that Grant hadn't seem much of the lass as of late, except during their secret project trials. Even then, there had been a dozen dragon-shifters present and Grant had never had the chance to talk with Faye alone. However, judging by the healthy glow of her skin, she was almost completely recovered from her accident last year.

He'd have to make a point of testing her abilities later. For the moment, he debated how to use her. Her family would tell Faye to sit on the sidelines because they didn't believe she was fully healed. But Grant knew Faye's spirit would slowly fade if he kept dismissing her. Faye was a warrior and always would be.

His dragon spoke up again. *She's stronger. Let her help.*

Always you bloody suggesting her.

We're thinking the same thing. Stop overanalyzing everything and go with your gut.

Grant eyed Faye's flushed cheeks and even breathing. "We have some unknown dragons approaching. I want you to run to the bunker and watch over whoever is there. If it comes to a fight, I need someone on the ground who can take charge."

She raised her brows. "Does this mean I can tell you what to do, like in the old days?"

The corner of his mouth ticked up. "Aye, it might. But hurry. If the battle is over before you reach the bunker, you'll lose the chance."

Determination glinted in Faye's gaze. "Oh, I'll make it. And someday, you'll acknowledge that I'm faster than you again."

Before he could reply, Faye raced out of the room. For once, he wished he could follow her and have that race. But he was head Protector and the clan needed him.

Grant focused back on the security camera feed. The dragons were flying at a gentle pace, which signaled it probably wasn't an attack. Of course, it could just be the cold January temperatures slowing the beasts down.

He pressed a button that connected him to the security post at the front gate. "Shay, I want you to spare as many of your staff as possible and have them shift in the sheltered landing area. I want them ready on a second's notice."

Shay replied, "Aye, consider it done."

Grant moved his gaze to Brodie, one of the males in the room. "Take the B-squad and do the same. The sooner we start warming up our muscles, the sooner we can fly without injury."

Brodie nodded and the B-squad members in the room followed him.

Grant studied the screen and wondered who the hell the red dragon was at the front of the formation. Since Grant knew every Scottish dragon by sight, and most of the English ones as well, the mystery dragon-shifter worried him.

His dragon huffed. *Why? We can hold our own. We defeated the dragons holding the hospital hostage a few months ago.*

Aye, and they were older dragons in their fifties, sixties, and seventies. These ones are young.

Faye would never back down.

Grant mentally growled. *I'm not backing down, you bloody dragon. I'll let you out when I need you.*

He created a complex mental maze and tossed his beast inside. As soon as his mind was quiet again, he gave the orders for his special surprise. If he were lucky and the strangers attacked, he might be able to lower the number of Lochguard casualties with his top secret maneuver. No doubt, the old-timers who had abandoned Lochguard would frown upon his surprise, but Grant would do whatever it took to protect his clan.

Moving his gaze back to the security feed, he waited to see what happened.

~~~

Gina half-ran and half-waddled to the entrance of the warehouse. She was definitely not fit for running at this point in her pregnancy.

Huffing and puffing, she somehow made her way into the entrance with Fergus right behind. They were greeted by Fraser's neutral expression, which made her stomach drop. She'd never seen Fraser so serious.

Fergus's twin nodded toward the door. "Come. The dragons are drawing nearer. We need to get you two inside."

Gina's heart thumped inside her chest. "Do we know who they are yet?"

Fraser shook his head. "No, but there's a video feed from the security cameras downstairs. You can take a look and let us know if any of the dragons are with BroadBay or not."

Fergus placed a hand on her back. "Regardless, you're safe here, lass. We won't let anyone try to take your or the bairn."

Gina looked up at her dragonman. "Even so, I want to see the feed. If it's BroadBay, I might recognize them. That could give you an edge over them."

As they moved down the stairs, Fergus frowned. "I thought you never saw them in dragon form."

"Not many of them. But I would recognize Travis anywhere." The pupils of both the MacKenzie twins flashed. Before either could speak, Gina did. "I want you two to promise me you won't try to kill him. No matter what he did, I won't have his blood on my hands."

173

They remained silent and Gina poked Fergus's chest. "Promise me, Fergus MacKenzie."

Fergus growled out, "Or, what's the threat?"

She shook her head. "There's no threat. I'm asking you to do this for me."

Fergus remained silent a second before answering, "Aye, I promise. But if he attacks you or anyone from the clan, he's fair game."

"That I can live with," Gina stated.

Fraser opened one last door and they entered a room decked out with high-tech equipment—flat screens, touch controls, and a lot of gadgets and buttons she didn't recognize. There was a male and female dragon-shifter manning stations toward the front, but despite looking like siblings with the same black hair and blue eyes, neither one of them were familiar. She'd just have to trust Fraser and Fergus that they were trustworthy.

Then Gina's eyes fell on the video of the dragons beating their wings in the sky in several V-formations.

Fergus pressed against her back. "Well, lass? Are any of them with BroadBay?"

Scrutinizing the dragons for any familiarities, she finally answered, "I don't think so."

Fraser spoke up. "It's probably the traitors, then. I'll let Grant know."

Gina held up a hand. "It still could be them. I've only seen a few members of Clan BroadBay in dragon form."

"Aye, well, we know the bastard isn't there, nor is the clan leader since we do have a picture of Steven Roberts on file. It's a start. I still need to tell Grant. Any and all information will help."

As Fraser went to the front, Gina leaned against Fergus's side. She murmured, "Is it wrong of me to hope it's the traitors and not the American clan?"

He hugged her tightly against him. "No, but it's a bit early to be celebrating. For all we know, they might be working together."

She raised her head. "Do you know something I don't?"

"I might."

"I know your work is classified and I never would ask for you to put your clan at risk. But is there anything at all you can tell me? Please, Fergus, if they're coming for me and my baby, I need to know."

Fergus stared down at her. One beat passed and then another. Finally, he replied, "There has been some chatter about British dragon-shifters talking with American-sounding ones over the last few days. While all of the witnesses are human and might have misjudged if the subjects were indeed dragon-shifters, I'm not about to dismiss it so casually. Neither has the DDA."

"Will the DDA help us?"

Fergus sighed. "I don't know, lass. Part of Finn's mission on Stonefire was to convince them to help us concerning you."

She blinked. "What?"

"Aye, Finn's in England to try and secure your future here."

~~~

Keeping Finn's true purpose from Gina had nearly torn Fergus in two. But his cousin's line of reasoning made sense—offering a safe haven before a deal could be made was foolish. Gina had suffered so much already and Finn didn't want to raise her hopes only to dash them. So, Fergus had agreed to keep the secret.

Gina turned to face him. "But Finn never asked me if I wanted to stay."

His dragon snarled in the back of his mind, but Fergus ignored it. "My cousin is fairly good at reading people. Was he wrong that you wanted to stay here?"

Fergus's heart skipped a beat at Gina's silence. He refused to believe Gina didn't care enough for him to stay.

Or, had he yearned too much for a mate that he'd constructed the image inside his head?

No. Fergus knew Gina cared for him.

His dragon growled. *This is why we needed to tell her we love her. Your caution may have cost us our mate.*

You're wrong, dragon. Saying the words too soon would've spooked her.

His beast huffed. *We'll find out soon enough.*

Thankfully, he didn't have to wait much longer. When Gina answered, her voice was strong. "You know, that's why I wanted to talk with him, actually. And also why I was so irritated that he kept canceling." She stood on her tiptoes and whispered, "I didn't want to give you false hope until I knew my future."

Fergus's dragon chimed in. *Ask her if she wants to stay with us.*

If Fergus were rational, he would save this conversation for a later time. But between his dragon's roaring and his own curiosity, he asked, "So you've thought about becoming my mate?"

Last week, the word had caused panic to flare in her eyes. But in the present, Gina's gaze was only full of hope. "I've been warming up to the idea."

176

He placed his hands possessively on her hips. "That's not a good enough answer."

She smiled and laid a hand on his cheek. The soft touch of her fingers eased his tension a fraction. "I thought you were supposed to be the patient MacKenzie?"

Leaning down, he nipped her bottom lip. "I am, except when it comes to you, lass. It's as if I become a whole different person around you."

She tilted her head. "Is that a bad thing?"

"Yes. No. Hell, it's both." Tightening his grip on her, he pulled her closer. "But I wouldn't change a thing, Gina MacDonald. You're everything I never knew I wanted."

Her eyes watered and his beast snarled. *Don't make her cry.*

Sometimes, tears are happy.

I still don't like it.

Gina wiped her eyes with the back of her hand and murmured, "I wish I knew if Finn had found a way for me to stay. There's so much I want to say."

"Then say it, lass. Because even if I have to leave here to follow you, I will. And not just because I'm your Guardian or because you're my true mate. Life would be lonely without you."

Gina shook her head. "But you can't leave your family and I would never ask you to do so."

The corner of his mouth ticked up. "Oh, they'd find a way to sneak off and see me. My brother and I have secret hideouts all over the Highlands."

Amusement twinkled in her eyes. "Full of treasure?"

Fergus chuckled. "Maybe one day, you'll find out."

As they stared at one another, Fergus willed the lass to speak her mind. But before she could say anything, Fraser rushed over to them and said, "I'm sorry to break up the lovey dovey time, but we have a problem."

Fergus frowned. "Spit it out already, brother."

Fraser answered, "Iris radioed back. She's found several wings of dragon-shifters just beyond the Naver forest." Fraser switched his gaze to Gina. "The ones in human form are speaking in an American accent. A few have mentioned Virginia."

Gina's body tensed under his fingers. "BroadBay."

Fraser nodded. "Aye, we think so. What's worse, Roderick McFarland is with the Yanks."

Confusion flashed on Gina's face and Fergus filled her in. "Roderick is one of the traitors who not only left the clan rather than accept Finn's leadership, but he helped lead the attack on the human hospital and Holly a few months ago."

Placing a hand over her belly, Gina looked between the twin brothers. "So, what's going to happen?"

Fergus stroked her side. "We wait. It's in the hands of Grant and the Protectors now."

Gina answered, "But I don't want anyone to die for me, Fergus. And that's a possibility."

He growled. "If you think I'm going to just allow you to waltz out of here and turn yourself over, you're sadly mistaken." Gina opened her mouth, but he cut her off by asking Fraser, "Can we patch in a line to Stonefire from here?"

Fraser shrugged. "Probably."

Fergus narrowed his eyes. "Then do it. I want to talk to Bram Moore-Llewellyn."

Fraser didn't budge. "Are you sure that's a good idea, brother? Finn doesn't like it when we step on his toes and contacting the English clan leader will definitely be doing that. We should clear it through Grant in his absence."

Fergus shook his head. "No, there isn't time. What I need to ask of Bram isn't Protector-related anyway. Just get him on the line." Fraser remained silent and Fergus growled out, "Don't make me ask again."

"Fine," Fraser answered. As he walked toward the front of the room, he muttered, "But it's your funeral if Finn gets pissed off."

Gina's voice filled his ears. "What's so important that you need to talk to the Stonefire leader?"

Fergus met her eyes again. "It's not him so much as his mate, lass. But before they come on the line, I need your permission to share what Travis has done to you and the other females. If the DDA knows what BroadBay has been doing with the deceptive pregnancies, they may step in and help in a way that can prevent a battle and bloodshed."

Hesitation flickered in his human's eyes and he raised a hand to her cheek. "The information won't be public knowledge, Gina. Only those who need to know will. No one on Lochguard, outside of this room and possibly Finn and Grant, will know what the American bastard did to you. And if any of them brings it up, I will beat them to a pulp to defend your honor."

As his dragon paced in the back of his mind, Fergus held his breath and waited for Gina's answer.

~~~

Deep down, Gina knew she should just say yes and let Fergus share her secret. Yet as she tried to make her mouth work, memories of her so-called college friends calling her crazy for wanting to keep a dragon's bastard flooded her mind. Or, how her parents had told her that if she kept the child, they never wanted to see her again. They wouldn't have her younger sister associated with a dragon's whore.

Only her ailing grandmother had taken her in with open arms. But when she'd died a few months ago, Gina had been on her own in Scotland.

Everyone on Lochguard had been kind to her so far, but would they remain so if they knew the truth? Or, if protecting her ended up costing them the lives of their loved ones?

Fergus stroked her cheek and she forced herself to meet his kind, steely eyes again. He murmured, "I can't help you if you won't tell me what's going on inside that head of yours."

Swallowing the emotion in her throat, she whispered, "If the truth got out, then everyone would either pity me or look at me with disgust in their eyes. And if it came to a fight just to protect me and their family member died as a result, then they'll boot me out of the clan faster than you can say Lochguard."

Anger flashed in Fergus's gaze. "What in the bloody hell are you talking about?"

She frowned. "Don't yell at me. I've been here a week and I'm not even your mate. On top of that, I'm carrying another dragon-shifter's child and wanted by the American DDA. I know you'll say the clan took in Arabella despite the dangers and her past. But Ara is a dragon-shifter. I'm a human carrying contraband. I can't imagine any dragon clan wanting to protect me if it cost them their lives."

Finn's voice boomed inside the room. "Lass, then you don't know us at all."

Gina whipped her head toward the screen in the front, which displayed Finn and another male dragon-shifter with dark hair and blue eyes she'd never seen before. "Finn."

The Scottish dragon leader answered, "Aye, it's me. And this is Stonefire's leader, Bram. But enough with the introductions. Tell me now, Gina MacDonald. Do you wish to stay on Lochguard? And don't give me any excuses. Yes or no."

At the dominance in Finn's voice, she felt compelled to answer truthfully. "Yes."

Finn nodded. "Aye, well, that's good enough for me." He looked to the other dragon leader. "How about you Bram?"

The dragonman's reply was dry. "Does it matter what I say?"

A female voice from off-screen hissed, "Bram."

Bram sighed. "Okay, Evie." The English dragon leader met Gina's gaze. "I do have another question for you, Ms. MacDonald. Before my mate works her magic with the DDA, do you plan to mate Fergus MacKenzie?"

Fergus growled at her side, but she hit his chest lightly. "Stop it, Fergus."

Tightening his grip on her hips, he replied, "This shouldn't be rushed, Gina. You need to make the decision on your own terms."

She looked up at her dragonman. Fergus always put her needs first. Even in the short time she'd been on Lochguard, he'd always been kind, patient, and protective. In that moment, she accepted the truth—Fergus would never abandon her the way Travis had done. She trusted her dragonman completely.

Hell, she was half-way in love with him already.

Taking a deep breath, she finally answered, "I am making the decision on my own terms. I want to stay with you, Fergus MacKenzie, provided you want me to stay."

An emotion she couldn't identify flashed in his eyes before his pupils turned to slits and back. "Of course I want you to bloody stay, Gina. If you don't know that by now, then maybe I need to do a lot more convincing and show you."

He leaned down to kiss her when Finn's voice interrupted them. "Right, then you're going to mate each other right now, but in the condensed version with me and Bram as witnesses."

Gina blinked. "What?"

Finn asked, "Are you having second thoughts, lass? Because it's now or never."

Fergus muttered, "Gina deserves more."

Finn raised his brows. "You can do a romantic, pull-all-the-stops ceremony later. I know you've been planning one since you were in your early twenties, cousin. We'll let you have your dream later."

Before Gina could reply to Finn's revelation, Fergus growled out, "Fine. But you're going to pay for that later, Finn."

Finn shrugged. "I can handle that." The dragonman motioned toward them. "Hurry up and state your claims. The sooner it's done, the sooner we can see if the DDA will help flush out the traitors and Yanks near Lochguard."

Fergus turned her body fully toward him. "Are you ready, Gina?"

Placing a hand over her belly, she nodded. It was time to embrace her choice and chance at a future. "As you Scots say, aye, I am."

CHAPTER FIFTEEN

Both man and beast were still reeling from Gina's answer. In a few short sentences, Gina would be their mate.

His dragon growled. *Then hurry up and say the words. The human has no idea what to do.*

Fergus took Gina's hands. "I, Fergus MacKenzie, wish to take you as my mate, Gina MacDonald. You're stubborn, clever, and are always out to push my buttons. You'll make a fantastic mother and addition to the clan. With you by my side, I will be a happy dragonman. The only question is—will you accept my claim?"

Gina smiled. "I suppose so." Fergus growled and Gina laughed. "Okay, I do. We don't want to rile up your dragon."

Fergus opened his mouth to reply when Finn interjected, "Do the same, Gina. And quickly. I need this done."

To his human's credit, she merely nodded. He loved the fact she could focus on what was important, even if it meant taking an order.

Squeezing his hands, Gina stated, "I wish to take you as my mate, Fergus. Sure, you're hot and muscled, but you're so much more than the outer package. You're really smart, loyal, and kinder than most anyone I've met. To be honest, I sometimes wonder if you can read my mind because you understand what I need so well. I also think you need someone like me to help you relax and force you to take a break once in a while." Fraser snorted to his side, but a quick glare shut up his brother. Gina continued, "Together we fit and I guess all I need to know is if you accept my claim on you?"

Fergus tugged Gina gently against him. "Of course I do, bloody woman."

She grinned up at him and Fergus leaned down to kiss her. He'd barely nibbled her lip and slipped his tongue into her mouth when Finn's voice boomed again. "Right, it's done and witnessed." Fergus broke the kiss. He and Gina turned toward the screen. "Bram and I will see what we can do here. In the meantime, stay in the bunker. I don't know what they have planned and Grant is only starting to put together the pieces."

Fergus spoke up. "Let me help, Finn. If I reach out via mobile phone to some of my contacts in the area, they may have extra information."

Finn nodded. "Aye, do that. But stay in the bunker and protect your mate. Speaking of mates, where's Arabella?"

Fraser answered, "She's resting in one of the back rooms with Holly, Mum, and Ross standing guard. Ara's thrown up twice today and is exhausted."

Concern flashed in Finn's eyes. "I want you two to help Holly look after her."

Fergus replied, "Of course."

Finn clapped his hands together. "Brilliant. Then hang tight until—"

Faye burst into the room, her face flushed from running. She noticed Finn on the screen. "Hello, cousin."

Bram finally spoke up. "Finn, are you finished with the family business? Evie is going to need our help if we're to secure the human's future on Lochguard."

Fergus spoke up. "Wait, there's something you need to hear, Finn."

Finn pierced him with a stare, but Fergus didn't so much as bat an eye. "Then say it, Fergus. There's much to do and not much time to do it. "

Gina squeezed his hand in encouragement and he explained about Travis's bet and what the bastard had done with Gina and the other nine females.

Finn and Bram both cursed. Finn was the first to speak. "I'm truly sorry you had to experience the worst of dragon-shifter kind, Gina. I'm going to do everything within my power to make sure BroadBay and that bastard in particular pay. "

Gina leaned against Fergus. "Thank you, Finn. But all I want is to ensure Travis doesn't hurt anyone else."

Finn looked between Fergus and Gina and back again before asking, "Anything else we need to know?"

As soon as Fergus shook his head, Finn glanced at Bram. "Let's get to work."

The screen went blank.

Fergus put an arm around Gina's waist and waited to see who would speak first.

Faye surveyed the room. "What did I miss?"

At a later time, Fergus might have to hug his sister for not bringing up Gina's past.

Fraser winked. "Oh, nothing important. Just your oldest brother being mated."

Faye's gaze moved to Fergus and Gina. "What?"

Pulling Gina tighter against him, he wrapped his arm around her shoulder. "Aye, you have a new sister."

Faye grinned. "I'm happy for you both." She turned toward the two Protectors manning the technology at the front. "Fill me in on what's happening."

185

As Faye engrossed herself in her work, Fergus rubbed Gina's arm and murmured, "Come, lass. We could do with a moment alone."

Something beeped on the front console and a voice came over the line, "Rogue dragon overhead. Prepare for an attack."

In the next second, the ground shook under them and Fergus angled his body to protect Gina as they fell to the ground.

~~~

Everything happened in one long second. The ground shook, the lights flickered, and she was falling.

At the last second, Fergus moved his body to take the brunt of the fall and Gina twisted to spare her stomach.

Still, as they crashed down, a pain reverberated from the side of her abdomen and she cried out.

Fergus asked, "What's wrong, Gina? Tell me."

Another boom prevented her from saying anything. Faye and Fraser were yelling in the background, but she couldn't make out what it was.

Fergus turned her around to lay on the floor and he leaned over her body on his hands and knees. "Gina, are you okay?"

Taking a deep breath, she focused on her belly and baby. But while there had been a pain originally, there was just a sore spot on the lower left. "I think so. I just had a scare."

He leaned his head down. "Don't be strong right now, lass. If you hurt anywhere, tell me."

"I think I'm okay. But once we figure out what the hell is going on, we can have Holly and the doctor check me and our son out, okay?"

Fergus stared at her a second before leaning back and taking her hands. As soon as he hauled them both upright again, he barked at his sister, "What's happening, Faye?"

"Give me a bloody second, Fergus," Faye answered before bringing up the security feed.

The screen was blank for a moment before it changed to a scene of dragons flying over Lochguard's land and a few were dropping large bundles. They all watched as one fell and exploded on impact.

The blood drained from Gina's face. "Why are they bombing us? Isn't that illegal?"

Faye answered, "Aye, it is." She did something to the controls and a few seconds later, Grant's picture appeared. Faye asked, "Is the DDA going to help?"

Grant nodded. "They're watching the footage, but it's still going to be fifteen minutes before the first helicopters land."

Fergus cursed. "By then, we might not have a clan left."

Grant met his gaze. "I already garnered permission to fight back." Grant's eyes moved to Faye. "I need you to lead a squad with the maneuver we've been practicing."

Fraser growled. "Faye is not bloody going out in this. She can barely fly straight."

Grant's voice was steely. "She can and she will."

Fraser opened his mouth to reply, but Faye glared at her older brother. "If you trust me at all, Fraser, let it go. Each second we spend arguing is another second someone could be dying."

Grant added, "She's right. Your sister is fit to fly this maneuver. You have my word on this."

Faye moved toward the door. "I don't need your permission anyway. Take care of everyone here."

187

Faye left and all eyes moved to the screen. Grant raised an eyebrow. "Stay put. If any of you try to leave, my men there have permission to take you down."

The screen went blank and the room fell silent. Gina raised her gaze to meet Fergus's. "Is there anything we can do to help?"

Fergus squeezed her tighter against his side. "Aye, stay put."

Fraser walked up to his twin. "That's a bloody stupid idea, Fergus. We should be helping."

Holly emerged from a side hallway. She rushed to Fraser's side and poked him. "Don't even think about going out in this. You were lucky at the hospital, but this is much worse."

Fraser ran a hand through his hair. "But I can't just stay here and do nothing, honey. Every fiber of my being wants to join the fight."

Holly leaned against her mate. "We can do something. Get Dr. Innes and Layla on the line. We can start organizing a medical response team so that as soon as Grant and Faye take care of the threat, we can leap into action."

Fraser gave Holly a brief kiss. "There are so many reasons I love you, lass."

Holly kissed him again and then shoved him toward the console. "You get started. I'm going to check on Gina first."

With a nod, Fraser barked orders and the men up front listened.

At the talk of dying and injuries, Gina buried her face against Fergus's side. It was highly likely that all of this was her fault.

Rubbing her back, Fergus whispered, "Even without you here, the attack was bound to happen sooner or later, Gina. Don't beat yourself up over this.

She raised her head. "That's easy for you to say. But without the Americans, the attack would be a lot less powerful."

Fergus nodded. "Aye, you're probably right. However, if Lochguard crumbles at a new challenge, then we aren't worthy of being a clan in our own right. Trust me, lass. We've been through wars, clearances, and assassination attempts. A few Yanks with shiny toys aren't going to be the ones to stop us."

Holly finally approached them. "He's right, you know. I may not be a dragon-shifter, but tales of Lochguard's survival have been passed down through the ages even over in Aberdeen. They're nearly as hearty as the human highlanders."

Fergus grunted. "We're heartier."

Holly rolled her eyes. "I'll say yes just to end the debate." She met Gina's eyes. "Trust me, hen. If Lochguard took me in and welcomed me as one of their own after the fight at the hospital in Elgin, then they'll do the same for you. A dragon's true mate is a rare thing, so when one of the clan finds theirs, they work together to ensure their clanmate's survival."

"Really?" Gina asked.

Holly bobbed her head. "Aye, but it's up to you to earn their respect and trust after the fact. And somehow, I think you'll do fine." Holly motioned toward her stomach. "May I examine you?"

Gina murmured, "Sure."

As Holly moved her hands around her abdomen, Gina only hoped the woman was right about Lochguard accepting her. Gina wasn't sure she could survive yet another rejection by those she'd come to think of as friends.

189

~ ~ ~

Fergus was torn between comforting his mate and reaching out to contacts in the area for help. But as much as he cared for Gina, he couldn't stand by and do nothing for his clan.

Kissing her forehead, he said, "I might have some contacts who can help us. Is it all right for me to leave you with Holly for now?"

Gina raised her chin. "Of course. I'll be fine. If you can do anything to help them, then do it, Fergus."

He wanted to tell her how much he loved her spirit, support, and, hell, everything about her. But it wasn't the time.

His dragon spoke up. *Protect the clan and we can take Gina to one of the back rooms and show her all the ways we love her.*

Bloody beast. We're being attacked and Gina just suffered a fall. Stop thinking with your cock.

His dragon huffed. *I never suggested that.*

Ignoring his beast, Fergus placed a gentle kiss on Gina's lips and moved to the front. He asked Fraser, "Did you contact Dr. Innes?"

His twin answered, "He's not picking up his mobile. But Layla is already assembling a team. As soon as we get the all-clear, I'm going to help her airlift any injured dragons to her makeshift surgery."

Fergus frowned. "Innes not answering his phone worries me, brother."

"Me, too. But we're stuck here until the intruders are taken care of. Layla is going to try and see if Stonefire's doctor can come up and help."

Fergus took out his mobile phone. "I might be able to help, too. I'm going to reach out to Seahaven."

Fraser looked askance at him. "Are you sure that's a good idea? You've only established communications with them in the last few months. They're still quite bitter about the former leader tossing them out."

Seahaven was a small clan of former Lochguard dragon-shifters. Under Duncan, the clan leader before Finn, anyone who had a human mate had been told to leave. They'd been granted a small parcel of land fifteen years ago and lived in harmony with the local humans. Fergus had spent the better part of a year trying to get the leader, Euan MacKay, to visit Lochguard. While it still hadn't happened, the leader would at least take Fergus's calls.

If Fergus were lucky, Euan might help them out with the attack and recovery, too.

He dialed Euan's number and said to his brother. "I'm going to try."

After three rings, Euan's voice filled the line. "Fergus?"

"Look, Euan, I'm going to be quick. You may or may not know, but Lochguard is under attack."

The Seahaven leader was quiet a second before replying, "Aye, I know. But if you're calling and asking us to help, the answer is no."

His dragon growled and Fergus kept his beast contained in the back of his mind. "I'm not asking anyone from Seahaven to fight, but—"

Euan cut him off. "Look, lad, I know what you're trying to do. But we're a fraction of the size of Lochguard. If your traitors come here, we won't stand a chance. I have a daughter to protect."

Gripping the phone tightly, Fergus kept his voice calm. "Let me finish and then turn me down, aye? I just want to know if we can borrow your doctor for a few days, once the battle is over.

We've been talking about swapping medical information and this would be the perfect time to try that."

Fergus waited for an answer. As much as he wanted to tell the leader to hurry the hell up, that would only push Euan away. Exchanging medical practices and help was one of the points Fergus had been working on with Seahaven.

Euan finally answered. "Let me talk to Dr. Daniel Keith and I'll call back."

The line went dead and Fergus lowered his phone. Fraser didn't waste time asking, "Well? Did ol' Euan turn you down?"

"He didn't say yes but he didn't say no. We'll have to wait and see." Fergus looked at the screen, which showed Lochguard's dragons beginning to engage the intruders. "And for more than Seahaven's response."

Fraser gripped his shoulder. "Aye, I'm worried about Faye, too. But she's out there and all we can do is believe in her."

Fergus sighed. "As much as it pains me to say it, you're right."

Fraser cupped his ear. "What was that? I didn't hear you?"

He growled. "I'm going to check on my mate."

Fraser winked at Fergus and turned back toward the control panel.

CHAPTER SIXTEEN

Faye MacKenzie stretched her wings one last time and deemed her muscles were warm enough to use without injury. Or, at least, without further injury.

Her dragon growled. *We will be fine. Let's take down the bastards and help our clan.*

We will. But if we're not careful, we'll undo all the months of hard work and physical therapy.

You worry too much. Our muscles are warm. Let's go.

Looking over the bright blue hide of her shoulder, Faye touched the tips of her wings together. The other dragons behind her followed suit, confirming the command to fly.

She made sure to clutch the plastic canisters in her front claws firmly but not hard enough to break the seal. If any of the special powder touched her skin, it would be game over. Worse than that, she'd let Grant down. After his belief in her and support, she would rather die than fail.

Her dragon growled. *Then don't fail. It's simple.*

Crouching down, Faye leaped into the air. The first few beats of her wings were the hardest since the bones in her right wing ached with a pulsing pain. But once she was high enough to take advantage of the wind currents, the pain and the knots where her wings met her shoulders eased.

It was time to protect the clan and take down the intruders.

Her beast grunted. *Yes, so hurry up.*

She ignored her dragon and took in the scene. Faye and her wing of dragons had taken off from a hidden area at the back of the clan's lands. All of the attacks seemed to be focused on the front gate and the main living areas, which was where Lochguard's Protectors were trying to defend the clan.

At the edges of her vision, a few other dragon intruders let loose their bombs on other big structures dotted around the clan. The great hall was already partially destroyed and still under attack.

Remembering all of the events and celebrations held in the great hall over the years, Faye narrowed her eyes and headed for the dragon attackers near the hall.

She barely noticed the tightness in her back muscles as she flapped her wings faster. Timing and surprise was the only way the secret maneuver would work.

Right before her wing of dragons would collide with a group of enemies, Faye and her team spread out to form a line. As they hovered in place, the enemies screeched and half of them turned to charge Faye and her compatriots. Yet Faye didn't blink; they all held their line. It came down to timing.

When she could see the black slitted pupils of the dragon coming at her, Faye tossed one of her canisters at him. From the corner of her eye, she saw the others in her team doing the same.

The plastic cracked against the red dragon's hide and the powder inside dispersed over the enemy dragon's scales. The intruder looked unimpressed and reached out his forearm to attack when he flashed into his human form for a second, then his dragon, and human again as he sped toward the ground.

All of the dragons hit with the canisters had the same reaction; the brief flashes of returning to a dragon allowed each target to slow down their descent with their wings. They might be injured when they crashed, but they should survive it.

The modified periwinkle and mandrake root concoction was working.

Not that Faye had doubted it. After all, she had been part of the test group with Grant and a few others. She knew firsthand that being forced to flash between forms bloody hurt. It was as if one's bones and skin were stretched and then crumpled together, the cycle repeating itself for ten or fifteen minutes.

Her beast growled. *Stop dawdling. It's time to finish the others.*

Snapped back to her task, Faye dove down to another group of enemies releasing bombs on the hall. She released her other canister before pulling up at the last moment. The capsule broke and soon, the same flashing between forms happened.

Faye waited to see how the other intruders would react before making the decision to retreat and reload.

The intruders farther away finally noticed what was happening. The leaders gave the signal to retreat and they turned around. As they fled, Grant and his wing of Protectors pursued them.

She had always loved watching a group of dragons beating their wings with purpose as they dove and rose in their practiced maneuvers. When she'd been head Protector, drills had been top priority. Of course, the role had been taken from her when she'd been injured and unable to lead. Grant McFarland had taken her place.

Even a few months ago, Faye would've burned with jealousy that Grant was performing her role and protecting the clan. But as she watched his retreating green dragon's form, she admired his strength as he nipped one of the intruders and sent the enemy crashing into a tree. He was no longer the young male

195

who'd done everything in his power to put her down or undermine her.

Grant's belief in her after her injury had changed things between them.

Her beast huffed. *I don't understand why. His dragon is too cocky.*

You say that, yet you challenge him every chance you get. You're like a school child teasing on the play yard.

Am not. Go secure the traitors.

Satisfied she had won against her beast, Faye dove toward the flashing dragon intruders on the ground. Some of Lochguard's Protectors were already there, securing them.

Landing in a large open spot nearby, she imagined her wings shrinking into her back, her snout morphing into her nose, and her scales changing into skin. Ignoring the chilly January air, Faye started barking orders. She'd rather die of hypothermia than allow one of the intruders to escape. Grant and the clan were counting on her.

If she had any say in the matter, Faye MacKenzie would never let either them or herself down ever again. It was a new year and she was ready to seize control of her life once more.

~~~

Gina debated sitting down in the bunker's command room when Fraser yelled, "Bloody hell. Look at Faye."

While Gina couldn't identify many dragon-shifters in their dragon forms, she watched the group of dragons as they tossed something at the intruders. Within seconds, they flashed from dragon to human and back again. "What's happening?"

Fergus rubbed up and down her arm. "It's a new thing Faye and Grant have been working on. It's a combination of periwinkle and mandrake root that forces a dragon-shifter to shift back."

She leaned against Fergus. "Of course you knew about it. You seem to know everything."

Fergus chuckled. "I'd be careful with those words, lass, or my dragon will grow cocky."

She smacked his stomach. "You know what I mean. But why are they flashing? I thought that special powder prevented a shift for days."

Fergus placed a finger under her chin and raised her face to meet his eyes. "And how do you know that?"

Even a week ago, Gina would've hesitated. But no longer. Fergus was her mate and she needed to trust him. "I may have purchased my own vial as a form of protection."

The corner of Fergus's mouth ticked up. "So, that's how you planned to stop me."

"Hey, don't dismiss me yet. You should seriously train your younger Protectors better. One of them let me carry it right onto Lochguard. All I had to do was say it was some kind of special pregnancy tea mixture."

Fergus frowned. "I'll have a word with Grant later. His Protectors should know better than to fall for a bonny lass's charm."

Before Gina could think of how to reply to Fergus's roundabout compliment, Fraser's voice filled the room. "Shut it, you two. There's an incoming video call from Stonefire."

Finn and Bram's faces appeared on screen. Finn spoke without preamble. "Since Faye and Grant are otherwise occupied, I need you lot to coordinate clean-up."

Fergus asked, "While we've been watching the security feed, we can't see everything. Are you positive there aren't any more dragons with bombs nearby?"

"Aye," Finn answered. "Iris has the surrounding area contained and the DDA is already working with her to clean-up any threats within a ten-mile radius of Lochguard. I know these types of drills aren't your usual duties, but I trust you two. And right now, I need to be careful of who I trust."

Gina blurted out, "Why?"

Finn didn't miss a beat. "They knew our location and vulnerabilities a little too well. The warehouses are new, and it makes me think someone is sharing information."

Bram muttered at his side, "Always the bloody traitors in the midst."

Finn glanced at Bram. "Not for long." He met Fergus's gaze again. "Once everyone injured or homeless is taken care of, I want you to come up with a list of those who would never betray the clan." Finn waved toward the two dragon-shifters manning the console. "Ian and Emma MacAllister I handpicked along with Grant. Everyone currently in that bunker is cleared. The sooner you can put together a list, Fergus, the better."

Gina looked to her mate and he nodded. "Consider it done."

Finn sighed. "Right, then I need to get back to wrangling with the DDA. I'll check back in a little while."

The screen went black.

Without thinking, Gina whispered, "Finn trusts me."

Fergus squeezed her shoulders gently. "It appears so, not that I'm surprised."

She wanted nothing more than to lean against Fergus and revel in the safety of his arms. But to do so in that moment would be selfish. With great effort, she leaned back until Fergus released her. "Go help your brother."

He lightly caressed her cheek with the back of his fingers. "Are you sure, lass?"

Standing taller, Gina motioned toward the front. "Go and help the clan. I should check on Arabella and your mother anyway."

Fergus looked as if he wanted to say something, but instead, he leaned forward and kissed her. When he pulled away, he murmured, "I'll come to you as soon as I'm done."

As they gazed into each other's eyes, Gina's heart warmed. Not caring that his brother was listening, she said, "I'm glad you swooped down that day to check on me. If I were still living at my grandmother's cottage, I might be captured or worse."

Fergus's pupils turned to slits and back. "But you're alive, and you're my mate. Anyone who tries to take you away will face the entire collective wrath of Lochguard. Never doubt that, Gina MacDonald."

"After today, I'm starting to believe you."

He smiled. "Stubborn female." He gave her one more quick kiss and added, "I should help my twin. Go to Ara. She's probably bored of my mum's chatter by now."

With a nod, Gina moved toward the hall. "And I might just mention your words to your mom."

Fergus growled and Gina laughed. Not wanting to delay her dragonman any more, she dashed down the hall to the only door not open. She knocked. A muffled, "Come in" made it through the door and Gina entered.

Inside, Arabella was upright on the sole bed, watching Lorna and Ross. The pair didn't even notice Gina standing in the doorway.

Lorna frowned. "You try to leave this bunker and I will drag your arse back to this room and tie you to the chair."

Ross took a step toward Lorna. "I'm not an invalid and I want to help."

"You've only stopped the treatments a few weeks ago. Don't be daft, Ross. You're staying."

"I have four years on you, Lorna MacKenzie. You should listen to your elders. I'm going."

Lorna snorted. "Idle threat, human. I may be female, but even a dragon-shifter female is stronger than a human male."

Motioning Lorna forward, Ross replied, "Then try me, woman."

Arabella met Gina's gaze and rolled her eyes. Apparently, Arabella had tried to stop them to no avail.

As Lorna geared up to charge Ross, Gina rushed between them and held up her hands. Thankfully, they blinked and didn't try to run over a heavily pregnant woman. Gina pointed to one and then the other. "Stop it. Finn ordered us to stay put. Are you really going to defy him?"

Lorna crossed her arms over her chest. "Tell that to the human. He's the one who wants to leave."

Ross growled. "I was a volunteer firefighter as a young lad, when I lived in the country before moving to Aberdeen. I can help."

Gina interjected, "How about this? The next time Finn touches base, you can ask him if you can help?"

Ross frowned. "Is there nothing I can do right now? I don't like cowering in this bunker."

Lorna rolled her eyes. "You're sixty-five, Ross, not a young man."

Gina jumped in again. "Ross, sir, how about you go out and see if Fergus, Fraser, and Holly need your help? They're coordinating the clean up and medical teams. I'm sure they have something for you to do, if you ask."

Ross grunted. "As long as they don't dismiss me as an old man, as Lorna does."

Lorna walked up to Ross. "There's nothing wrong with admitting your age—"

"Save it, Lorna. We can discuss this later," Ross replied before moving to the doorway. "But you have my word that I won't try to leave until Finn gives permission."

With that, Ross left.

Arabella sighed. "I never thought they'd stop. Thanks for coming to the rescue, Gina."

Lorna harrumphed. "I'll let that slide as you've been quite ill today. Besides, it's not my fault. That blasted male lives to irritate me."

Gina fought a smile. "I'm sure you'll be irritating each other for many years to come."

Lorna waved a hand. "Leave it, child. I'm not in the mood to suffer your teasing. Tell us everything that Finn said."

Gina looked to Arabella. "He didn't call you?"

Arabella answered, "I got a very brief call to make sure I was okay, but that was it."

Gina grunted. "That's not very devoted of him, given how sick you've been."

Arabella shrugged. "He's clan leader. If all he did was dote on me, then Lochguard would be vulnerable to attacks and possibly be eradicated." She patted an open spot on the bed next to her. "Come sit, Gina. You're pale and I don't like it."

The adrenaline from the attack was fading, not that Gina would admit it. After all, who knew how many Lochguard clan members had been injured or worse, and it was partly because of her presence here.

However, she needed to keep healthy for her son's sake. She'd already tumbled over once today; she didn't need to do it again. Gina moved to the bed and sat down. "Finn didn't say much, I'm afraid. But you should've seen Faye."

Gina explained Faye's actions in battle and Lorna spoke up. "I want to believe Faye is hearty and whole, but I don't like her out fighting just yet."

Arabella looked to Lorna. "Faye is clever. She never would've risked the clan by going out if she wasn't ready."

Lorna sighed. "I know. But she's my baby girl, and I just want her safe."

Gina nodded. "I know, but she'll be fine." She paused, and then added, "Oh, and I forgot to tell you. Fergus and I are mated now."

"What?" Both women demanded at the same time.

For a split second, doubt clouded her heart. Pushing it away, Gina sat up tall. "We are. And while you haven't known me long, I will take care of him."

Lorna snorted. "Fergus has been taking care of himself and everyone else since he could walk."

Gina frowned. "You know what I mean. I care for him and he for me."

Studying her, Lorna murmured, "Aye, and I bet it's more than mere caring."

As Gina tried to think of how to respond, her cheeks flushed. She cared for Fergus, she really did. But it had only been a little over a week. There was no way she was in love with him.

Sure, she was falling, but they had so much to learn about each other.

Scrambling her brain for how to respond, pain ripped across Gina's abdomen. She cried out and closed her eyes.

Lorna's comforting hands landed on her shoulders. "What's wrong, hen? Tell me."

Gritting her teeth against the pain, Gina couldn't form a response. It was in that moment, her water broke.

CHAPTER SEVENTEEN

Once Fergus settled Ross into his role of keeping track of the injured, he took out his phone and dialed Euan MacKay's number. Dr. Innes had been found lying under some bricks, shielding a child. The doctor was alive, but unconscious. Cassidy Jackson from Stonefire was coming, but Lochguard needed help from Clan Seahaven, too.

Euan finally answered. "Fergus, I'm still talking with my doctor here."

Fergus decided the time for roundabout pleasantries was over. "Look, Euan, our head doctor was hurt and our junior doctor is overwhelmed. If ever there was a time we need your help, it's now."

Euan paused a second and asked, "And what does Finn say of this?"

"He gave me full control over relations with Seahaven. This is my call. If anything goes wrong, the responsibility is mine."

"Give me a second." The line went silent for about thirty seconds before Euan's voice came over the line again. "Daniel Keith will go, provided he returns tomorrow."

Fergus would take what he could get. "Done."

"Right, he'll fly in. I'll send a picture of his dragon, so your Protectors know who to look out for."

Fergus should let it drop, but his curiosity got the better of him. "Why did you change your mind?"

"Daniel is a distant cousin of Gregor Innes. Regardless of the past, he can't turn his back on family, no matter if others have."

Euan's words were a stark reminder of Lochguard's former leader and his harsh edicts to those with human mates or immediate family with human mates. "Thank you, Euan. I'm sure this will be the first step toward mending relations."

"I wouldn't hold my breath," Euan muttered before the line went dead.

Fergus looked to Fraser. "It worked. Daniel Keith of Seahaven is coming. Euan is sending his picture so we know it's not another traitor."

Fraser clapped his shoulder. "Your patience and diplomatic crap has its uses."

"Fraser, let me remind you of how many time my 'patience and diplomatic crap' has saved your arse."

Fraser opened his mouth to reply just as Lorna raced into the room and grabbed Holly's hand. "Come, child. We need your help."

Holly frowned. "What's wrong?"

Lorna met Fergus's eyes. "Gina's in labor."

Fergus's dragon woke up from dozing and roared. *She needs our help.*

Fraser spoke up. "Go, Fergus. With Ross here, we can coordinate everything fine."

He glanced to his brother. "Thanks, Fraser."

Not waiting to hear what his twin said, Fergus rushed down the hall and followed Holly and his mum into the far room. Gina lay on a bed with her eyes closed; Arabella held her hand at the bedside.

Fergus tried to reach Gina, but Holly waved him away. "I know you're concerned, but I need to see her first. Talk to her. That will help."

"Gina, lass." His mate opened her eyes and his dragon growled at the pain he saw there. "Your bairn has impeccable timing, I'll give him that."

"Now is not the time to tease me, Fergus MacKenzie. Even if it's not your sperm that created our son, I'm still going to blame you for him."

Both man and beast stood taller at that remark. "Then do your worst, lass. I can take it." She raised her middle finger and he chuckled. "I'm not sure if that's the first thing you want the bairn to see on the way out."

Arabella released Gina's hand and stood up. "Sit down, Fergus." He hesitated, not wanting to deprive Arabella of a seat. She rolled her eyes and pointed behind him. "I can sit over there. Will that appease your protective male nature?"

He grunted and Arabella scurried away. Not that he could blame the lass—she would be going through the same process herself later in the year, except three times. Gina's pain would only remind her of what was to come.

At least Arabella was a female dragon-shifter and should have an easy enough time. With humans carrying a dragon-shifter child, it could go smoothly or turn dire.

His dragon chimed in. *She will be fine. Gina is young and strong. Age makes little difference compared to genetics.*

His beast huffed. *Stop being rational for once and think positively. Gina will sense your unease and doubt, which might worsen the situation.*

THE DRAGON GUARDIAN

Admitting his dragon was right, Fergus slipped into the seat and took Gina's hand in his. He used the other one to smooth her brow. Even though he was looking at his mate, his question was directed at Holly. "How far along is she, Holly?"

Holly answered, "Farther along than I'd like, given our lack of resources. But we're going to make the most of it."

Fergus tried not to focus on Holly's 'lack of resources' comment. Instead, he kissed the back of Gina's hand and willed his strength to flow into his female.

Gina smiled at him. "Promise to stay with me."

He nodded. "Wild dogs couldn't drag me away."

She gave a half-laugh. "I still say I need to test that theory."

Fergus opened his mouth to reply, but a contraction washed over his mate. Gina gripped his hand as she growled. Leave it to his stubborn lass to not yell out at the pain.

When it passed and Gina's body relaxed, Fergus chanced a glance at Holly. To strangers, her face was calm and collected. However, Fergus spotted the tightness at the corner of her eyes, which signaled Holly's worry.

He debated how to broach the subject without scaring Gina. However, his lass spoke up first. "What aren't you telling me, Holly? I can sense something is bothering you."

Fergus forced his gaze to his brother's mate as she answered, "The delivery could be tricky if your dragon-shifter hormone levels spike or your blood pressure gets too high. The hard part will be monitoring them here instead of at the surgery."

Lorna chimed in from behind Fergus. "Is there nothing here we can use? I know the bunker wasn't quite finished, but surely there are supplies stashed somewhere."

Holly bobbed her head. "Fraser mentioned how they started stocking supplies last week. If we're lucky, they started

207

with the medical supplies first." Holly looked to Lorna. "Can you find out what we have here? Fraser should know where they're located. There should be a box or two labeled 'maternity kit.' If so, bring it."

"Aye, I'll find out," Lorna replied before exiting the room.

After a beat of silence, Gina's voice filled the room and Fergus focused back on his mate. "Fergus, tell me one of your stories about you and Fraser getting into trouble. I could do with a distraction."

Not hesitating, he gently squeezed Gina's hand. "Aye, that I can do. Have I told you about how I helped Fraser create a Nessie sighting?"

She smiled. "No. Tell me everything."

As he regaled the tale from his late teens, Fergus secretly wished with his whole heart that his mate would survive the birth despite the less than perfect conditions. With Dr. Innes unconscious and Layla looking over the rest of Lochguard, Gina might not have a doctor on hand to help if things went wrong. Holly was a bloody good midwife, but she might not be able to save Gina on her own.

Tightening his grip on his mate's hands, he pushed aside his worry. His stubborn lass and son would pull through this. They had to.

~~~

Dr. Cassidy Jackson clenched her fingers as the DDA helicopter sped toward Lochguard's land.

She hated flying.

Some might consider it odd for a dragon-shifter, but Sid's dragon had gone silent during her adolescent years. Flying only reminded her of what she'd never be able to do on her own. On top of that, she was at the mercy of a giant machine.

Both reasons made her heart pound and palms sweat.

Yet as they approached Lochguard's landing area, the smoke billowing up into the sky chased away her past and fears. The Scottish clan needed her help and she was going to give it to them. While she'd never met Dr. Gregor Innes in person, his reputation was well-known as a good doctor dedicated to his clan. It was Sid's duty to help out while he recovered; she might one day need the same favor.

The helicopter hovered for about a minute before retreating to a smaller landing area further inside the clan's boundaries. The second it touched down, Sid let out a breath. When it came time to return to Stonefire, Sid was going home by car.

The side door opened. Unbuckling her restraints, Sid grabbed her medical bag and jumped down. She moved quickly away from the twirling blades toward a female dragon-shifter with black hair, brown eyes, and an olive complexion. The female had put in a brief call to Sid earlier. She was Layla MacFie, Lochguard's junior doctor.

The doctor motioned toward a makeshift surgery tent not far away. "This way. I need you to man the tent and look after Gregor."

Sid easily switched to work mode. "How many are injured?"

"About fifty. The only saving grace is there were only two fatalities."

The two females approached the largest of two tents and Layla led the way. She continued, "The other tent has the ones injured in dragon form. There aren't as many since most were hit while in human form. If you can handle this tent, I'll handle the dragons."

Sid had a feeling Layla was sparing her feelings with the division of tasks. But as she saw the bleeding and groaning people inside the tent, she forgot about everything but tending to the hurt. "Just introduce me to the nurses and they can show me the ropes."

Layla picked up a two-way radio and pushed the side button. "Dr. Jackson is here."

Sid shook her head. "Everyone calls me Dr. Sid."

"Dr. Sid then." Two females and three males with disheveled hair approached them. Two of them had a fair amount of blood on their tops. When they were close enough, Layla motioned toward Sid. "This is Dr. Sid. Help her get settled. I'm trusting her care to you."

One male nodded and answered, "We'll be fine, Layla. Go. I know you have a surgery to perform."

Layla brushed a stray dark hair behind her ear. "Right, then. I'll check in with you when I'm done."

Sid pointed toward the door. "Go. I'll be fine."

As the young female exited the tent, Sid turned to the five nurses. "Is triage completed?" The same male from before nodded. Sid continued, "Right, let me quickly check Dr. Innes and then we'll work our way down the list. Unless anyone is hanging on by a thread?"

The same male shook his head. "No. Layla already took care of those. We mostly have burns, scrapes, and broken bones needing casts left. And a few panic attacks."

"Good. What's your name?" Sid asked.

"Logan Lamont."

"Okay, Logan. You take me to Innes and the rest of you go back to work. Don't hesitate to holler if something goes wrong."

Logan handed her a spare radio. "This is for you. They're easier than mobile phones."

Sid took it and the four other nurses rushed back to their sections of the tent. As Sid and Logan walked toward the back, she looked at the younger male. "Who were the casualties?"

Logan's face turned grim. "A mother and her child. A bomb hit their house before they could escape. The only good bit of news is that the father and other daughter were out when it happened."

The mention of the family's tragedy stirred a memory from Sid's own past. But she pushed it aside. "It's rare for a family to have two female children."

"Aye, but the Innes' have a rare track record of birthing more females than males."

Sid faltered. "Innes?"

Logan put out a hand. "No, Gregor never found another mate, let alone had a child. But his sister and her youngest child were the ones to perish."

Sid had dealt with her fair share of tragedies. From losing humans who died when birthing dragon-shifter babies to reckless teenagers who ended up tortured by dragon hunters; Sid had seen them all.

But Gregor Innes's past was well known among the dragon-shifter medical community because of his year's leave over a decade ago. The man had already lost his wife in childbirth and it'd taken him a year to regain control of his dragon.

Taking a deep breath, Sid fell back on her years of medical practice and training. She needed to be calm and collected for the sake of her patients. She'd handle Gregor Innes when he woke up.

Speaking of the male, they entered a curtained-off section. Her eyes fell on the unconscious dragonman on the bed.

Even pale with bruises on his face, he was handsome. His dark blond hair was a tad bit too long and a light scruff donned his cheeks. The laugh lines at the corners of his mouth told her he was a man who had eventually overcome his past to find some degree of happiness.

Sid didn't even realize she'd been staring until another male to her left spoke up. "Who's this, Logan?"

Forcing her gaze away from the male who had to be Gregor Innes, she met the eyes of the red-haired, brown-eyed male holding his sleeping four or five-year-old daughter. "I'm Dr. Sid, from Stonefire. And you are?"

"I'm Gregor's brother-in-law, Harris Chisolm." The male hugged his sleeping daughter tightly. "And this is my daughter, Fiona."

"I'm sorry for your loss, Harris."

The male's voice cracked. "Thank you."

"I hate to be indelicate, but I need to check Gregor and then attend to the other patients. My recommendation for you is to find something to eat and then take some rest with your daughter." She looked to Logan. "Can you assist them while I quickly check Gregor?"

Logan nodded. "Aye." He looked to Harris. "Come with me, Harris."

When Harris merely followed, Sid had a feeling the male was feeling defeated. She was usually pretty good about keeping her feelings partitioned when it came to tragedy and death, but Harris's case was too similar to another one.

Not now, Jackson. Sid pumped out some antibacterial gel from its receptacle and rubbed it into her hands. Pulling down the sheet, she was greeted with Gregor's bare chest. The light dusting of hair and muscles told her that even the doctor took time to remain fit and healthy.

She placed her fingers on the side of his neck and was surprised at how warm his skin was. Not too hot, but warm in a way that made her want to lie on top of him and drink it in.

Blinking at the randy suggestion, she looked at her watch and focused on each beat of his heart. The rhythm was steady and nothing to be concerned about. After checking the responsiveness of his pupils, she felt his neck and then ran her hands down his chest and sides. Sid had done the same procedure a thousand times before, but she found herself lingering at his waist. It was almost as if she didn't want to let go.

Maybe Evie was right and Sid needed to start enjoying life a little more. Sid couldn't remember the last time she'd had sex. Even without a dragon-half to demand it, the release would ease some of the tension she stored up because of her occupation.

Thinking of sex, her eyes trailed down Gregor's chest to the light line of hair just below his navel. The sheet stopped her from finishing her perusal. She hesitated, but then assured herself that she needed to check all of him. It was her duty as a doctor.

And it was most definitely not because she was curious about what was under the sheet.

With a deep breath, she tossed back the sheet. Gregor Innes hadn't been maimed in the lower half of his body. All the long inches of his penis were lying intact.

What are you doing? Sid was a doctor. She'd never had the slightest interest in gaping at one of her patients before. Maybe it was just because she didn't usually treat Lochguard's clan members.

Her eyes moved to his face and Gregor's chiseled cheekbones and strong jaw. Whatever it was, it was highly unprofessional of her. Sid needed to get her shit together. There were injured and dying people who needed care.

Tossing the sheet back over the lower half of his body, she examined his head. The large bump was probably the reason he was unconscious. Considering all of his other vitals were right on target, she would just need to wait for him to wake up.

With one last glance at the rise and fall of Gregor's chest, Sid took a deep breath and exited the partitioned room to dive into the fray. Thankfully, as she examined one patient after another, she never had another inappropriate thought. Only Gregor Innes has that effect on her and Sid refused to think of the reason behind it.

She would do everything in her power to steer clear of the doctor once she left Lochguard. That should protect her from any dangerous feelings of hope.

After all, solitude was the best chance for a dragon-shifter without a dragon to avoid losing their mind and going insane.

CHAPTER EIGHTEEN

Gina relaxed after her latest contraction. All of the books and articles she'd read hadn't prepared her for how much birthing a child hurt without drugs. To be more accurate, they should say, "A contraction is like someone gripping your uterus and twisting it until you think you'll break in two."

Sweat trailed down the side of her face, but Fergus wiped it away with a cloth. She looked over at her dragonman. While his eyes were calm and collected, the tightness of his jaw told her how he was worrying for her on the inside. Squeezing his hand, she murmured, "I'm glad you're here."

He kissed her forehead and lingered. When he finally pulled away, he answered, "Me, too, lass. Me, too."

Holly's voice cut through their moment. "You're fully dilated, Gina. So far, you've been brilliant. On the next contraction, I need you to push as hard as you can, okay?"

Gina nodded. "I'll try."

Holly looked over to Lorna at her side. "Is everything set up to check the babe once he's here?"

"Aye, it is. And if he's anything like my own kin, he'll be in a rush to get out."

Even though there was no blood relation between Lorna and Gina's son, Lorna acted as if they were. Tears prickled her eyes. "Thank you."

Lorna raised her brows. "For what? You're giving me my first grandchild, hen. The sooner he's here, the sooner I can spoil him rotten."

At Lorna's comment, Gina burst into tears and Fergus hissed, "Mum."

Not hearing their ensuing argument, Gina tried to stop crying. But the MacKenzies were kinder than she could've ever dreamed of. More so than her own family.

Her grandmother's words echoed inside Gina's mind: *Not all dragon-shifters are bad, Gina. Don't let one clan's actions close off your heart from the rest.* At the time, Gina had wondered why her grandmother would say such a thing. Now she knew—her grandma had probably foreseen Gina seeking out the Scottish clan's help.

Fergus kissed her tear-stained cheek. Then his strong-yet-kind voice filled her ear. "Let's just get the wee man out and deal with my mum later."

Gina sniffled. "But I'm crying because I'm happy, Fergus."

The corner of his mouth ticked up. "If you're happy now, about to push out a bairn, then wait until later. I'll show you happiness you couldn't dream of."

She smiled. "I can't tell if you're being cocky or sincere."

He grinned. "You'll just have to wait to find out."

Damn, Fergus was too attractive for his own good when he grinned with mischief dancing in his eyes. Maybe she could coax that grin out more often.

Gina opened her mouth to tease him when another contraction hit. Pain cut across her lower abdomen and she barely prevented herself from cursing out every person in the room.

Holly commanded, "Push, Gina!"

Gripping Fergus's hand, she pushed as hard as she could, stretching parts of her she didn't want to think about. The pain was finally too much and she screamed. *Please let this be over soon.*

After what seemed like an hour, the contraction finally ceased. Gina relaxed onto the bed with a huge sigh. She wasn't looking forward to doing that again.

Holly ordered, "Don't push again until the next one, no matter how much you may want to do so."

Fergus mopped her brow with a cloth and Gina managed to ask, "Is he nearly here? Please tell me he's nearly here."

Holly smiled at her. "I see the crown of his head. I think he might be a ginger."

"I'd been hoping he would," Gina replied.

Fergus brushed her brow and met her eyes. "Who needs the Three Musketeers when we can be the Three Gingers?"

She tried to laugh, but it hurt and Gina sucked in a breath. Holly's voice filled her ear. "Don't make her laugh, Fergus." Fergus mumbled something Gina couldn't interpret and Holly continued, "Gina, getting back to your son. You're a strong lass. I think one more push should do it."

Fergus kissed her hand. "Nearly there, Gina."

Between Holly and Fergus's calm, steady voices, Gina prevented herself from yelling, crying, or who the hell knew what at the thought of pushing a tiny person out of her vagina.

At least she no longer felt the urge to simultaneously punch every man in the dick while also wanting to hold Fergus close and draw on his strength. She was merely determined to be done.

She couldn't wait to be not pregnant anymore. And not just because she yearned to hold her son in her arms—Gina wanted to regain her true self again without the influence of hormones.

After a few deep breaths, Gina answered her mate. She needed a distraction until the contraction finally came. "Speaking of our son, I've been thinking about his name."

"Oh, aye?"

"I want to call him Jamie, after your dad."

A soft sound escaped from near the bottom of the bed. Looking down, Lorna had her hand over her mouth. Clearing her throat, Lorna lowered her hand, "Wait until you meet your son, first, child. Jamie may not even suit him."

Everyone always spoke of Lorna's strength, but in that moment, Gina saw a flicker of longing and loneliness. Lorna MacKenzie missed her husband still.

Maybe she could help the woman find happiness again. After all, Gina was fairly certain she and Ross had a connection.

Before she could think any more on it, another contraction twisted her insides.

Hearing Holly's, "Push," Gina fought past the pain to push with all of her might. *It's time to join the world, son. Don't keep us waiting.*

She barely heard Fergus murmuring reassurances and focused every iota of her being on getting the giant child out of her body. She didn't care if he was the smallest baby ever birthed on Lochguard—he was fucking huge to her right now.

She alternated between screaming and gritting her teeth. *Come. Out. Baby.* After who knew how much time had passed, the baby slipped from her body. The next few seconds of silence were the longest of her life until a small cry filled the room.

Holly worked quickly and soon held up her boy. "Your big, braw son has arrived."

Blinking back tears, Gina held out her arms. "Can I hold him?"

Holly moved toward the head of the bed. "Aye, for a minute. Then I need to check him over. He seems hearty, but he is a wee bit early."

Gina could barely nod as Holly placed the small bundle in her arms. Her son was pink faced and wrinkly with wet red hair plastered to his head. But to her, he was the most beautiful thing in the world.

Kissing his forehead, she whispered, "Welcome to the world, Jamie MacDonald-MacKenzie."

~~~

Fergus was close to crying himself as Gina whispered the greeting to her son. His beast growled and Fergus corrected himself—their son.

With a huff, his beast gloated at the sight of the wee bairn. *He is strong and hearty. He will make a great Scot.*

Fergus mentally snorted. *He's actually American.*

I refuse to acknowledge that. Born in Scotland. That makes him a Scot.

Ignoring his dragon, Fergus reached out a finger and lightly traced the lad's cheek. "Hello, lad. I'm your dad."

Gina laid her cheek against his and Fergus simply enjoyed the moment. He'd yearned for a family of his own for so long. Even a month ago, he never would've imagined he'd have it. Yet there he was, with both a mate and a son. He would give his life to protect them.

His mate spoke up. "You should hold him, too, Fergus. I want him to know you from the beginning."

As he gently picked up the wee bairn, he replied, "Why? Are you planning on hiding him from me for a while?"

"Don't even joke about that, Fergus MacKenzie. I'm just trying to create a memory."

He stared down at the wee one in his arms, kissed his cheek, and then met Gina's eyes. "Believe me, lass. I will remember this moment for the rest of my life."

His mate looked about ready to cry again and he scrambled with what to say. He knew it was the hormones in her body making Gina emotional, but he still didn't want to upset his lass.

Thankfully, his mum came up to him. "Let me take wee Jamie, Fergus. Grandma needs a turn."

Glancing to Gina, she nodded and he handed over his son to his mum. Lorna smiled down at the baby and murmured, "That's right, Grandma has you."

His mum walked away and Fergus nearly went after her. Without thinking, he growled out, "I wanted a longer turn."

Gina gave a weak laugh. "I'll keep that in mind when Jamie starts crying at all hours of the night. I don't want to deny his daddy time."

Fergus grunted. "Joke away, but I will always be there for him." He cupped her cheek. "And for you."

He swore she whispered, "I love you," but Holly's booming voice made him unsure. His sister-in-law said, "While I prepare Gina for the afterbirth, why don't you tell Fraser the good news?"

He was about to shake his head, but Gina spoke up. "Go, Fergus. Fraser is more than your twin—he's your best friend. I want him here, too."

"But I don't want to leave you or Jamie."

Even tired and sweaty, stubbornness glinted in her eyes. "I can handle a few minutes alone, Fergus. Go. The sooner you leave, the sooner you can come back."

Glancing over to where Lorna was cleaning up his son, his mum turned her head and motioned toward the door. "Fetch Fraser. And also make sure Arabella is okay. I don't know where she is."

Fergus hadn't even noticed Arabella's absence. His dragon spoke up. *Finn asked us to protect Arabella.*

But Gina needs us.

She is strong. Besides, if we run, it will only take a minute.

Fergus asked Holly, "Are you sure Gina's out of danger?"

Holly stated, "I can't ever guarantee 100 percent, but Gina has survived this as if she were a dragon-shifter. I think she'll be fine, and that's my professional opinion."

For a split second, he wondered about the wheels turning inside Holly's head—he'd bet his life his sister-in-law was going to find out why Gina had had such an easy birth for a human. But he quickly pushed it aside and focused on his mate. "I'll be back in less than a minute."

She smiled. "Okay. Ready, set, go!"

Cursing her with love, he raced out of the room. Thankfully, Arabella was sitting in the main control room, albeit toward the back. Satisfied the dragonwoman was okay, he looked at Fraser and yelled, "My son is here! Come see Jamie MacDonald-MacKenzie."

Fraser snorted. "That's a lot of 'Macs.' Maybe I should call him Mac-squared."

He gave his twin the double finger salute. "Mum wants to know what's going on. You've been summoned."

Without another word, Fergus rushed back into the room. Both man and beast mentally sighed in relief to see that Jamie was back with Gina, and both were healthy.

Rushing to Gina's side, he murmured, "I did it in less than sixty seconds, lass. What did I win?"

She met his eye. "A family."

He kissed her and then his son. "I couldn't ask for a better present."

Fraser's voice filled the room. "I don't know, brother. I'd ask for her to do some kinky things in the bedroom, once she's healed."

Lorna growled, "I'm standing right here, Fraser Moore MacKenzie."

"Tsk, Mum. No yelling around Mac-squared."

Fergus glared at his brother. "You're not calling him that."

His brother moved toward the head of the bed after blowing a kiss to Holly, who was preparing for what Fergus assumed was the afterbirth. Fraser said, "What do you think, Gina? Every child should have a nickname."

Lorna answered, "You can talk about bloody nicknames later. Is Arabella okay?"

Fraser shrugged and looked to his mother. "I think so. She's sitting quietly in the back."

Lorna rolled her eyes. "Do you know Ara at all? Quiet isn't good." Lorna leaned in and touched Jamie's cheek. "I need to check on Arabella."

Gina nodded. "I understand. I would talk with her if I could."

"Rest, Gina. And Grandma will be right back, wee Jamie."

Lorna exited the room and Fergus moved to pick up Jamie. Gina shook her head. "Let Fraser have a turn. Holly says we don't have much time until she needs everyone out but you."

Fergus's dragon growled. *We should have another turn. Jamie is our son.*

Since when do you dismiss Fraser? He's our brother.

His beast huffed. *I just want to hold the baby again.*

Soon. We have a lifetime with him. Fraser can have a minute or two.

With a grunt, his dragon fell silent.

Gina squeezed his hand and he looked down at his mate. But she nodded toward his brother before either one spoke. Gently lifting Jamie, Fergus turned toward his brother.

~~~

Gina watched as Fergus tenderly handed over Jamie to Fraser. Witnessing the tall, cocky dragonman coo at her son made the corners of Gina's mouth tick up. She never could've imagined anyone from BroadBay acting the same way.

Wanting to focus on the happiness of the present and not dwell on the past, Gina pushed aside all thoughts of BroadBay. There might still be trouble ahead, but in that moment, she celebrated the birth of her first child.

And if everything went to plan and she could stay on Lochguard, she might even find a way to bring over the only person missing from her special moment—her sister, Kaylee.

Fraser broke the silence. "Just wait, Mac-squared. I'm going to be your favorite uncle. We'll get into all kinds of trouble."

Fergus growled to his brother, "Right now, you're his only uncle."

Fraser grinned. "All the better. It makes me the best."

Fergus sighed and motioned with his hands. "You've held him long enough. Give me my son."

Fraser shook his head as he offered Jamie to Fergus. "Gina is going to have to balance out your protectiveness. Otherwise, you'll create a wee rebel."

JESSIE DONOVAN

Fergus cuddled Jamie close. "Not that it would matter. I think his uncle would plant the ideas in his head first."

Holly's voice interrupted the pair. "Fraser, love, I need you to leave for a bit."

Fraser saluted and blew a kiss. "I know the drill by now. But come find me when you're done, honey. There are some pregnant females who are worried and could use your assurances."

Holly nodded. "Aye, as soon as I'm finished here."

Fraser touched Jamie's cheek one last time and exited the room. Fergus sat next to Gina on the bed and leaned his head against hers. "Thank you."

She frowned. "For what?"

"For being bloody wonderful. Whether you realize it or not, you've scored brownie points with my mum today by naming wee Jamie after my father."

She raised her brows. "And what about with you?"

He adjusted wee Jamie's swaddling. "Since you mated me and gave me a son today, I think you've earned a few."

"Good. I plan to collect in a few months' time."

As Fergus and Gina remained silent, they stared at their baby boy and leaned against one another. Gina knew reality was waiting for them above ground and they'd face it soon enough. But for the moment, she simply enjoyed the heat and scents of the two most important men in her life and branded it into her memory. After the events of the day, Gina was ready to fight for her place on Lochguard. Not just for her son's and her own safety, but also for the man she loved. Fergus MacKenzie was hers in more ways than one and she was never giving him up.

224

CHAPTER NINETEEN

Grant McFarland ignored the stabs of pain in his injured shoulder and walked into the Protectors' central command. Thanks to the structure and reinforced design of the building, it still stood.

Other Protectors and select staff darted in and out of rooms. Grant trusted his people to take care of recovery and clean-up. He had a more important job to take care of before he could help them.

Striding into the main command room, he spotted Faye MacKenzie sitting in his chair, giving orders. Despite the events of the day, the corner of his mouth ticked up at the lass's actions. Faye had fallen back into her old role of head Protector; she might even challenge Grant for his spot before long.

Faye finally turned her head. The relief in her eyes warmed both man and beast. His dragon spoke up. *I like that she waited for us.*

Aye, I suspect you'd like any bonny lass to be waiting for you.

His beast growled. *Faye is better than the others. She is strong as well as beautiful.*

Grant resisted a frown. *If I had the time, I'd ask for more detail. As it is, keep quiet. I need to work.*

In the next second, Faye's eyes darted to his shoulder. Her lips parted and she stormed over with a frown. "Of all the bloody stupid things to do, Grant McFarland. Why wouldn't you get your injury tended to? If it festers, the clan will be at a loss."

Desperately needing a moment of levity after recent events, Grant raised an eyebrow. "Why? I'm sure you already have a plan in place to take over my position."

Faye shook her head and turned to pick up a first-aid kit from a nearby shelf. "Now is not the time to joke, Grant. Lochguard would suffer if you were lost."

"I'd almost say you'd miss me."

Faye turned. Studying him, she finally answered, "Maybe."

His dragon hissed. *She would.*

Ignoring his beast, he resisted the urge to tuck a wisp of curly brown hair behind her ear. "Regardless, I need to find out the prisoners' secrets. The DDA could come to collect them at any time and I might be able to persuade them to talk. My injury can wait."

Faye poured a disinfectant onto a cotton clump. "Then stop interrupting me and I'll have this done in less than a minute."

Before he could answer, she dabbed the wet cotton along the slash on his shoulder. Clenching his teeth, he resisted hissing in a breath.

Faye's ministrations were gentle yet firm. She worked quickly and efficiently, much like she'd done during their time in the British army.

Not wanting to remember what his young, immature self had done, he blurted out, "You were brilliant today."

Picking up a gauze pad, her eyes flicked up to his for a second. "Says the male who chased down the last of the intruders on the clan's land. I was able to watch some of it. While good, I have some suggestions."

"Of course you do."

226

She placed the gauze over the worst section of his cut with a little more force than necessary. "You give me suggestions all the time. I wish you'd stop being so male when I do the same. I haven't forgotten our agreement."

His beast huffed. *Why are you irritating her on purpose? She will never kiss us if you're an arse.*

Grant answered slowly, *Since when do you want to kiss her?*

Since when have you wanted to do the same?

His eyes fell on Faye's pink lips. At one time, he'd done everything in his power to insult the female in front of him. Yet in the moment, he wished everything was taken care of, the clan was safe, and he could pin Faye against a wall, let loose her wild, curly hair, and persuade her to kiss him.

Faye finished wrapping his slash and stepped away, reminding him it wasn't the time. He murmured, "Thank you."

She tilted her head. "I never thought I'd hear that from your lips."

Shit. If he were overly nice to her, Faye would try to figure out why. Grant fell back on his head Protector role. "I put it down to blood loss." Grant looked over to his staff at the front of the room. He directed his question to Cooper Maxwell, his second-in-command. "I'm going to question the prisoners. You and Faye can keep things under control."

Cooper nodded. "Aye. I'll let you know if the DDA approaches."

Grant nodded. "Right, then I'm off." He looked down at Faye. Her whiskey-colored eyes were inquisitive, but she remained silent.

Having dawdled for too long already, Grant turned and exited the room. As he strode down the long corridor, he carefully placed a mask of indifference on his face. If he appeared too eager, the prisoners would sense they had the upper hand. Grant needed to convince them he couldn't care less if they shared information or not.

He gave one final command to his dragon. *Stay quiet in there unless you sense something of importance in their mood or scent.*

Of course.

Interrogations and battles were the only time his beast was cooperative.

Grant knocked on the assigned room and his best interrogator, Brodie, opened the door and motioned him into the small, soundproofed observation room. Grant asked, "Anything new?"

Brodie shook his head. "Not since the last update ten minutes ago. The Lochguard traitor refuses to say anything except he's old and won't betray his true clan. The American merely asks for Gina MacDonald."

Grant frowned. He was one of the few who knew the details of Gina's past. "Do you think it's Travis Parker?"

"I don't know. We haven't found a clear picture of him to compare."

Regardless, anyone associated with a bastard who would impregnate females to fulfill a bet didn't deserve any sort of respect from Grant. "Let me try while we still have the chance. Stay here and monitor the situation."

Brodie nodded and Grant focused on his objective. Mentally prepared, he entered the small, windowless room and locked the heavy door behind him.

He eyed the male. Since he was in human form with scrapes and a broken leg set in a makeshift cast, he probably had been one of the dragons hit with the mandrake and periwinkle powder capsules.

However, the male's relaxed posture and smug smile told Grant volumes. The bastard wasn't afraid.

Grant didn't condone torture, but he was more than on board with mind games. Crossing to the empty chair on the far side, Grant sat down and stretched out his long legs in front of him. Removing a knife from his boot, Grant casually cleaned his nails.

After about sixty seconds, the male's American accent echoed inside the room. "I know you can't hurt me and anything you say is bullshit, so don't try any intimidation techniques with me. They won't work."

Grant flicked his gaze to the American. "I don't believe in wasting my time with lies. Or, in you trying to out-alpha me. Let me save us both some time and say I have all the time in the world."

"By law, the DDA will come to collect me and you must hand me over into their care."

He raised his brows. "Do I? My people didn't give a final prisoner headcount yet. In all of the commotion, it's easy to overlook one or two."

"And risk your clan? I somehow doubt it."

Grant shrugged. "This is the Highlands, lad. We tend to do things our own way and the humans barely take notice. My people will back my decision, no questions asked."

The man studied him and crossed his arms over his chest. "Which explains the illegal weapons and drugs."

All of the captured prisoners had been injected with a mandrake root and periwinkle concoction to prevent them shifting into a dragon for at least a day. "Says the man who helped bomb an entire dragon clan."

Grant went back to cleaning his nails. The shuffling of the male's feet signaled his plan was working.

Five seconds passed and then ten. Grant's dragon paced at the back of his mind, anxious to do something.

Flicking his wrist, Grant sent his knife sailing through the air to land just behind and above the American's head. Grant met the male's eyes. "Next time, I'll aim lower. I'll try not to make you a eunuch, although I can't guarantee it."

Slowly rising and walking over to the Yank, Grant tugged out his knife. The male visibly gulped. The dragonman wasn't as well-disciplined as Grant's team.

Taking five steps back, he tested the weight of his weapon. Just as he held the blade between his fingers and pulled his arm back to throw, the male blurted out, "Stop."

Grant paused. "Is there something you want to tell me? You have five seconds to spit it out."

The male nodded as he pressed his legs together and lifted his knees to try to protect his cock and balls. With his ankles chained to the floor, he didn't get far enough. "Roberts doesn't like to be denied. He wants the female and her baby."

Stephen Roberts was the leader of Clan BroadBay. "There must be more to it than that. Not even Roberts would risk an international incident over a mother and child."

"I don't know anything beyond the fact Roberts wants them both alive."

Grant took a step forward, the blade still between his fingers. "Tell me the reason."

The male remained silent and Grant swung his arm forward. The male yelped even as the blade clunked into the wood of the wall behind Grant.

Grant leaned down to the male's eye level. "My fingers must've slipped. To guarantee it won't happen again, I may just have to swing my blade upward into your balls."

Turning to pick up his knife, the male finally said, "All I know is the female is special. Something about her blood. I swear that's all I know."

Grant looked over his shoulder. The male was scrambling to lift his legs.

Casually strolling over to the American, he swept the chain connected to the male's ankles and forced the traitor's feet to the floor. "How would they even know anything about Gina's blood?" The man began to shake his head and Grant yanked the chain hard. The man screamed as his broken leg jarred and he nearly fell off the chair to the floor. Grant added, "I'd suggest saying something when it's just you and me. If I just happen to chain you at the edge of the woods and let slip your location, there are plenty of journalists willing to snap your picture and paste it all over the news. How long do you think you'd survive once the DDA found you and put you in jail? From all accounts, your clan members aren't as honorable as mine. I give you a week, tops."

"You'll just tell them anyway and I'm good as dead."

Grant shrugged. "Tell me everything, and I mean everything, you know and I'll turn you over with the other prisoners. You can tell them you were having your leg checked out."

Grant waited. The dragonman was clearly weighing his options.

The Yank let out a sigh. "All I know is they drew her blood to confirm the pregnancy. A few weeks after that, the entire clan was alerted to find the human female. When we received a tip from one of our Scottish contacts, we came as fast as we could. You know the rest."

Assessing the dragonman, Grant's dragon finally spoke up. *I think he finally told us the truth.*

So you don't think he knows anything else?

No. But what he told us is valuable. Now, knock him unconscious. He's taken enough of our time.

Grant stepped back and dusted off his hands. "You're going to wait here a while longer."

"But—"

"We're done." With that, Grant exited the room, locked the door behind him and looked over to Brodie at the monitor. "Reach out to the medical team once things start to die down. I want to know what's hiding in Gina MacDonald's blood."

Brodie nodded. "Aye, though it could be a day or two before we have enough staff to do it."

"That's fine. Take care of the clan first." Grant motioned toward the monitor. "Keep an eye on him. When word of the DDA retrieval team arrives, visit the American one last time just to ensure he's not hiding anything. I left my knife out of his reach in case you need it. Then hand him over with the rest."

"Of course," Brodie answered.

Exiting the room, Grant headed back to command central. He would eventually need to talk with Finn in private and let him know what the American had said. But in the meantime, he pushed away the information and focused on the list of things to be done. The fighting might be over, but ensuring his clan's welfare had only begun.

CHAPTER TWENTY

The next morning, Fergus lay beside Gina as she tried yet again to nurse Jamie. Despite Holly's busy schedule assuring pregnant females and new mothers that everything was okay, she'd come back to help Gina as often as possible.

And both man and beast noticed how every time Holly looked at Jamie, she smiled. His dragon spoke up. *Just ask her.*

We should ask Fraser first.

He's busy doing work for Finn above ground. I want to know. Our son could use some cousins.

Fergus debated bringing up the topic considering Holly's miscarriage last year. However, before he could convince himself to ask, Jamie finally latched on to Gina's nipple and suckled.

Gina scrunched her nose. "That feels weird. Good, but weird."

Holly nodded. "You may get sore as well. But I'll leave some special cream, just in case you need it."

Everyone watched Jamie for a few seconds. The nine-pound lad was hungry.

While never taking her eyes off Jamie, Gina reached out her free hand and took Holly's. "Before you leave, tell me why you keep smiling when you look at Jamie."

Fergus's beast snorted. *Gina has the bollocks you lack.*

Shut it, dragon.

Holly cleared her throat. "With everything going on, it's not really the time."

Gina looked up and smiled at Holly. "Of course it is. In times like these, happy news is direly needed."

Holly brushed some imaginary dust off her arm. "I also don't want to jinx it."

Gina grinned. "I knew it. You're pregnant."

Holly's eyes darted to the door and back to Gina. "Keep your voice down. Fraser and I don't want Lorna to know until the last possible moment."

Fergus eyed his sister-in-law. "That's why you're wearing a new, stronger scented lotion. To mask the scent."

"Aye. The last thing I need is everyone treating me like a delicate flower. My work is important and I can't disappoint my patients."

Fergus shrugged. "If Fraser allows it, then I'm not going to go up against him."

Holly raised her brows. "Oh, aye? So I have no say in the matter?"

Fergus was quick to answer. "Of course you do, although Fraser is going to become overly protective as you progress. You mated a dragonman. You knew that would happen."

Holly sighed. "I know. But just promise me you'll keep it from Lorna for now."

Absently stroking Gina's hair, he answered, "I will. You helped my mate through her delivery. I'm deeply in your debt for that."

Holly waved a hand in dismissal. "It's my job. And the easiness of the birth makes me think there's a reason behind it. Once everything settles, will you allow me to ask you some questions and draw some blood, Gina? If I can make it easier for humans birthing dragon-shifter children in the future, it will save a lot of heartache."

Gina nodded. "Of course. Although I highly doubt I have some super-secret ingredient in my blood. Sometimes humans give birth to dragon-shifter babies without any complications."

"Sometimes, but it's rare." Holly gently touched wee Jamie's head. "Right, then I need to go. Arabella's missing Finn and trying not to admit it."

In deep talks with the DDA, Finn couldn't risk being out of range while he traveled to Lochguard. There was also worry that Finn could become a target if he traveled back too quickly. Grant and the other Protectors were still searching the area for any lingering enemies.

Fergus motioned toward the door with his head. "Then help her."

Gina spoke up again. "Tell her to come visit. I could use the company when Fergus has to help Fraser, Grant and Faye."

"I told you I can stay here another day."

Gina raised her brows. "I'll be fine. The clan needs your help more than I. You can only find out so much from the control room."

Holly gathered her supplies and placed them in her medical kit. "Let's see if I can get Arabella here first. Her behavior...worries me."

Fergus chimed in. "Finn will be home soon. If anyone can get it out of her, it's my cousin."

"Aye, I hope so," Holly said. "I think she's depressed about the triplets. Maybe if I can get Melanie Hall-MacLeod on the phone, she can help. From all accounts, Mel has a way with Arabella."

Fergus replied, "Well, Dr. Sid is here. You could always have her try to talk to Arabella."

"That might work." Holly picked up her bag. "I have my mobile phone on. Call if there's an emergency."

Left alone, Fergus kissed Gina's cheek. He watched their son nurse a second before he placed his hand over hers. "I wish I could stay here forever."

Gina snuggled against him. "Me, too. But you have that conference call. And I have an idea I want you to run past Jane Hartley."

"The former reporter? Why?"

"Because we might be able to turn this disaster into something positive."

"I thought you were supposed to be exhausted."

The corner of Gina's mouth ticked up. "I'm tired, but often my brain goes into overdrive when I'm really tired. When I was trying to take a nap before Jamie woke up, I had an idea."

"Aye? I'm listening."

"Well, in addition to marketing, I studied a lot about public relations. Much like when you want to invoke an emotion or a need to buy something when advertising, the same can work for a principal or law. After Stonefire was attacked, the public moved to support them. As a result of that and Melanie's efforts, Stonefire has been granted special privileges. Dragonmen can petition for a special license to mate a human. Yet they're the only clan allowed to do so."

"They are, but I'm not sure I follow."

"If I could've mated you, I would've garnered the protection of the DDA. The attack most likely wouldn't have happened."

Fergus frowned. "I don't know about that. The traitors are determined to see Lochguard crumble."

"But the DDA would've acted quicker. Or, at least listened to any grievances Lochguard had."

Fergus grunted. "The DDA rarely helps unless they're forced to do so."

Gina adjusted Jamie at her breast. "Even so, if we could prevent another woman from worrying about her future if she falls for a dragon-shifter, that would help."

"Aye, you're right. But what do you expect Jane Hartley to do?"

Gina met his gaze. "She could put together a special report with footage of the clean-up. Do you think Finn will allow that?"

His dragon stood tall. *Our mate is clever. She will keep you on your toes.*

You're only realizing this now?

Ignoring his beast, he answered Gina. "I'll run it by Finn first, if he has the time. Remember, he's working hard to ensure you can stay here. I want that finished first."

"But Fergus, since when do you put your own wishes above the clan?"

He hugged his mate tighter. "When it comes to you, lass, I'll do anything to keep you. Not just because you're my true mate. I love you, Gina MacDonald, and I'm never letting you go."

Gina met his eyes. "Fergus."

"Is that a good, breathy 'Fergus' or a bad one?"

The corner of her mouth ticked up. "A good one."

He leaned down to her lips and murmured, "Care to tell me why?"

"Because I love you, too, Fergus MacKenzie."

She raised her head until her lips met his. He devoured her mouth and let her know how much he cared for her. He only hoped Finn's charm worked on the DDA. Gina deserved a proper home and to be loved. He never wanted her to be on the run again.

Or, to be stolen from him.

Fergus deepened the kiss, claiming her all over again. No matter what it took, he was keeping Gina MacDonald and wee Jamie. And no one was going to stop him.

~~~

Sid finished her latest round of visiting the long-term care patients. While one male had lost a leg and another an arm, no one had died apart from the two females during the bombing.

She'd like to think it was because she refused to let them die. But she also didn't want to let her clan leader, Bram, down. Sid wanted to strengthen relations between the doctors in the UK and abroad. Bram would never allow her to leave the clan again if she didn't give 100 percent and try her damnedest to save every life.

Well, that might not be completely true. Bram trusted her. Sid had earned it over their lifetime. There was another reason.

Glancing over to the partitioned section in the back of the tent, deep down she admitted she didn't want to let Dr. Gregor Innes down, either. It was stupid, really. Sid was in her late thirties and had long ago picked her career over a mate. She didn't know the first thing about Lochguard's doctor. For all she knew, he could be a controlling, dominating prick.

Tell yourself that, Sid. Everyone spoke highly of the overprotective doctor and his tragic past. Most of the unattached females also had dreamy looks in their eyes when they spoke of him. A few times, she wanted to walk away rather than deal with the jealousy that flared deep inside herself.

After drinking some water, Sid placed her cup down and headed toward the section at the back. She'd put off checking on her last patient long enough. There'd been no change, according to the nurse's report an hour ago. If she were quick, Sid could check his vitals, jot them down, and be off duty in five minutes for her scheduled lunch break. Then she would have some time to try and clear her mind of him. Again.

She slipped through the opening and blinked. Gregor Innes was sitting up with his back to her, flipping through his chart.

For a second, she admired his broad shoulders and trim waist. Then she shook her head, and switched into doctor mode. "Gregor Innes, what the bloody hell are you doing? Lie back down."

Gregor looked over at her, his brows frowning over his grey eyes. "You're English. Who are you?"

She walked over and plucked the chart from his fingers. "I'm your doctor. My name is Cassidy Jackson."

His pupils slitted. "The Stonefire doctor."

"Yes. Now that's out of the way, lay down and let me examine you."

His eyes flashed again. "Where's Layla?"

Sid wasn't a novice when it came to stubborn dragon-shifter males. She pointed toward the bed. "Last warning. Lay. Down."

They stared at one another for a second and Sid debated the best way to get Innes into bed.

An image of her lying on top of a naked, toned Gregor flashed into her mind. Before she could banish it, her heart thumped double-time. What the hell was wrong with her?

The corner of Gregor's mouth ticked up. "I can see how much you want to examine me, doctor. I'll be a good patient."

Sid rolled her eyes. "They say doctors make the worst patients and I'm starting to think it's true."

Gregor's chuckle was a rich, warm sound that sent a wave of longing over her. For some odd reason, she wanted to hear it again.

Then Logan's voice came over the radio and broke the spell. "You have a new patient to see you, Dr. Sid."

Picking up the radio, she pressed the button. "Is it urgent?"

Logan answered, "Not particularly, but I wouldn't want to keep Finn's mate waiting."

Arabella was here. "Give me a few minutes and I'll be there."

Lowering her radio, Sid motioned with her hand. "Lay down. I have shit to do and flirting with you isn't one of them."

Gregor lay back, covering his lower half with a sheet. While unusual considering dragon-shifter didn't think twice about nudity, Sid let it pass. Moving to his side, she gently touched the bump on his head. It was half the size of the day before. "The bump is healing and should be gone by tomorrow. Since nothing showed up in your earlier scans, you can start helping Layla later today. Her other helper, Daniel Keith, left this morning."

Gregor's voice was more neutral when he asked, "What about the clan? How are they?"

Sid looked at him askance. "Most of them did fine." She paused, and finally decided to just spit out the bad news. "Your

240

brother's mate and eldest daughter were the only fatalities. I'm truly sorry, Gregor."

All signs of his earlier humor vanished, replaced with a frown and flashing eyes. "Where are Harris and Fiona?"

"I sent them home to rest. I'll have a nurse call them in here soon."

Gregor put up a hand. "Don't disturb them. I know from experience that he'll need some time to pull himself together enough for visitors."

As a doctor, Sid shouldn't push for personal details that could upset a patient. But she blurted out, "Because of your mate and son."

"Aye."

Gregor never broke eye contact. Sid didn't know how long they stared at one another, yet she didn't want to be the one to look away. There was hidden pain in his eyes, probably much like there was in hers. They each had different pasts, but had more in common than Gregor would ever know. Both of them understood deep loss.

Logan's voice came over the radio again. "Dr. Sid?"

She finally forced her gaze away to answer him. "I'm on my way." Looking back to Gregor, she added, "I need to go."

"Aye, I reckon you do. Thanks for helping, Cassidy."

No one had called her Cassidy since she'd lost her dragon. Only through sheer force of will did she prevent her eyes from tearing up at the memories of when she'd been Cassidy instead of Sid.

Still, she couldn't bring herself to correct him. She almost wanted him to say her full name again, which was ridiculous.

Then she remembered Arabella and her duties. "You're welcome. I'm sure I'll see you again before I leave."

Sid turned. As she exited the room, she heard Gregor murmur, "Aye, we will, lass. That we will."

Pushing aside her curiosity at his statement, Sid rushed toward the front of the tent. One look at Arabella, and Sid forgot all about Gregor. Wrapping an arm around the female's shoulder, Sid ushered her into an empty partition. The second they were alone, Sid demanded, "Tell me what's wrong, Arabella MacLeod."

Arabella remained silent for a few seconds before she turned to Sid and hugged her. Taken by surprise, Sid patted Arabella's back. "Ara? Tell me. Nothing can be as bad as the dragon hunters." When Arabella remained silent, Sid lowered her voice. "You can tell me anything. I won't tell Bram unless there's a threat to Stonefire."

"There's no threat," Arabella murmured.

"Then stop stalling and tell me. I have a feeling you don't want to appear weak in front of Lochguard. I understand that. But I've seen you at your lowest, Ara, and I've seen you at your strongest. There's little you can say that will surprise me."

Taking a deep inhalation, Arabella finally answered, "I don't think I can handle three babies. When Finn's here, I can borrow his strength. But when he's gone, I just can't. And I know he's clan leader and I don't want him to put Lochguard at risk. But I need him or I'm going to fail."

Sid took Arabella's shoulders and forced the woman back to meet her eye. "You're not going to fail, Ara. You have family in two clans now who can help. No one would begrudge a mother of triplets asking for help."

"But that means I can't handle my own children. I don't want to become 'poor Arabella' again."

Sid had known Arabella her whole life and had been one of the few who'd talked to the female after her torture. Arabella had come so far and she wasn't about to allow her to regress. "That's it, we're calling Finn."

"No—"

"I know he's busy, but if he knew I'd seen you like this and I didn't tell him, he'd never allow me back." Sid put out her hand. "Give me your mobile. I want to talk to him first."

Arabella hesitated a second before complying. Sid dialed Finn's number. He answered on the first ring. "Arabella? What's wrong, love?"

"Finn, this is Sid."

Finn jumped in before she could say more. "Is Ara okay? Did something happen to the bairns?"

"The babies are fine. But you need to talk to Arabella and it can't wait."

"Then put her on," Finn ordered.

Sid held out the phone and whispered to Arabella, "Talk to him. Finn may be busy, but he'll always have time for you."

Arabella gingerly took the phone. Taking a deep breath, Arabella's voice cracked when she said, "Finn."

Wanting to give Arabella privacy, Sid stepped outside the tent and stood guard. Her lunch could wait. Arabella needed her.

Yet as her eyes scanned the room, her gaze fell on the back section. Gregor stepped out of the partition, fully dressed in scrubs and a white coat. She should yell at him to rest, but Sid understood his need to help the clan. All good doctors made the clan their first priority.

His eyes met hers and a spark traveled down her spine. For the first time in a long time, she wondered what it would be like to lean on someone else when things turned difficult.

But Gregor looked away and rushed toward the opposite end of the tent, away from her, reminding her of her silly fantasies. Sid was half a woman without her dragon. While she was stable for the present, she might not be so in the future. She needed to focus on helping others while she still could. There was nothing to be done about helping herself.

Her dragon half would never return.

CHAPTER TWENTY-ONE

Two days later, Gina stepped into the fresh air for the first time in days and cuddled her baby against her chest.

Parts of the warehouse lay in rubble, whereas one section had miraculously survived. It only made Gina wonder what the rest of Lochguard looked like.

Fergus squeezed her shoulders. "Come, lass. Let's take wee Jamie home."

Gina tore her gaze away from the wreckage and whispered to her son, "Let's not make your daddy worry too much. Come on."

Fergus grunted. "It's bloody freezing out here. The lad doesn't need to catch a cold."

They started walking. "He'll be fine. I swear you wrapped him in five blankets. Besides, I could do with a little Vitamin D from the sun."

It was a rare clear, sunny day. "The lad is half dragon-shifter. He doesn't need it. And you can take some vitamins."

Gina rolled her eyes. "Your mom was right—you're going to drive me crazy."

"Aye, and proud of it."

They walked in silence for a minute and Gina reveled in the normalcy of the act. However, as much as Fergus tried to act strong, the tenseness of his muscles spoke volumes. She looked over at him. "I'm sure Finn has good news."

"If he did, then why wouldn't he tell us over the phone?"

Gina shrugged. "He has his reasons. Maybe there's something sensitive he didn't want to leak out."

"There isn't any wire-tapping on Lochguard."

"That you know of."

Fergus sighed. "Not this again."

Gina raised her brows. "Hey, why not? You're clever and I love you, but a super-spy could sneak onto the land and set them up. Considering most of your enemies used to live here, it's entirely possible."

"With heightened security, no one will sneak onto Lochguard. Not even from the sky."

"Only because the DDA is still in the area watching out for enemies, but the DDA won't stick around forever. Same with the supporters out front."

A few pictures had been leaked to the press of the destruction on Lochguard. It'd been a calculated risk, but the supporters out front and the messages sent to their clan from the people of Scotland, especially from the Highlands and Islands, had been extraordinary. Memories were long and many still remembered the Scottish dragons helping during the Highland Clearances in the 18th and 19th centuries. Not even Dougal Munro's harsh treatment of the locals—Dougal had been the leader before Finn—had completely erased the Scottish humans' gratitude for past deeds.

Fergus squeezed her tightly. "One day at a time, lass. We've rebuilt before and we'll do it again. Now, stop dawdling. Our son needs to be inside."

Rolling her eyes, Gina complied. "Has anyone tried reaching out to the supporters?"

"Aye, I've been trying. Most are unwilling to give their addresses or phone numbers, but keep asking if we have a social media page."

She glanced over at him. "You know, that wouldn't be a bad idea. If we're to get Jane Hartley's video podcast up and running, we'll need to set them up."

Fergus scrunched his nose. "I'll leave that to you. If I look at a computer too long, my dragon gets antsy. I much prefer paper copies. How Arabella can stare at a laptop for hours when writing code, I have no idea."

"Each person is different. Look at you and Fraser. Your brother hates beating around the bush or being diplomatic, yet you excel at it. Maybe Lochguard needs some more humans to help round out the clan and be able to relate to and reach other humans."

Fergus met her gaze. "You staying is my top priority. The others can wait."

Smiling, she leaned against Fergus. "We'll make it work somehow, Fergus. We'll make it work."

As they continued to walk, Gina became lost in her thoughts. A tiny part of her worried about Finn's announcement, but she refused to let it overwhelm her. Even in the darkest hours of being disowned by her parents, Gina had remained determined and optimistic. She would remain so even with her future uncertain.

Staring down at wisps of red hair that had escaped Jamie's swaddling and lay on his forehead, Gina smiled. She was a new mother, but she already wanted to make the world a better place for him. Once she figured out how to balance a lack of sleep with taking care of her son, she would tackle that future with everything she had.

They neared the main living area and Gina sucked in a breath. While she'd seen the destruction via the feed, it was more severe in real life.

Some cottages lay in rubble, whereas others only had holes punched into a wall. A few others had lost part of their roofing. Families were already at work, patching up the damage that could be repaired. On the sites of the destroyed cottages, groups of men and women were clearing the debris and most likely preparing to build again. Since Fraser was the clan's head architect, he had his work cut out for him.

Which reminded her—she needed to talk with her brother-in-law later. The new houses should have bunker-like basements to protect the families in case of emergency. Gina sincerely hoped there was never another attack, but she'd rather be safe than sorry.

Fergus squeezed her tighter against his side as they walked. No doubt, her mate was also thinking of how to make Lochguard stronger for the future. While Fergus had tried to hide it, she'd heard his late-night phone calls to Seahaven and his other contacts. Most of the calls had ended with Fergus hanging up and cursing, but not all. Change was coming, but she had no idea what kind.

They finally approached the old Sinclair place. It stood mostly intact, except for one broken window out front. Fraser was removing the old frame, but turned at their approach. He raised a hand. "There you are. I wasn't sure how much longer I could keep the surprise."

Fergus frowned. "What surprise?"

Fraser grinned. "Come and I'll show you."

Fergus growled. "You do realize we have our days-old son with us, right? No pranks."

Fraser placed a hand over his heart and shook his head. "Always thinking the worst of me, brother." He looked up again. "But hopefully this surprise will help change that."

Gina looked between the two brothers and decided to step in. Otherwise, they would go on forever. "What's the surprise, Fraser?"

Fraser turned and cupped his hand around his mouth. "Holly!"

The door on the right side of the divided house opened. Holly stood there with a smile. "Come, let's get you two out of the cold."

Gina looked toward the door on the left side. "But we live there."

"Aye, you do," Holly answered. "But Fraser and I live here."

Fergus blurted out, "What?"

Fraser walked up to them and weaseled his way between Gina and Fergus. Placing a hand around each of their waists, he gently pushed them forward. "Deep down, I know you miss me, Fergus. We were one egg, once. We should never be far apart."

Fergus sighed. "I don't think I ever missed your ridiculousness."

Fraser slapped Fergus's shoulder. "And think about it—us together, protecting our mates and bairns is better than trying to do it alone. Thanks to years of dares and tricks, we're pretty good in the sky, especially as a team."

Gina leaned forward to look at Fergus's face. Her mate was battling a smile. Fergus's voice finally filled the area. "Aye, we are."

"Good, then it's settled."

They arrived on the stoop and Holly motioned them inside. "Come, let's try to warm you up before we head to Finn's announcement."

Fraser pushed his brother in front of him and led him to the kitchen. Holly gently bopped Jamie's nose and whispered to Gina, "I hope it's all right. As the only human females in the clan, I figured it couldn't hurt to stick together. It might also get our overprotective mates off our backs."

"That would be a bonus." Handing Jamie over to Holly, Gina removed her coat. "But what about your dad? Is he going to live here, too?"

Holly snorted. "I doubt it. He's quite taken by Lorna, even if he won't admit it."

Holly offered Jamie back, but Gina shook her head. "Hold him for a bit. My arms could use a rest."

Looking down, Holly smiled and cooed at the baby. With her whole heart, Gina wished for Holly to have her own delivered safely.

That reminded her. "Did you find out anything from my blood sample?"

"Labs have been backed up, but I should have the results soon. Most of Lochguard's injured have been discharged and that should free up a lot of resources." Holly motioned toward the kitchen. "Come. We don't have a lot of time and you could do with some hot tea." She held up Jamie briefly. "And then I can change him."

"Are you sure? I love my son, but his diapers are pretty gross. I can do it."

"No, let me. You're still healing. Cuddle with your mate and enjoy it. There won't be a whole lot of alone time in the coming months."

Guilt flared. Gina loved her son, but she wished she could have time with Fergus. As it was, they couldn't have sex again for weeks. Even then, the frenzy might come on and Gina wasn't sure if she wanted another child straight away. Not because she didn't want another one, but she looked forward to not being pregnant for a while.

Especially if she and Fergus had to leave Lochguard to fend for themselves.

Holly lightly nudged her arm. "I'm sure Finn will have good news."

"Everyone keeps saying that, but we have no idea."

Holly adjusted her grip on Jamie. "Well, we'll all find out in about an hour. Until then, just enjoy the moment. If you look down or depressed, Fraser will only try to make you laugh. And believe me, he will pull out all the stops to make it happen. I wouldn't put it past him to do some kind of half-arsed interpretive dance, which you'll never be able to unsee."

As they entered the kitchen, Fraser raised his brows. "I heard that, honey."

Holly tilted her head. "Did I say anything that wasn't true?"

"No," Fraser grumbled.

Holly laughed. "Right, then. Put the kettle on and let's warm everyone up before we have to trek to the ruins of the great hall."

At the mention of the great hall, everyone suddenly kicked into gear. Holly went to change Jamie and Fraser saw to the tea.

Fergus walked up to her and engulfed her in his arms. His voice was barely audible when he murmured, "Sorry about my brother moving next door unannounced. I hope it's okay."

Pulling back to meet his eyes, she cupped his cheek. "It's fine. You may deny it, but you love him. Besides, after spending months by myself in that cottage along Loch Shin, it's nice to be surrounded by people I care for."

Fergus traced her cheek with his finger. "And if I have any say in the matter, it's going to stay that way."

Wanting to treasure what little precious time she had with Fergus, Gina laid her head against his chest and listened to the thump of his heart. She'd found a man she loved and trusted with her whole heart.

She couldn't imagine a life without him.

Jamie's cry pierced the air and Fergus released his hold. "I'll check on him. You sit down."

Without another word, her dragonman rushed to their crying son. Sitting down, she memorized every detail—from Fergus's broad back to his soft baby voice to Jamie grabbing onto his finger.

In an hour, she would know the fate of her future.

~~~

Fergus stood near the front of the crowd with Gina under his arm, holding their son. Fraser and Holly were on their right side. His mum, Ross, and Faye on the other side.

All of the healthy members of the clan stood outside the ruins of the great hall. Not even the cold January air would keep them away.

A makeshift dais sat in front of the crowd. All they needed were Finn and Arabella.

Fergus had been trying all day to contact his cousin, but his calls kept going to voice mail. Since Finn wasn't a coward, Fergus assumed Finn's news wouldn't be too bad.

Or, so he hoped.

His dragon huffed. *Of course Finn will help us. Even if he lies to the DDA, he won't force us away.*

You say that, but the leadership contest for the head of the DDA is nearly over. If Jonathan Christie wins, he won't think twice about punishing clans who disobey the rules.

His beast swished his tail. *Rosalind Abbott is the more reasonable and experienced one. She will win.*

So you keep saying.

For once, push aside your need for hard data and just believe.

Fergus desperately wanted to do so, but it went against his nature. *We'll find out soon enough.*

Before his dragon could argue further, Finn and Arabella walked out, hand in hand. Whatever had been troubling Arabella must've passed; the female smiled and looked happier than he'd seen in a while.

The pair stopped in the middle of the dais. Finn raised his hand and the gathering fell silent. With a nod, Finn's voice boomed. "Thanks for coming. I don't want to keep you long, so I'll jump straight to the point.

"More changes are coming to Lochguard." The crowd murmured and Finn raised his hand again. When the noise died down, he continued, "Several months ago, we agreed to a researcher coming to stay with us for six months. That will still happen, although her arrival has been delayed. The reason is because in addition to the human coming to study us, she will accompany a group of potential sacrifices."

Someone shouted, "Why?"

Finn didn't miss a beat. "Because Lochguard is going to be the trial clan for a new sacrifice practice. Several females will visit the clan and interact with the single males. Our hope is that pairings will occur more naturally and leave less room for unhappiness or disaster. It will be beneficial to both parties. And if the pair like each other enough, they might even stay together."

Fergus glanced over at his twin and they exchanged looks. No doubt, the creation of the new practice had been influenced by the trouble with Fergus and Fraser over Holly.

Even so, Fergus thought it was a good idea. Forcing two people together had been necessary when the humans had feared the dragon clans. In the Highlands, at least, the humans weren't as fearful. The practice would be similar to what the clans had done in the past.

Finn's voice boomed out again. "To help encourage a broader pool of candidates, we will also implement the old practice of Guardians. Either a human relative of the sacrifice or a volunteer from our Protectors will watch over the sacrifice for a year, to ensure her best interests are at heart. If something vindictive happens to the sacrifice from within the clan, the Guardian will be punished. And if the sacrifice is caught breaking the law, she will also be dealt with by the DDA."

A random male shouted, "It sounds like less freedom to me."

Finn's voice was firm when he answered, "I disagree. I believe this path will lead to greater freedom, especially since the DDA has also given us leave to apply for special mate licenses. If, by chance, a sacrifice's relative or a local lass stirs a mate-claim frenzy and both sides wish to mate, the DDA will make it happen. Considering our recent problems, this concession will allow me to stop going gray before I'm forty."

A few clan members chuckled. Finn grinned. "And since I'm soon going to have three bairns to watch after, too, I'd rather save some of my blond hair for them. We all know three wee Stewarts running amok will turn all of my hair gray in a year or three."

Some of the tension of the crowd eased as more people snorted at Finn's comment. His cousin had always been good at diffusing situations.

Finn tugged Arabella to his side and wrapped his arm around his shoulder. "And one last thing—if anyone is interested in helping babysit the wee devils, then I might just set up a sign-up sheet. The both of us could use the help, although I'm sure it means they'll be spoiled rotten."

Shaking his head, Fergus murmured to Gina, "You think he's jesting, but he just found about a dozen babysitters without even trying. Finn has always been a sly one."

Gina smiled up at him. "That works for me. It means your mom can help us out more."

Fergus chuckled. "Aye, I do like the sound of that."

Finn addressed the crowd again. "I think that's enough announcements for the day. Ara and I will be visiting as many of the clan as we can today and the rest over the next few days. I'm determined to hear all of your grievances and see about fixing up Lochguard as quickly as possible. If there's one thing we Scottish dragons know how to do, it's pick ourselves up and come out stronger than ever before. We'll be having a celebration in the great hall before you know it."

The majority of the crowd cheered. With one last wave, Finn descended the stairs with Arabella beside him. The pair walked straight toward Fergus and Gina. When he was close enough, Finn brushed wee Jamie's cheek. "The lad looks strong." Finn looked at Gina and then Fergus. "Congrats to the pair of you." Finn looked at Gina again. "I heard about you choosing to name him after Uncle Jamie. Thank you, lass. It means a lot to all of us."

Gina snuggled against Fergus's side. "It's the least I could do, considering everything Fergus and your family have done for us."

Lorna spoke up. "Nonsense, child. It was nothing special."

Fergus knew it was special to Gina. But rather than waste time trying to convince his family of it, he met Finn's eye. "We'd better be the first visit of the day. I'm not sure how much longer I can wait to hear our fate."

Arabella frowned. "Didn't Aunt Lorna tell you?"

Fergus glanced at his mum. "No."

Lorna studied Fergus's face. "Are you sure I didn't tell you, Fergus? I'm pretty sure I did." She looked to Faye. "Didn't I?

Before Faye could answer, Fergus growled. "No, but how about telling me now?"

Ross stepped in. "Watch your tone, lad. Your mum has been under a lot of stress."

Fergus was on the verge of telling Ross to mind his own business when Gina pressed Jamie against his chest. Fergus took the bairn without question, although before he could say another word, Gina beat him to it. "We've all been under stress. How about you just tell us now?"

Finn answered, "Your mating was accepted by the DDA. You, and your child, will stay here."

CHAPTER TWENTY-TWO

Gina stopped breathing a second. She had a home, a family, and a future. She would also be able to help her son understand his dragon half; Fergus would ensure Jamie never turned rogue.

And who knew, she might be able to work with Lochguard and the DDA to prevent BroadBay or any other clan from hurting other women in the future.

For the first time in a long time, she was hopeful.

Turning her head to Fergus, she had to blink back tears to keep from crying. "We can stay."

Fergus maneuvered Jamie into one arm and pulled Gina against his side. After kissing her hair, he murmured, "I love you, lass."

A tear rolled down her cheek as she answered, "I love you, too."

Just as she raised her head to kiss Fergus, Finn interrupted. "I hate to break up the happy moment, but there are a few things you should know first."

Fergus growled out, "Then hurry up and bloody tell us."

Finn gave a shake of his head. "Not here. Come. This needs to be discussed in private." Finn looked at his kin. "Although you lot can come, too, if Fergus and Gina allow it."

Gina spoke before Fergus. "It's fine with me. I've had to keep too many secrets as of late." She looked up at Fergus. "I hope that's okay."

Fergus kissed her nose. "Of course." Her dragonman looked to Finn. "Just hurry up and take us somewhere we can talk."

Arabella walked a few paces and tugged Finn's hand. "Let's take them back here."

As the entire MacKenzie and Stewart brood followed Arabella's lead, Gina blinked to stop crying. No matter Finn's news, it wouldn't ruin the love and happiness running through her body. Her child would grow up among honorable dragon-shifters. Little Mac-squared would never turn out like his biological father; she'd make sure of that.

Arabella tugged open the door to a small building that sat about fifteen feet from the great hall. It was brick with two small windows. Judging by the moss and vines crawling up the side, it hadn't been used in some time.

One by one they filed inside. A giant hearth took up the far side. Several brick ovens were built into the fireplace. While empty of furniture, Gina had an idea of what the building was. "This used to be the kitchen for the great hall."

Finn nodded. "Aye, back before we installed a modern one in the hall." He pulled Arabella to his side. "These days, it's used for private moments."

Arabella smiled as she hit his side. "Now we'll have to find somewhere else."

Finn winked. "Good thing we have a long list of locations."

Fergus cleared his throat. "Cousin, tell us the news or I may have to pummel you."

Lorna clicked her tongue. "Fergus is right. Save your amorous escapades for later. Why are we here, Finlay Bruce Stewart?"

Finn's gaze moved to Gina. "It has to do with the results of your blood tests, lass."

Gina frowned. "Why? What did they show?"

Finn answered, "A mixture of human and dragon-shifter DNA."

She blinked. "I don't understand. My parents are human. Even if my mum had a dalliance with a dragon-shifter, I'd have an inner dragon since dragon-shifter DNA is always dominant. And I don't have one."

Arabella jumped in. "Finn is being overly dramatic. The mixture is normal for a human who has been injected with dragon's blood at some point in their lives. Are you sure no one in your family was a sacrifice and used it to save your life?"

Gina shook her head. "No. My whole family, except for my sister, hates dragon-shifters. All of my cousins are human, too."

Fergus spoke up. "Then the only logical explanation is your parents purchased dragon's blood from the black market, probably before you were old enough to remember."

Gina frowned. "I don't understand. Let's say my parents did as you said. Why wouldn't they tell me?"

Fergus answered, "A lot of humans are prejudiced against anything to do with the sacrifice system, which includes being injected with a dragon's healing blood. They wanted you to be free from scorn."

In that moment, her parents' past actions made sense. "For years, they did everything in their power to vilify dragon-shifters. When I still became fascinated, my mom tried even harder to make me hate dragons." She looked down at Jamie. "Despite everything, I still ended up tainted by association."

Lorna moved in front of her and lifted her chin. "Not tainted, lass. You're blessed."

Gina asked, "But how?"

Holly answered. "Because I have a feeling being injected at a young age with dragon's blood is the reason you had such an easy birth with wee Jamie. We might be able to try injections with other humans and see how it works."

Lorna looked to Holly. "Aye, starting with you, Holly MacKenzie."

"How did you—" Holly started.

Lorna cut her off. "I may be middle-aged, but my sense of smell is just as keen as when I was a young lass. You reek of Fraser."

Fraser growled. "Mum."

Lorna smiled. "Not in a bad way." She looked back to Gina. "Thanks to you, my other daughter-in-law might have a greater chance of living a long life, surrounded by a horde of children."

Holly murmured, "I don't know about a 'horde.'"

As Holly, Fraser, Lorna, and Ross started arguing about respect and talking back, Fergus leaned down and whispered in her ear, "Are you all right, Gina? It's a lot to take in."

"It is. I wish I knew more about why or how my parents had done it."

"You could ask them," Fergus stated.

A small part of her was tempted. But that would mean dealing with the scorn and disappointment all over again. "Maybe some day. But right now, I want to cherish my new son and my new husband."

He tucked a section of hair behind her ear. "Maybe if we sneak out now, they won't notice. I'd like to do a little cherishing of my own. Holding my son and mate beside me on the couch, with maybe your wee cat next to us, sounds like heaven to me."

"Oh, Fergus."

"Come, lass. Before they stop arguing."

Fergus tugged her hand and moved toward the door. He didn't get more than two steps before Finn shouted, "Not yet, you two. We have a few more things to discuss."

~~~

Fergus growled as he turned his head toward his cousin. "Then hurry up and tell us, Finn. I want to see my family settled."

Finn raised his brows. "But I think your mate will like this bit."

Fergus's dragon snarled. *If he doesn't get to the point soon, we should pin him to the ground and demand answers.*

You're aware he's leader, aye?

Right now, he's not clan leader—he's our annoying older cousin.

Lorna walked up to Finn and grabbed the top of his ear. Finn yelped. "What the bloody hell are you doing?"

Twisting his ear, Lorna narrowed her eyes. "In private, you're merely my nephew. Watch your tongue, Finlay."

Fergus bit his lip to keep from smiling. From experience, he knew his mum would grab his ear too, if given the chance.

Arabella sighed. "How about I just tell them, Finn? Otherwise, we could be here for another hour and I'm hungry for a change."

Finn looked at his mate with concern. "Are the bairns giving you trouble, Ara? You promised to tell me if they did, no matter what I'm doing at the time."

Arabella shook her head. "They're actually behaving, which means I'm starving." Arabella looked to Fergus and Gina. "What my dear mate wanted to say is that in addition to BroadBay being under constant surveillance to ensure they don't cause any more trouble or plan any more attacks, there was one other stipulation from the DDA."

Relief flooded Fergus's body. Unless BroadBay found a way to bribe the DDA, Gina and Jamie would be safe.

Fergus would whittle the details surrounding BroadBay out of Finn later. He needed to know what else to expect from the DDA. "A requirement beyond the changes to the sacrifice system?"

Arabella nodded. "Yes. That was something Finn hashed out with Bram. This next bit was a request from the American DDA office." Arabella smiled at Gina. "You're going to see your sister Kaylee sooner than you anticipated."

Gina clutched his hand and stood perfectly still. "Please explain what you mean, Arabella."

Arabella shrugged. "The American DDA is investigating BroadBay and the actions of their clan members. While that Travis bastard wasn't part of the attack on Lochguard, some other Broadbay members were. As such, the American DDA is afraid of retaliation against your family. Your parents and Kaylee were offered a relocation program, complete with new identities. The only catch is they could never contact you again."

Fergus adjusted his hold on his son and wrapped his arm around Gina's shoulders. "Something must've happened."

262

Arabella answered, "Correct. Kaylee refused. She wanted to be relocated here."

Gina's reply was breathy. "And?"

Finn chimed in. "I agreed to the plan. She arrived a short while ago and is waiting inside the Protectors' central command building. If you need some time to adjust before seeing her, she will stay with me and Ara until you're ready."

Gina took a step forward. "No!" She looked up at Fergus. "Can you take me there now?"

His dragon spoke up. *Do it.*

But what about Jamie? The temperature is dropping by the minute.

Lorna released Finn and put out her arms. "Give me my grandson. I'll wrap him up tight and follow you."

Fergus looked to Gina and nodded. "Please, Fergus. I just want to see my sister. Your mom will watch over Jamie and make sure he's okay."

He handed over his son without hesitation. "Just make sure he's warm enough, Mum."

Lorna adjusted Jamie's swaddling. "I raised you three and Finn, didn't I? Now, go. The sooner you do, the sooner we can welcome Kaylee MacDonald into our family."

Gina looked over at Lorna. "But you don't know anything about her."

"Aye, but she chose you, child. That's all I need to know." Lorna motioned toward the door. "Go."

Tugging Fergus along, he and Gina rushed into the fresh air. Before his mate could start running, he scooped her into his arms. "This way is faster."

As he half-jogged, Gina laid her head on his chest without complaint. The pair of them had come a long way from the first day back along Loch Shin.

His beast huffed. *Of course. I'm quite charming.*

Fergus mentally snorted. *Just because Gina thinks you're beautiful in dragon form doesn't mean that's how we won her.*

I guess we'll never know.

Oh, I know the reasons. Live in your fantasy, if you like.

His dragon turned his back on Fergus and walked toward the back of his mind. *Just hurry and make our mate happy so we can finally take her home.*

Picking up his speed, Fergus drew on every bit of strength he had. Much like how he was incomplete without his family, he had a feeling Gina was the same way with her sister.

It was time to fix that.

~~~

Gina closed her eyes and enjoyed the beat of Fergus's heart as he ran. A lesser man might take offense at a quiet evening alone being pushed aside in favor of welcoming a new sister-in-law. But not Fergus. Even though Gina had only mentioned her younger sister a few times, he instinctively understood her longing to see Kaylee.

She still couldn't believe her sister's choice.

True, Gina should be even more excited about BroadBay being under surveillance and investigation since it meant she and Jamie were safe. But in the present, she could only think of finally seeing her sister.

A sister Gina had believed she might never see again.

Fergus's pace slowed and his deep voice rumbled in his chest. "We're nearly there, lass. I'm going to put you down at the entrance."

Opening her eyes, Gina blinked to adjust to the fading light. Ten seconds later, Fergus slowed to a stop and gently placed her on the ground. He moved toward the door, but she placed a hand on his chest to stop him. "Thank you, Fergus."

He smiled and chucked her chin. "I intend to collect at a later date."

She raised an eyebrow. "So much for being noble."

He gave her a quick kiss. "I can be noble, but I'm also male. I have plans for when you're healed and naked." Gina blinked, but Fergus placed a hand on her lower back and pressed before she could reply. "We can discuss this later. Come. Your sister is waiting."

Each step only made Gina's heart rate increase. Kaylee had given up her life to come to Lochguard. She might be okay with that for now, but who knew about the future. Despite what her parents had done to Gina, they had been loving parents before Gina's accidental pregnancy. Kaylee may yet regret severing ties.

From time to time, even Gina longed to see her parents' faces again.

Fergus murmured, "Talk to your sister first and then decide if you need to worry."

She glanced up. "How do you know I'm worrying about anything?"

"You tap your fingers together when you're worried or nervous." He moved his from her back to her hand and threaded his fingers through hers. "We'll face her together, lass. Don't fret."

Drawing on the strength of Fergus's grip, she nodded. If Gina weren't sleep deprived, she probably wouldn't be worrying in the first place. She'd take Fergus's example of gathering the facts before making a conclusion. Kaylee might actually be happy to see her. Her sister also had a fascination with dragon-shifters, which could make the transition smoother.

They rounded the last corner and entered the main command room. Grant McFarland stood with a group of Protectors, discussing something she couldn't hear. At the sound of their entrance, Grant looked up. "I wondered how much longer you two would be." He motioned toward a side room. "She's in there with Meg Boyd."

Fergus snorted. "That's quite the way to introduce her to the clan."

Grant answered, "Aye, well. Meg volunteered before I could even ask. I think she's jealous of your mum and the human male and just wants something Lorna doesn't have yet."

Gina squeezed his hand. "Can we discuss Lorna and Meg's rivalry later?"

Fergus nodded. "Sorry, lass. Come, let's go before Meg Boyd talks her ear off."

Taking a deep inhalation, Gina straightened her shoulders for courage.

They crossed the floor. Fergus looked at her with love and encouragement in his eyes before opening the door. An older woman's voice met their ears, "And that's how I married off my second son. As you see, there are some tricks to catching a fine dragonman—"

Gina's eyes fell on her sister and she whispered, "Kaylee."

Kaylee's brown eyes filled with surprise and she jumped out of the chair. In the next second, she ran into Gina's arms. "Gina."

Closing her eyes, Gina released Fergus's hand and hugged her sister tightly. "I can't believe you're really here."

Kaylee squeezed gently and then moved back. Gina opened her eyes to meet her sister's gaze as she answered, "Of course I'm here. I've been trying to find a way to Scotland for months, but I didn't have enough money saved up. I wish you'd have let me come with you."

Gina blinked back tears. "I didn't want you tainted by association, Kaylee. You deserve better."

Kaylee shook her head, the short strands of brown, curly hair bouncing around her cheeks. "You always were an overprotective sister." Kaylee gripped her upper arms. "But in this, you were wrong. I missed you, Gina. Don't ever push me away again."

Meg Boyd chimed in. "Aye, she's right, Gina. Sisters should stick together."

Gina smiled. "You're right, as usual, Meg." Fergus sighed at Gina encouraging the older dragonwoman, but Gina ignored it and turned toward her mate. "Kaylee, I'd like for you to meet Fergus MacKenzie. He's my mate-slash-husband."

Kaylee elbowed her in the side. "You did all right, sis."

She whispered, "Kaylee."

Fergus chuckled. "Nice to meet you, Kaylee MacDonald. But I need to correct one thing—I'm the lucky one to have found Gina. I still can't believe she chose me."

The way Fergus stated the fact, as if it were the simplest thing in the world, made Gina smile. "Are you still working on earning brownie points?"

Fergus grinned. "Aye, maybe I am."

They stared at one another a second before Kaylee asked, "Did something happen to the baby, Gina?"

At her sister's worried tone, Gina moved her gaze to her sister. "He was born a few days ago. Would you like to meet Jamie MacDonald-MacKenzie?"

Kaylee nodded enthusiastically. "Where is he?"

The anticipation in Kaylee's voice warmed her heart. No matter the past, her sister would accept Gina's son without question.

Clearing the emotion from her throat, Gina answered, "My mother-in-law should be here shortly, if not already. Let's wait for her. I can introduce you to more people along the way."

Meg interjected, "But don't set your sights on anyone yet, child, until you've met my Alistair."

Fergus answered dryly, "I'm not sure Alistair would like to know his mother is trying to set him up."

Meg waved a hand. "He's had nearly thirty years to do it himself. If I don't try, he'll never find someone. He spends too much time reading. He should socialize more often."

Rather than answer, Fergus opened the door and smiled at Gina with love as she walked out with her sister. They would have a good laugh about Meg's antics later. Knowing what Gina did of Alistair, he wouldn't welcome his mother's matchmaking efforts.

Kaylee leaned over and whispered, "I keep pinching myself to make sure I'm not dreaming. Not only because I've found you, but also because we're on freaking dragon-shifters' land. I never thought I'd see the day."

Gina laughed. "I've been here over two weeks, and I still think it's a dream."

Fergus appeared at her other side just as Lorna rushed into the room with Jamie. Her son had to be wrapped in eight blankets by now.

Lorna stopped in front of them and looked between Gina and Kaylee. "Aye, I see the resemblance. The hair and eye colors are different, but the faces are the same."

Gina motioned toward Lorna. "This is Lorna MacKenzie, my mother-in-law. Lorna, this is Kaylee MacDonald, my younger sister."

Lorna smiled. "Welcome to Lochguard, child."

Fraser, Faye, Holly, and Ross rushed into the room. Ross was out of breath. "You move quick for your age, Lorna."

Lorna raised her brows. "Aye? I think you just need more exercise. Or maybe it's those four years you keep lording over me."

Before Ross could do more than frown, Kaylee pointed at Fraser and then Fergus. "There are two of you?"

Fraser wrapped an arm around Holly, but Faye was the one to answer. "I know. Sometimes I wonder why. One brother is more than enough to try my patience."

Fergus growled out, "Faye."

Faye shrugged. "What? I'm just telling the truth. With you two out of the house, I have better access to Mum's scones. We should've kicked you out years ago."

"You and the bloody scones. You should learn to make them yourself," Fergus muttered.

As much as Gina loved her in-laws, she didn't want Kaylee's first impression to be of them bickering for ten minutes, as they were wont to do. She put out her hands to Lorna. "Can I have Jamie?"

Lorna handed over a sleeping Jamie. Gina carefully removed four blankets before moving closer to her sister. "This is Jamie. Say hello to your Auntie Kaylee, Jamie."

Gina gently maneuvered her son into Kaylee's arms. Her sister smiled. "He's so tiny."

"Believe me, when he was coming out, he didn't feel tiny," Gina murmured.

Kaylee chuckled. "I won't argue with that." She touched Jamie's cheek and he moved for a second before settling again. "I can't wait to spoil you, little man."

Gina sighed. "Between you and the MacKenzies, I'm going to have to be vigilant if I want him to ever learn how to do things by himself."

Fergus came up behind her and wrapped his arms around her waist. She relaxed against her mate's chest as he answered, "I'll help you, lass. My brother is the one to watch out for."

Fraser ignored Fergus. He and Holly moved closer to Kaylee. "I think introductions are in order. I'm Fraser, the more handsome and clever of the MacKenzie twins. And this here is my mate, Holly." Fraser motioned toward Faye. "The annoying female over there with the wild hair is my sister, Faye."

Faye growled. "My offer still stands, Fraser. Let's shift and settle this once and for all."

Kaylee jumped in. "I wouldn't mind seeing a few dragons up close."

Thankfully, Grant stepped forward. "I think it best to use our energy on rebuilding. The fights can wait for later."

Faye murmured, "Killjoy."

Grant merely raised his brows and Faye looked away.

Fraser whispered loudly to Kaylee. "Speaking as an uncle to an aunt of wee Jamie, maybe you can help me."

Kaylee looked around the room. "How?"

Fraser grinned. "I'm trying to get a nickname to stick, you see. What do you think of Mac-squared?"

Kaylee paused a second and then laughed. "Because of MacDonald-MacKenzie."

"Aye," Fraser stated. "Are you with me?"

Mischief flared in Kaylee's eyes. "That depends. Will you shift into a dragon for me?"

Holly frowned. "Maybe you should ask someone else. I don't like other people seeing Fraser naked. Maybe Grant can do it."

All eyes turned to Grant. The head Protector answered dryly, "I have some things to attend to."

As Grant scurried away, Ross stepped in. "I'm Ross Anderson, Holly's dad. Maybe you should ask Lorna here. She rarely shifts for anyone, not even me. And I ask nicely."

Lorna sighed. "Not this again."

Ross grinned. "Aye, this again. I'm determined to see your dragon self at some point."

"You can keep trying, but you won't get anywhere, Ross Anderson," Lorna replied.

Ross asked, "Not even if I ask nicely and offer to do the dishes?"

Lorna shook her head. "No."

Ross took a step closer. "How about if I offer to cook, too?"

Lorna rolled her eyes. "And have you set the cooker on fire again? I think not."

"I'll find out what will trigger an agreement, Lorna, dear. Just wait," Ross stated.

Fraser shook his head. "Leave my mum alone. She has her reasons. You shouldn't push."

Ross stood taller. "This is between me and your mum, lad. Mind your business."

Fraser growled, but Holly jumped in front of her mate. Looking between Fraser and Ross and back again, Holly's tone was stern. "I swear I have to keep stepping between you two."

271

She looked to Ross. "Stop provoking a dragonman, Dad. Despite your bravado, you're not as strong as him." Holly looked to Fraser. "And you need to let your mum fight her own battles."

Ross and Fraser started arguing yet again about respect, boundaries, and keeping out of other people's business. Gina half-expected Fergus to jump in and defuse the situation, but instead, he leaned down to her ear. His whisper was so low she could barely hear it. "This is your family now, lass. Are you ready to run?"

Gina glanced at Kaylee, shared a smile, and then turned in Fergus's arms. She looped her hands behind his neck. "Never."

He pulled her tighter against him. "Good, because I'm never going to let you go. I love you, Gina MacDonald. Wild dogs couldn't tear me away from your side."

She tilted her head. "After this, let's find some wild dogs. I really want to test your hyperbole."

Fergus growled. "I have a better idea."

She played coy. "Oh?"

"I think I'm going to steal a kiss from my mate whilst I still have the chance." He nipped her bottom lip. "I love you, Gina, my lass. I waited a long time to find you, but you were more than worth the wait."

She touched his cheek with her fingers. "I love you, too, Fergus. I may not have thought so even two months ago, but I'm glad events played out as they did. Otherwise, I never would've found you."

With a growl, Fergus lowered his head and kissed her.

Gina reveled in his heady taste as she met each stroke of his tongue. A month ago, she'd been alone, on the run, and scared for both her life and her son's.

But now, she had a mate, her sister, her son, and a new family that would do anything to protect its own. Fate may have thrown a few wrenches into the mix, but Gina wouldn't have it any other way. Fergus MacKenzie was the man of her dreams and she would move heaven and earth to keep both him and their son by her side.

EPILOGUE

Two Months Later

Gina smoothed her hair down one last time, but her curls popped right back up and remained wild. While she preferred keeping it in a braid, Fergus liked it down. Normally, she ignored his wishes and kept it back for convenience. However, the upcoming evening was special—she and Fergus were ready to try having sex again.

In the intervening months since Jamie's birth, she and Fergus had been creative. But as much as she loved his tongue between her thighs, she wanted to feel his hard cock inside her.

And yet, Gina's stomach flipped. By all accounts, the mate-claim frenzy shouldn't happen as long as she was breastfeeding. However, that didn't mean it wouldn't happen.

Stop it, Gina. You trust Fergus. Even if it starts, he will rein it in. Taking a deep inhalation, she turned from the mirror and paced the length of the bedroom. Fergus should be back any moment from dropping off their son at Lorna's house. Jamie had definitely become Grandma's little boy.

Not that Lorna was the only one doting on Jamie. Fraser and Kaylee acted as if they'd always been brother and sister, resulting in more mischief than Gina liked. Only because she knew none of her family would ever do something to hurt her baby did Gina let it slide. Deep down, Gina admitted that Kaylee finding allies in the MacKenzies made her heart warm with happiness.

The downstairs door clicked closed. Fergus was home.

Undoing her robe, she slipped it off and sat down on the bed. It took everything she had not to fidget and pick at the scraps of clothing covering her body.

About thirty seconds later, Fergus opened their bedroom door and stopped dead in his tracks. His eyes roamed her shoulders, her breasts, and her legs. When his eyes met hers again, they were flashing. "How attached are you to what you're wearing?"

The approval in his eyes gave her the courage to be bold. Trailing her finger down her chest until it reached the small bow between her breasts, she asked, "You like it?"

Fergus took one step and then another, his heated gaze never leaving her face. "Aye." He was close enough to lift up a strand of her hair and rub it between his fingers. "And you wore your hair down for me."

She placed a hand on his lower stomach. "I did a great many things tonight. But I think you have something to do for me, first."

He ran a finger up and down her arm. "I say forget the silly games. My bollocks are blue from wanting, lass. Don't make me wait any longer by performing a strip dance."

Gina smiled. "Only if you promise to do it tomorrow."

Fergus grunted. "I'll promise to run naked through the local village tomorrow as long as you let me have you tonight, Gina."

The corner of her mouth ticked up. "I rather like that idea."

He lightly tugged her hair. "I thought you were possessive of me."

275

She tilted her head. "I am. But I also like pushing your boundaries. You have to admit, it's been fun."

"Buying my family a karaoke machine was a mistake."

"Only because I made you sing, too."

"I'd rather not remember that," Fergus grumbled.

She laughed. "Okay, okay. I think I know of a way to distract you from that memory." Gina scooted back on the bed and lay down on her elbows. "Undress me without ripping anything and you can do whatever you want to me, dragonman."

Fergus's pupils remained slitted for a few beats before growing round again. He leaned on the bed and covered her body with his. His lips were a hairbreadth away from hers as he whispered, "You think you're the clever one. But you'll be begging me to rip off your clothes before I finish."

Memories of Fergus's fingers between her thighs, on her breasts, and strumming her nipples all rushed back to her. Blood rushed to her cheeks at the same time as her heart beat double-time.

Aware her pale skin was flushed, she merely answered, "We'll see, Fergus MacKenzie." She lifted a leg to rub against his hard cock trapped in his jeans. Fergus groaned and she whispered, "I've waited nearly two months. Don't make me wait any longer."

With a growl, Fergus kissed her and thrust his tongue in her mouth. Each stroke was a claim.

She raised a hand to his hair and dug her nails in. He growled and took the kiss deeper. As he licked and nipped, it felt as if he was kissing her for the first time all over again.

As quickly as he'd started, Fergus pulled away. His voice was husky as he said, "I love you, lass, but the kissing is going to wait."

THE DRAGON GUARDIAN

Before she could nod, Fergus leaned back and traced the strap of her lingerie top. The roughness of his finger against her skin sent a jolt through her body. When the strap ended, he traced the edge of the lace cup holding her breast.

"Fergus," she breathed out.

Her dragonman let his fingers do the talking and he lightly strummed her nipple through the silky fabric. Each pass caused more wetness to rush between her thighs.

Hoping to encourage him, Gina spread her legs wider. Fergus chuckled. "My mate is impatient."

She raised an arm and lightly traced the outline of his hard dick. Fergus sucked in a breath and Gina smiled. "You can keep teasing me, but I'm only going to tease you back."

"Maybe I should've brought some scarves with me to tie you up. Then you'd be at my mercy."

She shivered at the idea of being naked and open to Fergus's every touch. "Maybe later." She spread her legs as wide as she could, her crotchless panties displaying her core to her mate.

Fergus's gaze zeroed in on her swollen flesh and he licked his lips. "My favorite sight."

Playing innocent, Gina scooped her breast out of its lace cup. "I thought this was?"

With a growl, Fergus leaned down and licked her nipple, and again. At this rate, she'd come before he was ever inside her.

~~~

Fergus was barely keeping control of his dragon. His beast roared inside his head. *We've played your games for two months. Hurry up. I want to feel her heat around our cock.*

277

She needs to be ready.

Look at her. Our mate is more than ready.

Fergus ceased his attentions to Gina's nipple and leaned back to stare at her pussy. His mate was pink and glistening, ready to grab onto his dick and wring every last drop from him.

Still, he restrained long enough to ask his dragon, *You're sure you can contain the frenzy?*

Yes. Now, hurry up and claim our mate.

Fergus met Gina's gaze again. The heat there caused a drop of precum to leak out. "I'll replace the lingerie later."

In the next instant, he ripped the tiny scraps of material from his mate's body. He ran a hand down her naked chest, breast, and stopped at her abdomen to trace the faint stretch marks. Even after all this time, Gina still shifted when he paid extra attention to the marks. Leaning down, he kissed them and murmured, "You are the sexiest woman alive to me, Gina MacDonald." He kissed her skin again. "Don't ever doubt it."

"Then show me or I may need to go through the things the pregnancy changed in me."

He grunted, ripped off his own clothes, and covered her body with his. Cupping her cheek, he answered, "As much as I love your games, lass, I only have one question before I claim you for the first time as my mate."

Gina searched his eyes. "What?"

"Do you want me to use a condom?"

She paused before answering, "No. I trust you not to start a frenzy."

He brushed her cheek with his thumb. "Even without the frenzy, you could end up pregnant again."

She wrapped a leg around his thigh. "According to Dr. Innes, it's less than a 2 percent chance while breastfeeding in the first six months. If it happens, it happens." She kissed him. "Claim me properly, Fergus. I've waited long enough."

His dragon hissed. *Now.*

Fergus took Gina's lips as he positioned his cock at her entrance. Inch by inch, he eased inside until she took him to the hilt.

Bloody hell, his mate was tight. He'd have to be careful not to hurt her.

Gina broke the kiss and moved her hips. "Stop overthinking. You won't hurt me, Fergus. I'm more than ready for you. And I mean all of you—both man and dragon."

His beast grunted in approval. *Do as she says. She wants us.*

Fergus moved slowly at first before increasing his pace. Judging by Gina's moans, he wasn't hurting her.

His dragon jumped in. *Stop holding back. Claim her. Hard.*

As his beast's lust and desire to claim flooded his body, Fergus's restraint faded.

Pinning Gina's hands above her head, he watched her small breasts bounce with each thrust. He moved even faster. While the frenzy was absent, every iota of Fergus's being itched to finally brand their female as their mate.

Gina arched her back and Fergus pounded harder, each movement a claim on Gina.

Rearranging his grip so he held her wrists with one hand, he ran his other down her chest, her abdomen, and stopped at her clit. Lightly brushing her bundle of nerves, Gina cried out, "Harder!"

Fergus didn't waste any time. The bed shook with each piston of his hips. Gina wrapped her legs around him and dug into his arse cheeks. Both man and beast thought, *Ours.*

But Fergus wanted to see Gina's green eyes as she came. He ordered, "Look at me."

Opening her eyes, she met his. The love mixed with desire stoked his dragon's desire. Fergus growled and he increased the pressure against Gina's clit as he rubbed back and forth. The sound of flesh slapping on flesh filled the room, mixed with Gina's moans.

His dragon snarled. *Our mate is ready. Take her.*

Pressing against her hard bud, Gina screamed right before she clutched and released his cock. Fergus never stopped moving, the pressure building at the base of his spine. Just as his mate came down from her high, he roared, "Gina," before stilling his body and releasing.

Each drop from his dick branded their mate and sent her into one orgasm after another. Gina arching her back as he made her come was a sight he'd burn into his memory.

When he'd spilled the last drop of his seed, Fergus let go of Gina's hands and collapsed on top of his mate. Gina moved her fingers to his back and lightly scratched his skin with her nails. Her voice was breathy as she said, "You're just as good as I remember."

Somehow he mustered the strength to raise his head. "You doubted me?"

She smiled slowly. "Well, I was pretty pregnant and my memory wasn't functioning at full capacity then."

He grunted. "I see through your games, lass."

"So if I asked you to take me at least two more times to make sure it's not a fluke, you wouldn't do it?"

With a growl, he moved his head to hers and lightly bit her bottom lip. "All you need to do is ask, lass. And I'll claim you as many times as you like. Unlike humans, I don't need much time to recover."

Gina moved her hips and Fergus sucked in a breath. "You will always have a claim on my heart, Fergus MacKenzie, but I think you need to claim my body a few more times for good measure. I can't have the other females doubting you're mine."

Pulling out, he thrust back into her core. "There will never be any doubt, Gina MacDonald. You're mine and I'm keeping you."

Taking her lips in a kiss, Fergus claimed his mate three more times before holding her close as she fell asleep. He was the luckiest dragonman in the world and he'd do whatever it took to convince Gina of that fact. Every day he expected his happily ever after to be taken from him, but Fergus would fight until his dying breath to protect his family. MacKenzies loved deep and hard; Fergus was no exception.

Dear Reader:

Thanks for reading *The Dragon Guardian*. I hope you enjoyed Fergus and Gina's story. If you're craving more of this couple, don't worry, they'll show up again in the future. Also, if you liked their story, please leave a review. Thank you!

The next story in this series will be *The Dragon's Heart*, which is a novella for Lorna MacKenzie and Ross Anderson. My goal is to release it Summer 2016.

To stay up to date on my latest releases, don't forget to sign-up for my newsletter at www.jessiedonovan.com/newsletter.

Turn the page for an excerpt from one of my other series.

With Gratitude,
Jessie Donovan

Reclaiming the Wolf
(Cascade Shifters #1)

Female wolf-shifter clan leaders are rare, but Kaya Alexie thrives on the challenge and can handle anything the men of her pack throw her way. However, when the male cougar-shifter who broke her heart ten years ago shows up on her doorstep with a dead wolf-shifter in tow, her whole world goes off-kilter. She's determined to ignore him, but when a virus threatens to decimate her clan, she has no choice but to work with her ex and his brother to survive.

Sylas Murray is sent by his brother to ask for the wolves' help in solving the mystery of a recent wolf-shifter attack. There are a few problems, however. Not only is he a cougar-shifter among a pack of wolves, the clan leader is also his ex-girlfriend. To say they had a bad break-up would be putting it mildly— Sy's actions nearly destroyed the truce his clan had with the wolf-shifters. But as a virus threatens the GreyFire wolves, Sy and Kaya must put aside their past to find a cure.

As they work together and race against the clock, Sy starts to wonder why he let Kaya go in the first place. Despite their past, will he be able to reclaim the wolf that captured his heart and start over?

Excerpt from *Reclaiming the Wolf*:

CHAPTER ONE

Cascade Mountains, Eleven Years Ago

Kaya Alexie kept crouched low behind the thick underbrush of the forest, careful to keep still in her human form, making no more noise than what it took to breathe. If the male cougar-shifter found her before she reached the target, she would lose, and she needed to win if she wanted to claim her prize. Only then could she get what she'd wished for these past few months.

She strained her ears for the slightest sound that might give away the male's hiding spot, but even though her hearing wasn't as good as in her wolf form, all she could hear was the rustling of the leaves and branches and the small scurrying of the ground mice. Apart from the occasional bird cry, nothing seemed out of the ordinary.

Maybe, just maybe, she had finally lost him.

Not that she would be celebrating anytime soon. She'd been secretly dating Sylas Murray, the cougar-shifter from a neighboring clan, for the last six months and she was well aware of how skilled he could be. His tracking skills were damn good, and definitely her biggest obstacle to winning.

Still, she wasn't too bad herself. She could outsmart the other eighteen-year-old wolf-shifters in her pack when it came to tracking and evading drills; it was only a matter of time before she could beat Sylas too.

Maybe even today.

A bird chirped and then flew right past her. She looked up into the trees, but since the sun had set half an hour ago, it was too dark to make out any recognizable shapes. If Sy had made his way into the branches up above, the sneaky cat would use his feline grace to pounce on her. She needed to move.

She itched to shift into a wolf and feel the wind against her fur, but they'd agreed to stay human to make the challenge more difficult. Of course, moving her nearly six-foot tall body through the underbrush without making a sound was no easy feat. Autumn was nearly here, which meant the thick foliage of the understory had turned into a maze of sharp sticks.

She finally broke through the last of the trees at the edge of the clearing and felt a sense of giddiness. Victory was nearly hers for the taking. If she could just make it to the big rock outcropping on the far side, she would win, and Sy would have to give her anything she wanted. That was their deal.

And she knew exactly what she wanted to ask for.

She was tired of looking over her shoulder or finding a way to sneak past her clan's guards and sentries to spend a few stolen hours with her boyfriend. She wanted to show off Sy to the world, and if she won tonight, she was going to invite him to her clan's autumn celebration next week.

Sy accompanying her to the celebration and facing the scrutiny of her entire clan was a big step. Interspecies pairings were still considered taboo among most shifter clans, Kaya's included. Yet, if Sy felt as she thought he felt about her, he wouldn't care about her clan's objections and old-fashioned bullshit. He would stand with her against anything.

But she was getting ahead of herself. First, she needed to make it across the wide-open clearing and be the first to touch the rock.

Kaya sprinted as fast as her long legs would carry her. She had ten feet to go when she heard a cougar growl behind her.

This was the border between her clan and his, and her heart skipped a beat as a million questions and worries raced through her head. Had someone from Sy's clan discovered them? What would Sy do if they had?

Stop being a chicken shit, and see who's following you. She took a deep breath and looked over her shoulder, only to find a naked Sy chasing after her. She stumbled at the sight of his broad chest and strong, lean muscles, but Kaya quickly regained her wits. They had both started this game dressed in clothes and his nakedness could only mean one thing: Sylas Murray was a cheating bastard who had shifted into his cougar form back in the forest.

Despite months of these little games, he'd never cheated before. His shift and disregard for their "human only" rule signaled that he was afraid she could finally beat him.

Her inner wolf growled at his deceit and her human-half agreed with that sentiment.

Well, fuck him. I'm still going to win. She pushed her body harder. It was just a few more feet to the rock, and now more than ever, she was determined to beat her man.

~~~

Sylas Murray noticed Kaya's glare and realized he might actually lose. The woman was beyond determined to beat him.

Normally, he loved the way she challenged him and tried to outsmart him. She being a wolf-shifter and seeing the world differently because of the wolf inside of her was part of the reason he loved her.

From raising her chin in defiance to her grand plans on how to improve relations between shifters and humans, he loved all of it. On top of that, just a hint of her scent drove both him and his inner cougar crazy. His body was always on fire for her, to the point he spent most of his time with a hard cock and a blood-deprived brain.

That was why he needed to win tonight because if he did, he could finally claim Kaya as his own. He was pretty confident Kaya would say yes to his request and allow him to finally make love to her.

As Kaya picked up her pace and raced across the clearing toward the victory rock, Sy drew on the last of his strength to run as fast as he could before he jumped and just barely caught her waist with his hands. As they tumbled to the ground, Sy was careful to take most of the impact. She might be tough, but the thought of her getting hurt because of him made his inner cat snarl.

Once they stopped tumbling and he managed to get Kaya pinned face-down on the ground, he leaned down and nuzzled her neck. He took a deep inhale of her womanly scent, and his already hard cock turned to stone.

Since he wasn't able to pound into Kaya's wet heat just yet, he settled for nipping her earlobe. When she didn't make the little noises of pleasure like usual, he knew she was angry. He wished he could shift into his cougar form and purr to calm her down, a trick he'd learned early on, but she would bolt the second he released her.

He nuzzled her neck again and gently kissed the place where her neck met her shoulder before he said, "Losing isn't the end of the world, Kaya-love. You nearly beat me this time."

Her body went tense below him. She turned her head and narrowed her warm dark chocolate eyes. "I would've beaten you if you hadn't cheated, Sylas Murray." Her voice went low. "Now, let me go."

He wasn't afraid of her cool, simmering anger; he was used to her notorious temper. He simply laced his fingers through hers and squeezed. She tried to tug her hand loose, but with him on top of her, she didn't have enough range to accomplish it. "Cede defeat, and I'll let you up."

She growled. "Why should I? You're the one who cheated. By all accounts, you should cede."

He decided truth was his best option. He gently bit her ear and whispered, "I wanted you too badly to play by the rules. Will you cede, Kaya-love? All I want is you naked and willing beneath me."

Kaya remained motionless under him, but he could smell her arousal. *She wants me, too.*

But he had hurt the woman's pride, and he needed to ease it a little before she would acknowledge her desire.

He'd planned to tell her tonight anyway, but if he told her he loved her, she just might let him off the hook. While he'd said the words a thousand times in his head, he'd been afraid to say them out loud.

Of course, some people, such as his twin brother Kian, would say telling a woman you loved her when she was angry and face down in the dirt might not be the best strategy. But nothing between him and Kaya had ever followed the rules. His gut said it was time.

He lifted his head and looked his wolf-shifter in the eyes as he said, "Please, Kaya. I want to show you how much you mean to me. I love you."

~~~

Kaya's anger eased a little as she heard the words she'd yearned to hear for weeks, if not months, and a plan started to form in her head. There was a chance they might both get what they wanted.

Still, she wasn't about to let her cougar off easy. If she said it was okay to cheat now, the male would do it again. She was going to make him work for it this time. "I don't know if I should believe you. For all I know, you're just trying to get into my pants."

He moved one of his hands from her back to her cheek. As his fingers stroked her skin, it became harder and harder to stay mad at him.

Damn the man and his warm, rough hands.

———————

Want to read the rest?
Reclaiming the Wolf is available in paperback

For exclusive content and updates, sign up for my newsletter at:

http://www.jessiedonovan.com

Author's Note

Here we are at the end of yet another Lochguard novel. I hope I did Fergus justice, especially since a lot of readers were sad for him at the end of *The Dragon's Dilemma*. (I'm a bit biased, but I think Gina suits him perfectly!)

I actually had the chance to visit Scotland last year and saw where Lochguard is situated. I try my best to create a visual for you all. If you ever have the chance to visit Scotland, I highly recommend it!

Next up will be Aunt Lorna's novella. She's been without a mate for so long; she deserves some happiness. Faye's book is after that.

Oh, and if you haven't had a chance to read my Stonefire Dragons series yet, I highly recommend it. Finn and Arabella's story is part of that series (*Healed by the Dragon*), as is many of the other Stonefire character we met in this book.

Thanks for reading! And I hope you'll continue to follow the stories of both Stonefire and Lochguard in the future.

ABOUT THE AUTHOR

Jessie Donovan wrote her first story at age five, and after discovering *The Dragonriders of Pern* series by Anne McCaffrey in junior high, she realized people actually wanted to read stories like those floating around inside her head. From there on out, she was determined to tap into her over-active imagination and write a book someday.

After living abroad for five years and earning degrees in Japanese, Anthropology, and Secondary Education, she buckled down and finally wrote her first full-length book. While that story will never see the light of day, it laid the world-building groundwork of what would become her debut paranormal romance, *Blaze of Secrets*. In late 2014 she officially became a *New York Times* and *USA Today* bestselling author.

Jessie loves to interact with readers, and when not reading a book or traipsing around some foreign country on a shoestring, can often be found on Facebook:

http://www.facebook.com/JessieDonovanAuthor

And don't forget to sign-up for her newsletter to receive sneak peeks and inside information. You can sign-up on her website:

http:///www.jessiedonovan.com

16334540R00174

Printed in Great Britain
by Amazon